Gulf Stream North

Books by Earl Conrad

HARRIET TUBMAN, Biography
JIM CROW AMERICA, Criticism
SCOTTSBORO BOY (with Haywood Patterson), Autobiography
ROCK BOTTOM, Novel
MR. SEWARD FOR THE DEFENSE, Novel
THE PREMIER, Novel
GULF STREAM NORTH, Novel
THE GOVERNOR AND HIS LADY, Novel
THE PUBLIC SCHOOL SCANDAL, Criticism
NEWS OF THE NATION, History
HORSE TRADER, Memoir
CRANE EDEN, Novel
THE INVENTION OF THE NEGRO, Historical Theory
THE DaVINCI MACHINE: Tales of the Population Explosion,
    Short Stories
MY WICKED WICKED WAYS (for and with Errol Flynn),
    Autobiography
BILLY ROSE: MANHATTAN PRIMITIVE, Biography
EL CRISTO DE MONTSERRAT, Novella
TYPOO: A Modern Novel
BATTLE NEW YORK: Mural of the Metropolis, Poetry
EVERYTHING AND NOTHING: The Dorothy Dandridge Tragedy
    (for and with Dorothy Dandridge), Autobiography
CLUB, Novel
ERROL FLYNN: A MEMOIR

Gulf Stream North

BY EARL CONRAD

SECOND CHANCE PRESS

Sagaponack, NY

TO MY WIFE ALYSE
for her faith in me, her sympathy and criticism
which have shaped me as a writer

First published in 1954 by Doubleday & Company

Library of Congress Catalog Card Number: 80-50244
International Standard Book Numbers:
            0-933256-13-2 (Cloth)
            0-933256-17-5 (Paper)

Although this book is based upon real incident, recent or remote, in
the menhaden fishery, all names and characters are fictional, and
any resemblance, which may seem to exist to real persons is purely
coincidental.

Manufactured in the United States of America

SECOND CHANCE PRESS, INC.
Sagaponack, New York 11962

First Day

JULY 11, 1949

CAPTAIN CROTHER, he stood on the bridge and talked down at the crew strung out around the galley and the port-deck rail. "Men, you-all thinking hard on me because we ain't catched no fish?"

All the fishermen sounded together: "Oh no, Captain, we don't never think hard on you. We think you a good captain," and like that. "You'll find us fish, Captain."

You got to crap up a captain now and then, that's the way the men feel.

I am the mate of the menhaden fishing ship, *Moona Waa Togue*. I was standing next to Captain Crother. I had told him he better talk to the men, they was a little restless. For five or six weeks we been fishing for menhaden, or pogy, the way some call it around here, but hadn't caught much, just a few loads. I winked at the crew very steady. That way they knew I thought they should pay him a little mind.

"Sometimes," he said, "most any way you go you'll find fish. But every few years we get a bad season like this. The fish don't flip . . . but the crew *does.*"

The fishermen laughed. Someone said up to the captain, "We ain't going to flip, Captain."

A bright look came on the captain's face. "The other boats ain't doing much better than we. The company done sent a half dozen of them up to North Carolina because the fishing been so poor hereabouts." Then his voice came on sad. "And till that bad spell breaks it just ain't going to be *no fish* in the hole and *no money* in the measure."

"We sticks with you, Captain Crother. We sticks with you."

"You an old hand, Captain. You know the game!"

The captain, he wanted to hear that. He been feeling in a serious way for days, for weeks. No fish, there's no good heart nowheres. And the company, the Merrick Thorpe Menhaden Company, they going to keep after the captain and just about fault him for the sea and the seasons.

"Captain," one of the men said, "we want you to fish us hard today. Fish us hard so we can get back in tonight in time for some fussing and doing and dancing."

The captain, he stood up straight as the mast.

Sometimes a man's face comes to be like the work he does. Captain Crother, he had a look around his nose like he was born smelling pogy, always lifted his nose as if he was sniffing something. He was only in his early fifties, but he been catching so many fish in his time, and he got so salty, his face was a net of wrinkles. Now he spread the net of his face and he made a promise:

"If it's one goddamn pogy out here under this Georgia sea we catch the sonofafish-bitch!"

"That showing the spirit, Captain Crother!"

"Let's get that po-o-o-ogy!"

"I swear by all the salt in the sea, Captain Daniel Crother going to lead you to fish today!" He said that, he knocked a hole in the air with his fist.

Captain Crother, he heeled around till he about fell off the steward's deck, he was in such a hurry to go up to the hawk's-nest to see out for menhaden. Old captain, he wasn't too good on his footing lately anyway. I gave him the flick of a wink as he went by, a right smart wink, let him know he done the right thing.

A mate can about go blind with the job he has to do with his eyes. Sometimes, between the left eye for the captain and the right eye for the crew, you wink your way through a bad day so much that by night your eyes are all a-pepper. Just from winking—and not even from looking at the sun on the water.

I stayed on deck to see would everything be more settled. But just when Captain Crother got up to the crow's-nest the men started in to bitching again, talked out thoughts as long as the coast line.

A half dozen bunt pullers, the two ring setters, and the two seine setters, they went aft and hung around the fish hole and the engine house. Broke up into twos and threes to play cards, read, smoke, and wait for the "Fish! Fish!" cry to come from the mast, and the sound of the bell over the forepeak to let them know it was set-making time.

Genty, a bunt puller, a man to give out with more than one fisherman's share of complaint, he said, "I never had *no* captain I had any love for." He argued he was on a ghost ship. "She showed up that way ever since this season began. Other ships been catching fish, we been seeing *some* schools, but the *Moona Waa Togue,* she just too damn ghostly!"

15

Fellow we called Fort, he came from Fort Lauderdale but his right name it was Jim Puttnam, he jumped right in behind Genty. "That's for sure we on a ghost ship. She got thirteen letters in her name, ain't she?" That's a strong argument, and the men don't like it any too well fishing on a ship with thirteen letters in her name.

Fort, he worked up the men over thirteen-letter boats he been on, the *Charles T. Eaton,* the *Arthur J. Hessie,* and the *Wilbert L. McCoy.* "They been men killed on all those ships and not one of them boats ever any good after that. Always been haunty. Catch no fish, just catch hell. Ought to sink all them haunty ones."

I picked him up on that. Told him where the *Wilbert L. McCoy* just last season brought in twenty million fish. "You got to make a sharp tack in your thinking between a bad-luck boat and a bad-managed one."

The bunt puller from Louisiana, they called him Bob or Louisiana, he was standing at the rail by the fish hole. He picked a sliver thick and long as a pencil off the rail, flicked it off easy; just rotten wood. He said, "Ought to sink *this* one. If they don't, it may could sink *us.* Look at *that!*" He pecked at more of the wood till they had to tell him to stop it, they needed a ship to fish from! "You can punch your fist through it anywhere," he said. The boat wasn't that wormy and rotten-wooded, but her maiden days was long before any of us been born. The *Moona Waa Togue,* she began life as a sailboat way back before 1865.

I told Louisiana he shouldn't low-rate the ship like that because *that* might just help sink it. If the men lose confidence in a boat, they going to neglect her, and that make her worse.

Louisiana said, "I didn't say sink her when we was *on* it. I said *they* shouldn't let her float no more."

I couldn't stir the men away from ghost-ship worry. Though I believe there is such, and been on plenty ghost ships in the menhaden fleet myself. Just this wasn't the time, when you are on one that may *be* one, to talk of it. That talk, it's best on the hill.

Morris, a seine setter from New Mexico, he been on a few pogy ships out of Gulf ports, said he was on the *Coast Traveler*, a converted oil tanker. "Ever since they brought dead soldiers back on her from Europe she ain't been no good."

Blu, the Florida ring setter, he asked Morris, was that the ship the cook took sick on and he died?

Morris said yes, that was the boat. "Could have been his own cooking killed him. And after he died all of us could hear him in the galley—from down in the forepeak. You could hear the dishes rattle too." He told how the crew got jumpy hearing all that back talk from the dead cook up there in the kitchen. "We'd run topside to see him and he'd be gone. But just as soon as we got out of the galley we heard the dishes rattle again and the pots and pans move, even when the sea was glass."

I knew about the *Coast Traveler*. No menhaden captain ever stayed on her for more than a week or two, because the crews walked off. They had to give her up for menhadening. Fishermen got a good instinct for a boat that can help them bring up fish or stand in the way of catching them.

Ghost-ship talk, that brought the rest of the crew aft in a pack right away. Everybody pitching in with what they knew about such ships all the way from Long Island up by New York down the coast and over the Gulf to Port Arthur, Texas. That's the two ends of the menhaden fishing world.

Pretty soon all that haunty talk had the men worked up against the *Moona Waa Togue*. Till Genty, he came back in it very important because he was the one had started it. "You see

17

what I done told you! This ship got a jinx! She ain't caught
nothing all spring and ain't going to! She been running the
sea too long! Time she was beached!"

Genty, he took a private fretful look around at each fisherman. His voice dropped a fathom. He stared down at the
bottom of the fish hole real worried till he said, "It could be
the fish know about a boat to stay away from just like everything in the world got it sensed into it to stay away from
something that's going to hurt it." Then his tone started to
surface. "Could be the menhaden just smell all the fish that's
died off in that hold, smell it a long ways off and know *to stay
away from this funky old bitch!*"

One or two others threw that out, said they didn't believe
pogy had that much sense and never known them to work
that way. But haunty talk ain't far from luck talk, and they
slipped into it. The danger of a man coming on board with a
black suitcase, and such. I've thrown many a black suitcase
overboard myself. This bunt puller, Ritchie, he hailed from
Texas, he said he never saw it to fail, any time anybody left
the hatch cover bottom side up the ship got into trouble. Another fisherman, he thought it wasn't no reason to worry about
that because they had a good cat on board and a good dog
to ward off such.

That's when Rev came into it. Rev was a ring setter, a good
man in a purse boat, been pulling bunt and setting rings for
twenty years. He was a preacher at the port when he wasn't
fishing. Preached on the ship too; but he did more to keep a
crew in the right spirit than any captain I ever known.

He stepped into the middle of the crew, held up his hands
like he was stopping the clapping before it began. Some fellows haunched up against the engine house, they pounded
on the engine-house wall. "Let Rev say!" They liked to see him
go from the sea to the pulpit and the pulpit to the sea.

Rev, he had a voice with bells, so that it proclaimed, like

from a steeple. "Now, you talking about the *wrong* things and
you just believing in the *wrong* things!"

He cast them a prophet's eye. "You follow *this here*," he
commanded. He held up a small cross. "This the compass that
carried me all up and down the coast, in the deep fathoms and
in the stony shoals, in gale and sun." He shook the cross at the
crew. "Fourteen ships in twenty years!" He let that sink in.
"This my first year on the *Moona Waa Togue.* I got no fear of
this ship because this here compass, it's going to bring me
through like it done brought me through other ships, other
years. This ship been bringing in pogy since the Indians and
she going to bring it in again!" His eyes showed with second
meanings after the first meanings rolled from his tongue.

"You follow good-luck cats, you wind up on top of the mast!"
The men laughed.

"Pay mind to the black suitcase, if you do, the man with the
black tie, he's going to carry you off—and I be the one, I'll be
there to say the last words for you!" They listened hard. He
was preaching now, hitting it.

"Don't you worry about the hatch top! You follow this here
compass of the Lord! Here's your true mast!"

The captain and the striker-boat man, both up in the lookout, they could make out every word Rev said. Like he used a
speaking trumpet, but his trumpet, it was just his big voice and
big faith.

Rev held the crucifix tight in his right fist. He pointed at
the arms of the cross. "This crosspiece, it means due east and
west, it's safe shipping. And this part"—he held onto the long
stem on which the Lord rested His back—"it means due north
and south. Hold to it like I do! Believe and you always catch
fish and make port!

"*This* one, it's the true compass—not the one *there!*"

And he pointed to the pilot's house on the steward's deck.
That's where Fitch, the white pilot, had the ship at this

minute . . . five miles off St. Simon's Sound, Georgia, in forty-two feet of water.

When a menhaden ship crew up the fishermen don't always get to know one another's real names or full names. You might ship with a fellow all season, never hear his first or his second name. A man fast on his feet, he might get the name Lightning, or High Man. When I was young and working out of North Carolina ports they called me Streak, Wings. Hardly nobody knew me as John Bixman, but it settled down to Bix or Mate. Nobody be giving anybody a nasty name, because a man won't stay with a nasty name. People don't mind being called something that grows out of what they are or do, or what they're like—if the spirit is right. On a menhadener, where it's twenty-two men, a big crew for a small ship, the feeling got to be good if fish going to be brought in.

Cooking Devil, his right name was Claude McNally, we was lucky to have him because he could have been the only good cook in the whole menhaden fishery. He stuck his head out the galley door. "Mate, this new mess boy sick. He ain't no good to me none. How I'm going to bake anything special in here?"

He talked at the bunt pullers hanging around the fish hole. "I'm trying to sweeten a big mess of yams, and this child here, he can't find his way between the stove and the table. He go around me like he think *I'm* the mast!" The wood mast, it was sixteen inches thick where it went through the galley and it could really be in the boy's way if he was seasick.

We been having mess-boy trouble for weeks. By this being a poor season, we not meeting much fish, and it's little money on deck, no mess boy wanted to stay. The mess boy, he's not counted as part of the crew. The fishermen take up a collection for him every two weeks on payday. We even had one or two grown men take the mess-boy job, men that couldn't get nothing else to do on the ship, but we rather have a boy like Roger. He was only eleven, he started with us this morning but got seasick as soon as we went out the jetties.

I had a bunt puller to take Roger's place alongside the cook and told a few of the others to do what they could for the boy.

Carters, Lift, Westley, Ronay, and Morris, they gathered around Roger by the port rail just outside the galley door. This bunt puller, Westley, he looked at Roger, then at the sea. Said he couldn't figure why anybody be sick on this sea, it was like glass, the ship on an even keel. "You must have a weak stomach, Roger." But the boy, he was too sick to carry an answer.

Westley, he turned to the others, said, "Poor little fellow, he may be no good for the sea." Young Roger didn't want to hear that. He wanted to help out at home, wanted to make out on ship. Acted like he was going to cry. The crewmen saw that, they put their arms on his shoulders, said now, now, take it easy, it going to be all right. They was sorry for him. The most had been through this themselves. But nobody had any feeling the lad was going to die. One or two even joked over it.

Westley, a fisherman that came from Alabama, he never been seasick in all his days, he started to show Roger how you should walk on deck. "You got to roll your body to the deck," he told the boy. "Like this: watch me!"

Roger watched with half a heart how Westley walked along the deck the same as always, like he walked on the hill.

But it didn't comfort the mess boy.

On the sea they got as many remedies for seasickness as on land the doctors got for the common cold.

Ronay, a Florida bunt puller, the biggest man on the ship, he had a young boy of his own on the hill the same age as Roger. He tried to be like a father, he said, "Son, what you got to do, do something to take your mind. Don't look at the water.

21

Watch me, I make some knots for you. If you going to be a menhadener you might just as well get to know the ship." Ronay showed the mess boy the bowline knot, the lover's knot, the slipknot. He spliced, he did all he could with a piece of rope. But a little list of the ship and Roger started to thinking of himself again.

Carters, a Georgia man, he pulled bunt too, he thought maybe he should get the boy to talk, maybe that make him forget, because the child wasn't sick enough to lay down. He asked Roger, "When you first began to feel sick, what you feel?"

Roger, he tried to help out, figuring *they* could help out. The mess boy said the first thing he felt, it was like the cook say, the mast was in the wrong place.

The fishermen, they talked that over very serious. Hardly a wink going on among them. All agreed on *this* boat that could be true, the mast might just could be in the wrong place and the child might not be so seasick if he figured that was what happen. "You can't be too sick," Carters said, "because anything can happen to *that* mast."

"Look, you going to ship out with us," Ronay said, "you got to know the ship." He pointed aft to the top of the engine house, called out what was what, the cable drum, the dunky, the triptail. But Roger kept looking out at the sea that been giving him so much trouble.

Ronay, he got a little short patient. "Here, Roger, I'm trying to teach you, and you looking out on the water! That's the worst thing!"

Roger, he tried to heed the big fisherman, and Ronay kept on: "You see them purse boats in the davits?" He pointed to the stern. "That net that go between them two boats, it's big enough to fence the world around."

But a very sick look came over Roger, like he was having a hard time to breathe.

Morris, he gave the mess boy a warning. "If you feel anything hairy coming through your teeth, don't spit that out! Be
careful because it might be your palate!"

Roger heard that, he looked up like the end come already.
But some others said to pay no mind to Morris.

Fellow we called Lift, a Virginia bunt puller, he been quiet
till now. Lift, he got his name from his good humor. The
fishermen want to work with a man like that because he wears
his even way with good color, like the ocean wears its big
green hat. Lift said, "Roger, I tell you what to do. You get a
piece of bacon about that big"—he made with his fingers a size
about an inch and a half—"and tie it to a piece of twine. You
swallow that, with the string hanging out of your mouth, keep
the string hanging out of your mouth, and you feel better."

The boy went into the galley and he did get from the cook a
piece of bacon and a length of string. The fishermen figured
the boy might just as well be busy doing something, anything,
even this idea of Lift's, as to stay by the rail suffering.

So they all watched the boy monkey with the bacon.

Roger, he tied the string around the bacon, then he put the
bacon into his mouth. Each time he felt he was going to
swallow it he pulled it back up. He was so busy swallowing
that bacon—and still not swallowing it—that maybe it helped
him forget his upset.

Yet in a half hour he was worse.

Ronay brought him some sweet coffee; he drank it, but that
made him sicker. He was tired, too, and he sat on deck up
against the galley wall. Still he didn't cry. Just looked bad.

The fishermen, they was all helpless. Talking, tricking, fun-
ning, nothing seemed to help. But Ronay knew that Roger was
real interested in everything about the ship and menhadening,
so he said, "If you lucky, Roger, you see us spin out that web
today. Once you behold that, you going to get right over being
sick, hear?"

Roger, he looked up. He was willing for anything that would ease his dizziness and quiet his insides.

I went by the boy, I heard Westley say, "I bet that kid don't never come back out for pogy again." Somebody else said about the same thing, that the child be better off on the hill.

But I seen judgments like that go wrong. "You can't tell," I said. "I was worse seasick than him when I first went out more than forty-five years ago—and I been out ever since."

Roger, he wasn't no boy to just sit. After a while he got up and went ahead with his own remedy. He walked fore, right to the stem, and he got to playing with a line and a bitt. The bitt is a timber fastened into the deck for tying ropes to.

He tied one end of this rope around the bitt and the other end around his ankles. Did a good job. Quite a few was watching him, still they had no idea what he was up to.

"Hey! Hey! *Stop that boy!*"

Somebody saw him all of a sudden try to go over the side. But they grabbed him, pulled him back on deck before he got over the rail.

Roger, he was smarter seasick than some in their level head. He thought if he could just cool his head off in the water he'd feel better.

"*What the hell you trying to do?*"

"That water might could just comfort my head some," he said.

Seasickness, it's like you drinking salt water, though you never tasted it. You sweating outside, inside, and topside. You want to walk, you can't. You want to run, you can't. You want to crawl, you can't. You want to just hang overside from a rope and cool your brow, they won't let you.

"*Goddammit*," I said to the crew. "*He like to have got killed! Watch that boy!*"

I went up to the crow's-nest to sit beside Captain Crother and the dry-boat man, help them look for the red line.

The captain, he was signaling the pilot every few minutes, go this way, go that way. Offshore, inshore, upcoast, and downcoast. We'd go a distance one way, a half mile the other. Hunt and hunt, stalk and stalk.

You don't exactly *fish* for menhaden. You hunt for it in a ship, stalk it along the coast with your eyes and a Diesel engine, capture it with the biggest net in the world, chase it up and down the waters like they hunt for game in a jungle.

Our jungle, it's the sea. The no man's land between the deep sea and the shore. On the incoast ledges, the coastal waters, a narrow way, where below it can be all traps of sand, hard coral, bars you not looking for, fans that stick up out of the mud, rocks to stove you in from under, all that can cut up your keel. Around these Georgia and Florida beaches, by the inlets and the sounds, where land washes out, shore lines change.

Sometimes we be in close till the crew can see through the water to the bottom, like you see tea grounds when you tip up a cup. The men be yelling to the pilot, "Hey, Fitch, deep water won't drown you." Telling him and the captain go farther out. Hunt for the fish where it's plenty depth under our old flatbottom crate of soaked-up wood.

But it's in close, in the shoaly part where you mostly find this oil fish that schools in hundreds of tons, like islands that move under water.

A menhaden school, it'll go in circles sometimes, like a dust storm in water. Till you see it wheel out in a straight course, then all of a sudden sound, the top of the waters be quiet. Then up they'll come, like a hill from beneath, each fish with his mouth open to catch the skim. A ton or two of fish may hit the top of the sea hard, splash so you can hear it a hundred yards away. Could be the weight and drive of the fish in the hulk of the school forces the top fish out of the sea. Another time you going to see an acre of pogy plowing ahead, like it's a piece of land with fins, then separate, be two islands furrowing the sea.

It's times a crew feel they know where to find them as well as the captain do. They'll be about the deck, like now, a bunch of sea lawyers. "Why don't the captain go in by Such-and-Such Island?" Or that way, or north, or southeast, or farther out?

But Captain Crother, he's got the make of his own mind about where the hunting going to be. Carib, the striker-boat man, he can't tell the captain. Neither can I. Captain Crother, he just tell the pilot which way to go, like a pilot fish lead a shark.

"Captain Crother," I said, "you keep twisting the ship every which way, you get the crew thinking you don't know where you going."

Captain said it might be as much luck going one way as the other. "And we been having poor luck."

"Don't tell yourself nothing about luck, Captain. You can bring bad luck if you think too much luck," I told him.

Every fisherman got his own ideas about the fortunes of the sea. "Luck's in *you*," the captain said. "You got it or you ain't."

I thought different, told him, "I believe luck is in the Lord, but the *conduct*, that's in you."

One or another, we been sitting in the mast ever since sunup. Sometimes two will be in the lookout, sometimes three. If you going to spot fish you should usually see them by nine or ten in the morning. That's if they're schooling regular in a good season. At times they'll school in coast waters according to the tide, but show better in ebb tide. You may spot red patches a quarter mile away. Get up on top of it, or close to it, it looks like a red line, you'll see thousands of menhaden feeding. Sometimes, when the moon been three or four days full, that seem to bring out the fish. Sometimes the wind drive them. Still other times all the signs you been following your whole life can fall out, and you'll see fish or you won't.

There's a wooden crosspiece for a seat in the lookout. The
captain, he sits in the middle, and the striker-boat man and
me, we sit to each side of him. You rest your feet on a horse-
shoe-shaped floor five feet wide. You come up into the lookout through a trap door. Close it and that wood falls back and
becomes part of the floor. You can even sleep on those boards
at night during a hot spell, and some men do it. But now the
three of us, we just sat on the cross-board spying on the ocean.

By this three-way sentinel's watch we can see all ways as
far as we likely to spot the red line.

The red line, that's the sign of the menhaden school. Actually
that pogy may show up in all colors, solid blood red to a
purplish black, sometimes ripple white as whitecaps. The sun
and the sea, they'll sandwich a pod of fish so as to split their
color up into any glint of the rainbow, but mostly those
crimson, brownish tones. You got to watch out for uncertain
colorings skipjacking along the surface of the water. Maybe a
brassy tinge, maybe silvery, or some color you not expecting.

Out here in the bowl of the sea the pogy can be painted any
color the ocean churn up for it. Then study it hard, shade your
eyes with your hand, because you may think it's a wave, a
trick of the sun, a cloud blotting out whitecaps. What it may
really be, it's that little herring-type fish moving in thousands,
hundreds of thousands, even schools of millions.

In our jungle you don't have trees for shade. Be up in this
hawk's-nest built around the mast, sixty feet over the deck,
combing the sea for pogy, you don't have nothing for shade.
Nothing between your skull and the South coast sun but a thin
white straw hat or a cotton cap. Right now it could have been
a little over a hundred in the shade on deck.

Only thing you talk about any more than women, money,
politics, and religion on a menhadener, it's the weather. You
can go without God on one of these ships, as a few may, but
not without the weather. Captain Crother, he was cussing it

out, and Carib, the dry-boat man, he outcussed the captain.

"No use tearing up the best thing the Lord gave us," I said. "Captain, why you don't order a shade be built?" Some lookouts have a five-foot wood or canvas shade on top, it helps.

The captain said he was going to take care of it as soon as we got back to port, he wasn't putting it off no more.

But Carib, he was a man to talk up to anybody, he poured the captain right back into his jug. "Captain Crother, you made that promise as many times as they's fish in a net!" Carib flecked sweat off his forehead, flipped it onto the floor of the lookout.

We all knew Captain Crother didn't speak up to Merrick Thorpe the way he should. Because the captain, he was none too happy working for the Thorpe Menhaden Company. Ever since he came to De Leon Beach and took over the *Moona Waa Togue* he been getting salty beyond his years in the fishery. A salty captain, that's a tough, tight, sour, hard-to-be-by man. He came here from Virginia. He been living there most of his life, made good money, had a good new-built ship, worked for the biggest menhaden company in the business. But something happened, nobody knew what. He broke with them and had to take this old boat and live in Florida. Captain didn't like it. Summer fishing off these shores, it was too hot for him, hard on his health. Besides, we heard it said Merrick Thorpe made him take less on each measure of fish than some other captains got, and he was debted to Thorpe too. Put it all together you could see why, with everybody got a sour side that's to show sooner or later, it would show sooner with Captain Crother. Still, he wasn't no evil man. Just a cussing, salty one. He'd sit by me in the hawk's-nest and tell me the sea been in his family and he been in the sea's family for a long time. "My grandfather ran a ship in the War of the States," he'd say, "and went into menhadening after the war closed out. That's how long us Crothers been combing these coasts." He'd shade his forehead so as his eyes could ride over the waters like a gull's looking for the red line, and then he'd get a bad twist in his voice. "I ought to own this boat. But I don't own it. My father should have gone into the meal and oil side of this business, like some other captains did. Instead he just ran ships and didn't leave me no boats and no factories."

So we used our hands for eyeshades. Each time a ripple moved our way, it carried our hopes; maybe the pogy be under it. That's plenty ripples, plenty hopes, but still it was no fish. They should have been in these waters by the million at this time of year, off Cumberland Island, off Jekyll Island. But how and when and why and even *where* the menhaden schools, it's a mystery. Only a few ships in the menhaden fleet been catching any the past few weeks. No fish, no money. The crew of a menhadener, we get paid only for the fish we catch. Don't have no wage paying. We sharecrop. We're sharecroppers of the sea. Catch no fish, get no share—and the company make nothing neither. So it's a real worry when you don't see the red line.

"Captain," I said, "they ain't even a gull following us."

Nothing but the quiet sea and the heat working harder than anything else. You'll drift like that for hours. Coast for miles. Sometimes no words pass in the nest for a full hour. You just look and you just think. Still you been long trained to spot a menhaden school. Like the eye of the fish that's always open, your eye is always open too. So that if it's the slightest hint there in the sea, it will break through your thoughts, and you going to wake up quick.

When he don't find fish in close a captain may start looking way off coast, where the line of big ships goes into the Caribbean, maybe to South America. A steady parade a few miles east of us. Happy-looking boats, fat around the middle, taking people on pleasure rides. Some ships with three or four smoke-stacks, with big heavy prows to make them look like bulldogs.

Freighters, tired-looking, the way washladies might be, too long on their knees. Sometimes, going low, fast, like tigers, the ships of the services, with guns looking at all faces of the sea. Speedy Coast Guard ships; and all around us, shrimp trawlers, each with rigging up in the center like a rope tent.

Mostly it's in between that parade of ships and the shore where we catch menhaden. But now, Captain Crother, he was looking east. He said, "Bix, I bet they out there. Let's go!" He gave the signal to the pilot to head due east for the deeper waters.

That time Captain Crother was right. About eleven o'clock, eight miles off St. Simon's Sound, the captain leaned forward in the lookout till I thought he'd go over. You couldn't see the beach from here. Nothing but sea about, and the stacks of a big ship farther out. Below the ship it was about fifty-five feet of water, hard gray sand on the bottom.

Captain, he was staring steady enough to hypnotize the fish, till he pointed and whooped, "*Fish hit! Fish hit!*" Sometimes his voice got a little music in it when he sang out a strike. He stomped up and down in the crow's-nest like a boy that they took his football away from him.

Carib pulled the rope that rang the gong over the forepeak.

Down on deck they was yelling and pointing off the starboard bow. "Fish! Fish! Strike!" Yell anything, everything. "There they play!" What we ain't seen in days, a brassy stretch of water, fish thumping at the surface. The color getting redder and redder as we got nearer. Each second more like blood color. Like red raindrops.

Captain gave orders. "Hey, below! To wheel—starboard!" Fitch put the wheel over.

Carib stood up, put the palm of his left hand over his eyes, got the sign of the red spot good in his mind, tried to figure which way the school of fish might be heading. Carib, he was

a South Carolina man, he may be the fastest man in the
Florida fishery on a ratline. Been on the sea since he was a
mess boy, he be bound to be a mate before long. Knew seamanship and fishing both. Sometimes the crew called him
"Little Boat." He's called the dry-boat man because he don't
get wet, like the bunt pullers do. He guides the purse boats
around the school of fish, shows them where to lay their net.
Stays in his small dory and stays dry, so they know him as the
striker man, or the dry-boat man, or the little-boat man.

Captain Crother called below, "Lower the dry boat!"

While the dry-boat man skinned down the rope ladder,
three bunt pullers lifted the rowboat off the deck and slid it
overside.

But by this being the first strike we had in days, Carib
could have been too anxious. He got three fourths of the way
down the ladder, he missed a step. He finished the rest of the
way sliding down the rope. Grabbed onto the ratline and
burned his hands bad doing it. He plunked down on the deck
full of as much surprise as something that comes out of a
jackpot. He stood up, held his hands out like to let them cool,
and looked around at the men that was watching him. But he
never let on he slipped. Wouldn't admit nothing like that. He
gave the fishermen as straight a face as the mast give the sea.

The two seine setters and the two ring setters, they were
already around the purse boats at the stern. Those are the small
boats that have the big net in them. You spread out the net
from those boats. The webbing itself, half of it is in one boat
and half in the other. The center of the net, we call it the bunt,
it straggles loose between both small boats as they ride in the
davits. If you could see that net stretched straight, out of water,
she'd be in a rectangle shape nearly a quarter of a mile long
and about a hundred feet across. But you don't never see her
that way. At the port you just see her rolled on big spools. Or
like now, she's craunched down in folds in those small boats

31

like a woman that keep her full nature from you, hides out from you, keeps you guessing what she fully is, what she really look like from head to foot.

But those purse boats, they ain't *too* small. Each about thirty feet long. The ring and seine setters popped these boats into the water from out the davits. On a menhadener there's no man-ropes to help you get on and off the big ship. You just jump from the mother ship—that's what we sometimes call the *Moona Waa Togue*—into the purse boats. Scramble off the big boat the best way you can and just make sure you land in the small boats, because it's a dangerous jump. The captain and nine men got into his captain boat, and seven men and me jumped into the mate boat.

Kirwan and Booker, the purse-boat engineers, they started the Lathrop engines, and we headed toward Carib. Both boats side and side, held together kind of Siamese-twin fashion by that net, with its bunt dragging in the water. The name bunt, it may come from the bunt part of a sail, the middle of the sail.

You have to get around up ahead of a menhaden school.

Carib, he was two hundred yards away. We had to wait on his signals before we could get over the fish. He was spinning his oar above his head. That meant don't come in too close, the fish moving around. He wasn't sure which way they going, which was the head part.

While us purse boats moved up slow toward Carib, the *Moona Waa Togue,* she slipped around the other side of Carib, but way away from him. The motor of the big ship, it can scare off a school of fish, so the big boat don't come in close till we get the fish in the net. Fitch knows how to handle the big ship while we make a set.

You got to be a bee to get the sweet out of a blossom and a trained menhadener to get these fish out of the ocean. Carib, he kept shooting us signals to halt or come in closer. Signaled

with his oar upside down, blade up to the sun. That meant the
fish sounding, going under. Anything can cause them to go
down, a motor sound, trouble with big fish under water that
may be eating on them, even a wrong move by the dry-boat
man.

Captain Crother, he was sitting on the bow plank of his
boat, getting anxious. "Come on," he said, "let's move up in
there!" The purse-boat engines picked up on the fuel.

But Carib heard us. He stood in his rowboat and signaled
us to stay back.

"What the hell ails him?" Captain Crother cussed. "He so
crazyass out there! What's he on?"

About now you begin to feel the heat. You can't move much
or easy in those purse boats. It's hot summer to begin with.
The sun is going to hit you directly, and the rays that hit the
water, they'll jump at you. The bunt pullers, they're all muscled
men, cordy wrists and bulgy forearms, knotty shoulders. So
that there's sweat crying through their skins already even
before the work begins.

Some palm-of-your-hand-size fish, the leader fish, he was
under there outsmarting Carib. Some head man just six to
eight inches long, but leading tons of fish, he was running
Carib just about ragged. The fish won't break in a flanking
movement, but go in a column movement; snake around in a
long line, play follow the leader. The leader, he can be tart as
a general, sense all kinds of dangers to the school—winds, currents, preying fish, boats, birds, spoiled water, cold water,
water with no food in it. If something don't sense right, that
leader be gone, and the pod of fish with him. You don't go for
the leader, you can't ever see or spot any one fish, but you do
go for the whole head part of the school, where it may look
like a thick rush of water.

Carib stood up, gave us the come-ahead sign with his hands
and wrists. "Here they pla-a-a-a-y!" In a few seconds our purse

boats got up by him till he motioned us to separate. "Let your net go!"

The captain, he steered his boat left. Me, holding the tiller of the mate boat, I went right.

When our boats separate the net slips overside, out of the purse boats. A ring setter in each boat, he helps the net out with a long iron shaft that guides the rings into the water. But the action of the boats moving away from each other, that does most of the spreading of the net.

Eight thousand pounds of netting and gear—rings, lead, corks, lines—all that starts playing out. That's the time to watch your net. Plenty that can happen because the net gets big and hard to handle. If you not careful with that net it can split your hands open. You make a wrong move, you can smash your legs against these steel purse boats. You can get killed too, because men have got killed.

All you can see on top of the water, it's the cork side, just a line of corks bobbing on top, making a circle around the school of fish. Each cork is four inches high and four inches wide. They're a few inches apart, the whole length of the net, till twenty-five hundred corks are going to form a circle over the school.

But the other side of the net, it slides under water as soon as it goes overside. That's because it's weighted down with one-pound rings the whole length, rings that carry a purse line through them. The purse line goes along under water, one end of it in the captain boat and the other end of it in my mate boat. At the center of the net, on the ring side, all along the bunt, there's one-pound weights to hold the net under. All that ring and lead weight carries the net down so that it's like a screen hanging slack all the way to the bottom.

But when we made half the circle the dry-boat man, he spotted a movement of the head of the fish tangenting off outside the radius of the net. He yelled to me to back up on my mate boat. I ordered Kirwan to cut the motor. Then had him to back up. We backwatered about fifteen yards till Carib called out for us to make a tack, told us when to bring her around. Then we started again, curving toward the captain boat.

"You got it made," Carib told us.

Now we went fast as our Lathrops would take us. Got to close that circle. Us two boats have to meet and come aside each other. While we finish wheeling the net around the fish Carib has to stay where he is, at the bunt of the net. He helps hold up the cork line on that side, so the fish won't try to get over it.

Till our captain and mate boats met, the quarter mile circle around the fish done.

The next job, it's Blu's. He's a ring setter, a little fellow, froggish, lots of spring in him. Got an eye fine as a needle. He's got to carry our end of the purse line over into the captain boat—that's a hard fast jump—and hook his line to a scratch block in the captain boat. The scratch block, it's attached to a purse weight. But mostly we call it the tom weight. That's a hunk of lead about two feet high, weighs five hundred and eighty pounds. It's got to be lowered by a hand winch, with the block and purse lines attached, so that down under, at the bottom, the force and weight of the tom helps close up that ring line.

A split-second trick. Got to be done fast because the fish can get under the ring line and get away before it's closed up.

Blu made his jump. He aimed to land on a piece of steel in the captain boat called the thought. It's the width of the purse boat and it's in front of the engine house. But our mate-boat engine, it was still running when Blu jumped. It should ought to have been off. By our boat still moving, Blu missed the thought. Instead his feet landed *boom*, right in the pickle bucket.

That bucket, it's supposed to be filled with salt that we

spread on the net to keep it cool, but this one was emptied out. The bucket is wide at the mouth, smaller as it gets to the bottom. Both of Blu's feet landed in the bottom, curled up in there.

Blu flopped so ridiculous trying to keep his footing that all in both boats laughed. Nobody ever saw that happen before. The man couldn't do it again probably if he tried. His arms flapped about like the wings of a shot bird and he hollered funny.

I laughed.

Captain Crother, he thought it was so funny, he slapped his thigh just below his shorts so it sounded like a wave frapped the hull. Maybe you couldn't help but laugh. Even Blu himself laughed, harder and louder than anybody, but a nervous, hurt laugh, like he was holding something, but laughing anyway. A man will sometimes laugh when he's in pain, the way Blu did. Because if everybody thinks it's funny, maybe a man don't dast feel pain.

Till it hit everybody at the same minute that the net hadn't been tommed. The purse line wasn't even in the scratch block. The lead hadn't been winched overside.

The fish poured out from under the net. They surfaced and some came right up by our purse boats, flipped white and foamy. A big rich school that could have got us a good day's pay.

Everybody's face dropped hard, like the crew was the tom weight going under.

They gave Blu serious looks. "Man, you could have tommed the net!"

The red in Captain Crother's face, red from the sun, it showed beneath his sweat. He banged his fist down on the gunwale, and he got like a philosopher. "*Almost* tommed the net don't make oil!"

By these fishermen coming from farms and plantations, and working in the fields in the winter and spring before the fishing season begins, they got two ways of looking at the world, sometimes like farmers, sometimes like seamen. They will mix sea water and cabbage sometimes, go from ocean language to farm talk, take a saying of the field and put it out to the pasture of the sea. They got regular words for good sets and bad sets.

"Man, you made a bull," someone said to Blu. That's when you make a tom stab at the fish and don't catch any.

"Man, that could have been a heifer if you'd have hooked your line!" A heifer, that's a successful set.

They cussed out Blu very general. I was against faulting him. Making sets, I am never surprised at anything to happen. Till this ring setter, he hushed them the way he should: "Well, you-all in this boat *with* me. You-all saw what happen! Some one of you could of grab that line from me and hung it to the block . . . *but you had to laugh!*"

The captain, he filled both purse boats and the whole inside of the cork line with his noise. "Get the nets back in the boats! We going to get them *sa-a-a-me* fish!"

He hollered at the bunt pullers. "Them damn fish should *never* have got away! We going to stay out till we get them!"

It wasn't no fault of the crew that the menhaden got away. The fishermen started tugging in the netting. A half hour's job. Had to get it back into the boats before we could make another set, because you got to circle around the fish all over again once you make a bull.

Captain Crother, he spit at the ocean. The sea just took that, like it take everything. He gave Blu a hard look. I saw it and others saw it. "Captain," I said, "you know if the Lord meant us to catch pogy he'd have birthed us with nets attached to our butt ends." The men laughed. I got to stick up for them when the captain get hard, but the first chance I get I'm going to wink at him.

I joined in with the men on pulling the net back into the boats. They like for a mate to do that, gives them a confidence in you. You don't wear gloves when you pull bunt. You *can't* wear gloves and pull that meshing. The little squares of linen thread, they're too small for that. You got to work fast, and gloves going to be in your way. Pull bunt and you get three ridges across your hands. One, it's across the middle knuckles. Another, it's at the base of your fingers where they join the palms. And the third gutter is across the palm of your hands. Those three lines, they're your real life lines.

A few of the crew complained of bunt pulling in the heat. Because in weather like today's your hands swell up from the meshes cutting up your fingers. Get home at night, you'll douse your hands in vinegar to limber them, take away rawness, cure the soreness.

Sometimes it's going to be so hot you can't make more than one set, then want to go in. But the captain, he seemed bound to make a haul today—and so was we all for that matter—so that I said, "No use crying in the ocean. Enough water in it now. Let's get in the net and chase them again."

Captain Crother's mouth rolled for a time, then stopped, like a wave that breaks at shore and foams out to nothing. He signaled the mother ship to come by.

The crew got the webbing back into the purse boats. We tied the small boats to the stern of the big ship. Once you get the purse boats lowered, you just haul them behind (unless there's a high sea), and it spares you having to raise and lower them for each set.

Pretty soon I was back with the captain and Carib in the crow's-nest, hunting again. "Them *sa-a-a-ame* fish!" the captain said over and over. "It must have been a *million* of them! They still here and we ain't going back to the beach till we got them in the hold!"

Carib and me, we uh-huhed that.

Captain, he roamed his eyes over that water like he was a bird of prey. Which he was. Which we all was. He made motions with the fingers of his right hand, tried to feel of the breeze, looked up at the sun, acted like he had the senses of a bluefish, tried to figure out which way those menhaden may have gone.

"I think they headed inshore," he said.

He signaled below to Fitch to wheel her straight west into thirty-forty-foot-depth waters, toward Sea Island.

It was high noon, and each of us in the nest, we shaded our eyes and helped the sweat off our bodies with flicks of our fingers.

You look steady at that sunny sea, try to spot the brass line, you'll get eyesmart. The dots dance before your eyes. Sometimes lights, or small little rainbows by the thousands, you'll see all that, and your eyes play you other tricks. You'll run your fingers into your eyes to ease the strain, shade your forehead, look down deck for a minute's rest. But it's no rest till you get to port and home. By evening your eyes may hurt like sand been blowing in them all day.

Still you look every which way to see what there's to see. Most that you see in through here, it's shrimpers and the other ships of the Florida menhaden fleet. The fleet is placed at De Leon Beach in northern Florida. The fleet goes out each morning, maybe twenty-thirty ships. Some go north as far as Savannah, some south to Daytona Beach. But a few been fishing, like us, right in through here. They'd glum by, a half mile off. Looked like starved sea dogs, all skin and bones. Mangy-hulled fisher boats with twisted deck rails like broken wrists, one with a slanted mast. They went by hungry, without fish in their holds. Barnacles ate on their old hulls, ate the undersides of these ships because the most of them, they were built back in the old sailing days, like the *Moona Waa Togue*. Boats doing duty on the farm of the coast, like horses around a barnyard working till they drop.

Look down the rigging, you can see our ship, like a fat, smoked cigar, stretched underneath. Funky as a smoked cigar, with a burnt-out look, because the *Moona Waa Togue,* she can remember Abe Lincoln.

See the crew strolling on deck, resting up for the next set. Some playing cards, a few reading, others hanging over the fish hole, one or two trying to spot the menhaden that slipped away, another studying a shrimper way out. The pilot busy at the helm. "I like it most of all," Fitch often said, "when I feel a breeze blowing on the back of my neck. Just tickling the hairs on the back of my neck." All quiet, crew, ship, fish, sea.

The *Moona Waa Togue,* she's been patched, scraped, painted, fixed, fiddled with so much she looks like the overalls of a country boy in a poor old farm shack. Just a mess of patch and rags—but she works. On the hill the way they put it, "If you don't have a horse to ride, ride a cow." That's about what we riding, but more like an ox than a cow. Still I wouldn't speak evil of this old menhadener. I been aboard her so much, she brought in so many fish, and I make my living by her, that I got a good feeling for her most of the time except when the crew work up that haunty talk. Then I get worried too. But you don't cuss the bridge that get you across, nor the ship that make shore, nor the fish you get in your net.

Menhadeners like ours, and those we could see from our lookout, you can see them a mile or two offshore almost any day in the summer, all the way from New York to Texas. Maybe two hundred and fifty ships be skimming the coast all through June, July, August, and September, year in and year out ever since a hundred and forty years ago. Some of those ships been new-built since the last war, but plenty are like ours, old-timers, started as sailboats, then made into steamboats, and now running by Diesel engine.

The *Moona Waa Togue,* because she began as a sailboat, her stem twists up a bit like a pretty gal's nose. But ain't much else about her that's pretty. She's a hundred feet long and about eighteen feet athwart at midships. One thing about a menhadener, they never had one called *The Sweet Pea.* Not as I know of. Fish don't make a pogy ship sweet. The fish she carried in her guts for so long, the water in her bilge all that time, you just about riding along with a smell all the time. Except the salt breeze, that'll sometimes bring fresh ocean salt to you, crowd out the *Moona Waa Togue's* past.

It's the mast, lookout, and rigging of a menhadener that gives her a look different from the cruisers, freighters, and government boats that pass us. Like we're not a modern ship, but don't belong no more to sailing craft either. All that rope, the cables, the lines everywhere, it give us an old-time sailboat look, like the whalers had. The whole ship bounded by a steel cable, the forestay, it goes from the bow at an angle up to the top of the mast, helps hold the long pole firm. Ropes from the gaff down to the engine house and over the fish hole. Ropes to hold the purse boats in the davits, hank lines along the rail to tie the bunt to the ship when we make a set, rope-mat hooks, anchor lines to dock the ship, a tangle of rope, like vines, from stem to stern.

No waste space on the *Moona Waa Togue.* She's made for use, like a truck. Every ounce of wood, each bit of space got its reason. A jammed ship, like a machine, every square inch in use, packed with gear and men moving about between the gear so that every minute it's a danger. Always got to warn green men to watch out for a swinging line if they don't want a broke hip.

That's the picture of us if you see us from the side, a slow-goer, sea-mule, tough, mixed-up, made-over ship, made for just our kind of fishing, freakish in her look. But maybe more serviceable than any other kind of ship would be in menhadening, for she can't be any bigger than she is and navigate in coastal waters. So she's a flatbottomer, slick for slipping through the slews, getting over the sand bars and the coral reefs. We're built for inshore work because the menhaden, it's an inshore fish—and that's where we headed now—inshore.

Soon we saw the foot of the hill.

The burned yellow summer they get hereabouts, it makes the shore a brown line. We were two miles off Pelican Spit, just a spit of land, hardly an island, just birds living there. Birds that make a bunch of over-water stones all white with their droppings. About thirty-two feet of water here, and below us hard sand bottom.

Maybe the captain guessed right. The fish at this time of year, they head in to the coast anyway. That's where they eat, eat the skim in the water, the small life you can't see. You can usually bet on them hugging the shore. There could have been a million or more fish in that school that got away, and maybe the fish we came on now could have been those same fish—or some other menhaden.

Carib spotted something off the port that looked to me just seaweed, with sun shining on it, then water drowning it. But all of a sudden it turned to a whole brownish tone, then reddish, in a long narrow diamond shape.

Captain Crother, he was no doubter where a chance for menhaden was, he hollered loud enough to scare the gulls circling around the mast. "Fish! Fish! Pogy-y-y-y! Port to whe-e-e-e-el!"

He spit the tobacco juice out of his mouth and started down the ratline, the fastest barrel that ever rolled out of a crow's-nest. This once he beat Carib out of the lookout.

I said to Carib, "Captain falling out the mast this time, hey?"

All of us piled into the purse boats from the stern of the

mother ship. You got to watch it because sometimes you have to jump over somebody that just landed in there before you. The crew will just about fall into those small boats like it's a football scrimmage. If someone is in your way when you making that jump you can't stop in mid-aid and say, "Move over." You got to fly right over him and land somewhere in the piles of netting, or on the hard steel bottom—or on the man himself.

This time, when Carib gave us the signal to circle the fish, we did it right. The tom weight settled underneath, the way it should.

The ring and seine setters, they hauled in slack purse line till they couldn't pull no more and it was tight and hard. That meant the rings at the bottom been pursed. Then the heavy work for the whole crew began. The seine and ring setters and the bunt pullers, they started to yanking up the whole line of rings. Had to pull up all those one-pound rings, in long tugs at the netting, till no more rings stayed in the water and all were in the bottom of the captain boat. Then half the rings and the meshing attached to it got switched over to my mate boat. That way we shared the weight of the gear between the boats and got them ready for the next set.

Nothing under the fish now but netting. No way they can get out. That's when the bunt pullers go to work, pull hand over hand, shoulder to shoulder. Lean over the gunwales with each pull and draw that netting back into the boat, throw it on the bottom. Then haul in another armful of netting. About sixteen or seventeen men be doing that at the same time. Purse-boat engineers, they help pull bunt too. Everybody pull bunt but the captain and the dry-boat man.

Everybody make the same forward and backward movements of their hands, arms, and shoulders at the same time. And they don't hardly ever do it without singing in the fish. The songs we sing, they could be the same chanteys that been sung in this work for the last hundred years or more because it's about the same words used by the crews all up and down the coast.

You put your eight fingers and your two thumbs in the meshes, you sing:

> *I want to see Lulu,*
> *Oh, oh, honey.*

Those words bring breath into your lungs because the music go up at the word "honey." Then they pull in a load of webbing and water, draw the fish closer to the boat.

> *I want to see Lulu,*
> *Oh, oh, honey. . .*

All quiet again two-three seconds while the whole crew in both boats haul two or three feet more webbing out of the water.

> *Oh, I want to see Lulu,*
> *See you when the sun go down.*

Like a choir on the sea when the men sing the Lulu song. Drums, violins, and pianos in their voices. Then the silent bar of their muscles when they pull.

Most of the net, it still sprawled big and baggy in the water, with the fish moving around in it, trying to get out. The more we pulled in the mesh, the more we formed them into the bunt, into the center. That's where the netting is tight and strong, the square linen bars small and close together.

You have salt water in your sweat now, taste it rolling into your mouth. Because you flip up a lot of water when you haul that linen. But the most of what you feel, it's there in your arms and shoulders, and in what you chant:

> *Oh, oh, Lulu,*
> *I'll see you when the sun go down.*

44

Those fish fight for water and space like a man would fight for air and space. They need water to move in because air is in it; but pulling on the net, that forces the menhaden close to each other.

We're throwing sixteen-seventeen men's weight against hundreds of thousands of pounds of fish. Against thousands of pounds of linen webbing. And against the weight of the water itself.

Soon your fingers going to get like tight sticks. The mesh, it closes off circulation in your hands, and you steal an instant between pulls to beat your palms on your thighs to get the blood back, the crink out. Your fingers may cramp, stay stuck out in the twisted way of a crab's leg. You can get cramped in the arms and shoulders too. A hundred ways bunt pulling can draw on your body.

> *I got a girl in Georgia,*
> > *Help me to raise them.*
> > > (Pull)
>
> *Oh, oh, Lulu,*
> > *I'll see you when the sun go down.*
> > > (Pull)

The main length of the net, it's made up of what we call wing webbing. The linen bars are a little bigger than they are at the bunt. At first you pull into the boats all that wing webbing, till you get the fish jammed into the center.

We got most of the wing webbing into the boats, began rolling the fish into the center of the net, and that's when the menhaden started moving toward the sun.

Why the fish move toward the sun they don't nobody know, but every pogy crew knows they'll do it. Whatever time of day it is, wherever the sun is, those fish may all of a sudden move toward it. That throws the sun into the eyes of the bunt pullers.

45

Maybe the menhaden know it, maybe they don't, but they make it harder for us when they go to the sun.

That happens, it seems like more is against you than the fish and the net and the water. Like the whole sea, along with the sun, helping *them*, not us. It could have been a quarter million fish in that net and *they* became the bunt pullers.

This shift of the fish around to the sun, it made the webbing about the captain boat get stiff and powerful. The net on our side, it got slack. The brunt of the work, it shifted to the men in the other boat. My bunt pullers, they jumped into the captain boat, formed one long line of men to hold the fish. They braced themselves against the steel ribbing of the captain boat and pulled the big bag toward them a yard at a time.

Captain Crother, he sat on the bow, sweated like he been doing all the work, waved his hands and put spirit in us. "Raise'm! Raise'm!" But never once put his fingers in the mesh.

In menhadening each man is a fisherman, a musician, a small-talk philosopher—and he got to be a teamworker if he going to catch fish. They got a special chantey that comes out of their farm work when the fish don't come in easy:

> *I got a mule on the mountain,*
> *Call him Jerry.*

We pulled hard.

> *Oh, I got a mule, mule on the mountain,*
> *Call him Jerry.*

Once more, God Almighty strong, get them fish in the bunt.

> *Go bring him down, O Lord,*
> *Bring him down.*

Captain yelled, "Hold the fish, men!"

> *If I go get him,*
> *Who the devil going to ride him?*

"PULL!"

> *I can ride him all day long, Lord,*
> *Lord, Lord, all day long.*

The fish in this big ball of linen mesh, they still moved inch by inch toward the sun. If we pulled them a yard our way, they pulled us, boat and all, a yard to them.

The sun like needle points in our eyes. The bunt pullers, their arms all knots now, like twisted ropes. One bunt puller, he just first came out with us today, he fell out, just laid down in the netting and couldn't do no more. The men on each side of him, they closed together to get hold of the meshing that slacked away from him.

The set, it was in a serious way now. Anything happen. I started my own chantey, the one the mate sometimes move in with when it's time:

> *Captain, I got trouble on the water,*
> *So low down.*

They pulled.

> *Boys, will you please help me to raise 'em,*
> *Will you please help me to raise 'em*
> *All day long?*

Fitch been wheeling the *Moona Waa Togue* around behind us over to where Carib was. We got to draw the bunt to the side of the mother ship, hook it to beckets, and get the fish hardened in the bunt so we can brail them on board.

We could see the menhaden moiling at the top of the water. They whupped up a foam all over the inside of the circle, same kind of a foam as the tide will whup up when it beats into shore. That foam made the men feel good, even with all that sun and sweat—a foamy, snowy sight, multiplying, like money. Which it was.

The net, it's filled with fighting fish. They're addled in there, pushing against each other, suffocating and dying against each other. They die quick, die when they don't have enough water to swim in, die when they're shoved against each other. The hard meshes kill thousands. Still, there's so many that the most of them are still alive. You keep hardening them, closing in on them. Forcing the water out of the linen bars, packing them in tighter.

The big bag of fish moved away from the sun. The mate-boat men, they switched back into my boat, and we drew the bunt from the two boats again.

Not so much singing now. The men don't have too much strength left for that; still they'll haul together.

Sometimes you can feel the big ball of fish raising and lowering, like they may be moving in one direction or another, trying to work as one fish. Which they do.

"Harden'm! Harden'm!" Captain Crother yelled. "Fitch, get alongside!"

The big boat slid up by our small boats. Fitch, he worked and maneuvered up close to us.

Till we got the purse boats up against the mother ship, next to the fish hole.

Me and Carib, we jumped on board, tied the cork line to the beckets. The small boats closed against the big ship like a triangle, with the fish in the middle of the bunt, trapped between our small boats and the side of the *Moona Waa Togue*.

But you can't take the fish aboard yet. The net is full of water. You got to get the water out of the net, just have fish in the net, get it hard enough so you could about walk on top of the fish.

48

That's tons of weight, with just human hands and muscles to
hold it on two sides and the ship's lines to hold it on the third
angle. Maybe it could have been a quarter million fish in
there. Hard to tell when they lay in your bunt, because you
don't know how deep down they are. They're packed in the
bunt, dying or flipping, like hard, snowy cigars, like the pogy's
winter. But us fishermen got a saying, "Don't count your pogy
till you get them into dock."

There's a critical minute in menhaden fishing, in every haul
of it you make. It's when the fish are in that bunt hard enough
to brail, just at that instant, they'll show their spirit. Show you
the spirit in everything to stay alive or die trying. If you're not
looking for this, you'll get scared when it comes, and a crew
of bunt pullers better be ready for it all the time. Sometimes
the fish will act like they have some talk among themselves,
make a last try. They'll tremble the net and the water all over,
make no splash, but just tremble it all around. The bunt and
the fish be a big ball bobbing up and down in that triangle. If
you hold the net you can usually stop it then and there. But
sometimes maybe the fish are stronger, or the men more tired,
something else happens.

Like now.

Sounded as if the fish was a charge of dynamite.

They thundered.

A real explosion that nearly swamped both the small boats
and shook the big boat.

The blast, it split that net like it was tissue paper. Blew out
the bunt part, blew it to shreds, ripped the whole netting out
of the purse boats and split it up so that the sea was a mess of
tangled web, corks, and lines. The mesh flew out of the boats
in folds that you couldn't see unfold, in a balloon of split net-
work.

The *Moona Waa Togue,* she rocked like a swell hit her.

A big shower of water, thousands of gallons, it went up

twenty-thirty feet high, came down into the purse boats, threw most of the men overside.

The four-thousand-pound captain boat, with the winches, it swamped down in the water and swung back on its keel three fourths filled with water.

The fishermen, some hung onto the purse boats. Most made for the big ship, grabbed at lines, beckets, the guardrail. A few untangled themselves from split-up webbing.

The menhaden swarmed over the broken net, went in rushes off from the big ship, under it, all around it.

When the thunder comes it will kill off a great many fish, tons of them. But most, those that live, they sound. They know safety lies down under. Same as on land a trapped animal that may get away, it will run deep into brush or woods, so the menhaden sound to the sea below, away from the danger on top.

In a few minutes, by the time the fishermen got back into the purse boats and started bailing out the water, you couldn't see many live pogy around. Just the white bellies of the dead ones up to the sun. All their rainbowish colors, the yellow and the green and the red, it flies from their backs when they die, like it's their soul gone, and the most of what you get to see, it's nothing but their white bellies.

And that was our big set of the day.

You won't make another set in waters like that. Because live menhaden will go away from that spot. They'll stay away a day or two, till it's no more dead pogy floating around.

Little fish are more apt to thunder than the big ones. Maybe the young got more life in them.

Sometimes, if you feel a thunder coming, you can slack up your net a few feet, enough to absorb that shock. This time we never felt the signals coming. This was a bad thunder and it just about scared the crew. Wasn't the first time I've seen

bunt pullers frightened back onto the big boat by a bad thunder. Because you can't monkey with deep water and blasts,
you can be blown under water and smashed up against a boat.
Have known many a crew to see that tremble a-coming and
sense a big one and get so cautious about it they'll let the net
loose. Have seen thunders where the fish walked off with the
net, rigging, cork lines, rings, leads, and all, and sounded with
the whole caboodle. Went under and gone. Left nothing but
some lonely corks.

I stood in my mate boat, and me and the men in both boats,
and Fitch and the captain on the mother ship, we watched
the white sea around us. Till I laid down the net of my thinking in the Bible, because that's an ocean too, and in trouble us
menhadeners draw on it. I looked at Rev and I held out the
palms of my hands, where the bunt cut into my fingers like
wire, and I said to him, and whoever else that cared to hear,
how the Book say, "Upon my back have plowmen plowed;
they have drawn long their furrows." This time the plowmen
was the menhaden itself, they drew furrows in our hands, and
they done whupped us.

But the crew, they just cussed out the thundering school.
Found words I wouldn't much care to remember. And the
captain, he was stomping on the deck of the big ship, doing
the same thing, because a net costs five thousand dollars. A
captain and a crew don't like to lose a net any more than the
company do. A net ought to last two-three months and bring
in ten-eleven million fish before it gets used up.

Yet we just lost a new net. And I could just about picture
Merrick Thorpe, the way he going to take it when we go
down-coast twenty-five miles and dock at De Leon Beach.
See him coming down to the pier ready to jump on the captain
and us crew. Because he going to want to know the whole
story, just how it happen, and he'll be there holding out his

hands like *he's* pulling bunt, and say, "Why didn't you slack the net—like *that?*" And show us how he'd have stopped that thunder.

I sang out, hoping the crew would pick up and join me:

> *Captain, I got trouble on the wa-a-a-ter-r-r-r!*
> *Help me to raise the-e-em-m-m!*

And they did catch up on my singing.

While we put the purse boats back into the davits and they hauled Carib's dry boat back up on deck, the bunt pullers strung out over the deck getting ready to go home (because you can't catch menhaden without a net), and they started a chantey.

But the *wrong* song.

They started to singing of Eveleaner.

Eveleaner, the men sing about her when they got a rough. Eveleaner, she ain't the sweet woman the pogy fishermen sing about. The sweet girl, the girl back on shore, she's Lulu. They'll sing about Lulu when it's all going good and they're bringing in a net of fish. But this was Eveleaner. She's the woman that mean trouble to the men and they mean trouble to her. I wouldn't know where the songs of Eveleaner come from. Maybe once some woman went on board a menhadener for a day or a season and her name was Eveleaner. Maybe the men fished her up out of the sea to wash their troubles on her. Eveleaner, she's the woman they sing about when it's gone wrong on board and nobody rightly knows what's next.

> *Oh, Eveleaner, the poor gal taken sick*
> *On the water,*
> *Oh, Eveleaner, the poor gal taken sick*
> *On the water.*

The men just singing their weariness now, their want to go back to port.

The poor child died,
*   O Lord, the poor child died.*
*   I'm so glad the poor child had religion,*
Oh, when she died,
O Lord, when she died.

The Eveleaner song got some other verses, very rough, and the right situation among the men, that'll bring them out.

Captain Crother, he knew that song, knew the men's mood.

He went up to the steward's deck, yelled in at Fitch so the whole deck could hear it: *"Fitch, old boy, take us home! Take us home, old boy!"*

I SENT the green man aft for the thromping horn. The green man, we called him Mister Grass, he went to Stovely, the white engineer down in the engine room, and said, "The mate sent me for the thromping horn."

The engineer, he looked up at the new man like it was a mighty serious matter and he said, "Did the mate tell you *I* had the thromping horn?"

"Yessir," said Mister Grass. "He sent me to *you*. You must have the thromping horn."

The engineer, he wouldn't overlook no chance to have a little fun with a new man in the crew. "I had the thromping horn yesterday, but somebody took it from me after we bungled that last set. Why don't you try the cook? Sometimes the cook keeps the thromping horn right there in the galley with him so it won't get wet."

Mister Grass, he went topside and started walking toward the galley. Everybody watched him because I let everybody know Mister Grass been sent for the thromping horn. Mister Grass didn't feel good in the guts. Ever since he came on board, even in yesterday's calm, the sea rolled up to his ears. He was dizzy in the wrong places; he just wasn't clear, and I thought it best to keep him busy. At first there ain't nothing you can do with a green man but put him through the wringer and see what he's made of and whether he's going to make a fisherman.

It was pitiful to see him walk, trying to keep in the roll of the ship. He only been with us a couple days, and today we was having a spell of rough water. We moved south along the coast in sea that was thirty to forty feet deep, headed for the Mayport vicinity. Not quite as hot as yesterday. A steady easter washed good-sized waves under us every minute or two, and the *Moona Waa Togue* got plenty slaps in her windward side. Nothing to worry about, but rough on a new man like Mister Grass.

It was no sign of fish. I was on deck and figured it was time the men had something to take their mind. Mister Grass had such a sorry look in his eyes; he kept rocking and saying to whoever he went by, "Oh, I wished I'd stayed to the hill. Oh, I wished I'd have tried to find work at the paper mill instead of to come out here. The Lord didn't give *me* no fins and a tail."

He got to the galley, poked his head into where the cook was busy. Cooking Devil, he was a rolly, fat man, like he ate his own cooking and liked it. He would stare you straight in the eye and tell you how good he was. "I don't dread nobody making a biscuit. I don't dread nobody in the cookbook." Mister Grass just about got sick looking at all that food; he didn't waste no time. "I want the thromping horn!"

"Who sent you?" Cooking Devil asked.

"Engineer sent me."

"Who-all sent you to the engineer?"

"The mate."

"Do the mate want the thromping horn or do the captain want it?"

"I don't know. Only the mate sent me for it. I guess he wants it."

The cook let his face drop serious. He wiped his hands on his white apron to give better attention to this situation. "I don't know why they always sending you green men to me for the thromping horn. I don't keep an important thing like that in the galley. What *I* would want with the thromping horn? I don't do none of the fishing!"

"The engineer said you had it!" The green man was just about trembling. He wanted to do his work right and he wanted to carry out orders. He didn't mean no harm to anybody. Just wanted to be the right kind of fisherman.

The cook lifted his voice high as he would a skillet to hang on his wall. "You just tell that engineer *I* don't have the thromping horn. The ring setter *always* keep the thromping horn. He's the one that uses it. Go to Mister Blu, the ring setter."

He found Blu up in the bow, hanging over the forward rail, looking straight down the Florida coast. Blu asked Grass who he been to so far. The green man said he had been to the engineer and the cook, and neither of them had it. Then Blu said, "Man, do you know what the thromping horn is?"

No, he didn't.

"Yet you will go and get something you don't know what it is. How do you expect to learn about fishing and the boat and the ocean when you do things that you don't know what you're doing?"

"What *is* the thromping horn?"

"The thromping horn is used to call in the fish!"

"*No!*"

"Yes! It ain't used often, but when the red line ain't showed for many days they get out the thromping horn and try to thromp in the fish with it."

"How?"

"They just blows on that horn and the menhaden hear it."

"Blow on a horn!"

"Yes, real loud. The fish sometimes comes in by the horn. Like a duck to a decoy, or like when a hunter gives the sound of a doe and a buck comes running up to get himself shot. The thromping horn is magic with the pogy."

"Well, you got it? The mate want it. He just must want to blow on it right now."

Blu made out he was exasperated with the man's ignorance. "Hell no, the mate don't blow on it. The dry-boat man, he's the only one that's *allowed* to use it. You got to go up in the crow's-nest and see him and ask him for it."

"Oh no, Mister Blu. I can't climb that ladder!"

"You *got* to climb that ratline! Ain't no other way to get to the hawk's-nest! Who sent you?"

"The mate."

"Well, see here, you on a menhaden fishing boat, Mister Grass. You got to follow mate's orders. You best get going."

And don't you know, Mister Grass started to going up that sixty-foot-high rope ratline. Step by step he went up; rung by rung, with the boat swaying like Grandpa's chair. Mister Grass got way up. Toward the top you could see him hanging onto each rope rung like it was his thread to life. Which it was.

Everybody stopped what they was doing, looked up, and hoped he wouldn't fall and kill himself.

Men with a little experience get a good strong feeling of power over against someone that is new to something; so green men have some rough minutes on menhaden boats. I seen one man sent to grease an anchor so it would slide overboard easier. He greased the anchor so good the captain said he was the best anchor greaser on the Atlantic coast. Saw another man run all over a boat to get the keelson key. "Hurry, we got to turn the keelson around," they told him. The keelson is a ridge on the bottom of the boat; nothing you can do with that or have to do with it. Sometimes a crew will take a new man and say, "You been to the anteroom?" Of course he hasn't. And the anteroom is anywhere they start on him. They may make him sing. If he don't do it in good spirit they may paddle him. If he does it like a man they say, "You okay, you'll make it." Poor Mister Grass, he was getting as good a boat-breaking as I ever saw.

The cook came out from the galley; the engineer, he peeped out from the door of the engine house; the bunt pullers down by the fish hole stopped what they was doing; and the pilot even got away from his wheel for a few seconds while he stuck his head out of the pilothouse and corkscrewed his neck around, looking up there at poor Mister Grass.

Toward the last five or six rungs, it looked real bad. You could see the whole ratline trembling with his nerves. Up above, in the hawk's-nest, Captain Crother and Carib looked down at him.

Captain Crother said, "What you want up here?"

"The mate want the thromping horn. They say the dry-boat man got it."

The dry-boat man wasn't going to be the man to break the spell. He stuck his head out from the trap door in the floor of the hawk's-nest. We could see his face sticking through the door. He said, "It must be some mistake. I gave the thromping horn to the mate this morning. You go back to the mate and remind him I gave him it."

You should see Mister Grass come down that rope. Each time he put his foot on the rung below him, his foot felt for the rope blind, like a fisherman who is playing with a fish twenty feet below water and trying to find the fish's mouth.

The laughing went like waves from stem to stern. It rolled over the boat like a sea wash.

Mister Grass came trembling before me till I said, "Don't tell me you coming back to me without no thromping horn."

"The dry-boat man said he gave it to you."

Just then a look came into Mister Grass's eyes like he knew something was wrong and *he* was what was wrong.

"Mister Grass," I said, "you have done learned the first lesson in pogy fishing. The thromping horn is something the whole menhaden industry is looking for and ain't yet found. When the time comes they can bring in fish with a thromping horn, they won't need you nor me neither. All they'll need is a place to put the fish. Now you go and lay down because you done your trick like a good fisherman."

Ten o'clock. The sun raised like an ax, but not high enough yet to chop down on us. No sign of fish, and the east wind not helping any. The wind we want around here is the southwester; it blows off the beach, makes it easier for the boat to stay in toward the coast, and if there's fish around they won't work in to shore so much.

I joined the captain and Carib in the crow's-nest. Sat on the seaward side, looked off that way for the red line. The ship dieseled along at ten miles an hour. That's as fast as she'd go. If we had a load of fish, that might slow her up to seven or eight. On menhaden boats we don't measure by knots, but miles. And because we fish in close to shore we mostly measure depth in feet instead of fathoms.

Everything on a pogy boat, it's not fish and fishermen. This time of year everything comes to the boat to get a little something to eat. Mosquitoes will be there all the time. You take them on board at the dock and they go out to sea with you.

They'll even get into your purse boats and bother you while you making a set. At night, if you stay out, they waiting for you down in the forepeak.

All kinds of flying things go right out on the water with us. Especially houseflies. They're around wherever there's fish— at the fish factory, at the fish stores in De Leon Beach, along the railroad yards, all over the river edge where the boats dock—and they have a ball dancing on the edge of the fish hole of the boat. Flies and fish go together closer than two ends of a sandwich. Plenty of flies been ground up for meal and oil too.

Bull ants, dark red-looking ants, but some good-sized black ones too, will crawl from the docks over the ramp, or across the ropes onto the ship.

Life draws life. If man catches fish, most other animals and all that flies, swims, walks, crawls is going to be willing to get close to fish too. Man competes with most everything that flies, crawls, and runs, for the catch of the sea. Roaches, those flying roaches that get into most parts of the South this time of year, some get into the menhaden boats, got to take a cruise. They're one-two inches long, they'll fly around your head, land with a snap on your arm. We used to have chinches, a small biter that got into our bedclothes. In recent years we been getting at a lot of that vermin with Gulf spread; that's an insect spray; kills off most of it. But that small life comes back, multiplies, and you got to keep spraying. When the time comes for me to set the crew to work with the exterminator I yell out, "Grab that Gulf spread. Hit the forepeak. Break the sixth commandment!"

Bats on this boat too. All of a sudden they'll fly out of the rigging. They found a way to get inside the hull somewhere. Maybe old menhadeners like ours, with rotted, dead, soaked wood in all her parts, attract all that. Some pogy boats, like the *Moona Waa Togue,* they set off from shore, they got as many animals and insects on them, in pairs—and in hundreds of pairs—as the Ark in the Bible.

For company and for luck we got a dog, Jubilee, and the cat we call Hester. They get along good, just stay away from each other. Hester, she's a big cat, colored gray like a mouse, and her eyes light green as the sea out there now. All day she's licking her chops because she has all the rats she wants. This ship is her paradise, so full of graycoats down there in the bilge. Hester sleeps during the day, and at night she marches.

The rats know she's on board, but they got to come out for food and take their chances like all of us. They'll go for the fish particles that stay in the creases of the fish hole, or find a fish that ain't been swept away, or even get into the galley. Then Hester picks them off, maybe four or five a night till she's got her fill. You can hear the rat squeal sometimes when Hester gets it; then he wish he'd never left the hill. Sometimes she has so many she'll kill them for fun, after she's eat her full; and in the morning you'll see one or two on deck that Hester has left around.

Put the lights out at night, they'll come squealing out, six inches to a foot long. So bad we have to set traps for them; only the rats, they're extraordinary, and all but eat the traps.

I have been on menhadeners where the rats were so bad that they ate the salt and grease and cut holes in the wood; and one once cut a hole in the bottom of a ship and helped fill the boat with water so deep we had to pump it out.

Rat snakes, once in a while they'll crawl on deck from the dock; they'll go for the rats on board a boat better than a cat will. But the men don't like to have that kind of company; if they catch a rat snake they'll see how far overboard they can throw him. You'll see a rat snake once in a while curled up there like a hunk of rope—but I never saw any man mistake it for part of the ship's rigging. It's not the commonest thing on a pogy boat, it's just that you will see it.

I have been down in the fish hole while they brailed pogy from the net into the hole. My job it was to pick up any food fish that would be webbed in and keep that out separate. Once I saw some kind of snake laying there on top of the fish, maybe a water snake, maybe an eel, maybe harmless for all I know. When he saw me he didn't know how frightened I was; he showed me he was more frightened. He dived down into the small fish, went under them like they were earth and he was a worm. I tried to get out of there, but I was knee-deep in fish and my legs were bogged down in that fish suction and water. Tried to make it to the ladder. Mister Snake came out from under the fish toward me. I set up a holler they could hear on the hill. I pulled out my dirk, cut at that snake's head till that thing vanished again down into these fish. I rushed to the ladder, got up out of that fish hole, and cussed off my fright. They made meal and oil out of that snake.

Most menhaden boats will carry an animal or two on them. Plenty carry chickens, hogs. The men want things like that for company. Most of the crew, they come from farms or small towns, a few may have a little earth in back of their houses, and they will bring something on board from what they own. The *Moona Waa Togue* has a small pen on the starboard deck, by the bridge. Just a few square feet. The men wash up the space in and around the pen, keep it clean, feed scraps to the pig, and watch her grow. When she gets big and before the season is out, we'll eat her. The men call the hog Ready Yet, because whenever they talk of her they ask, "Is she ready yet?" I've known boats to have raccoon and possum on them. The raccoon is a very clean animal, washes everything it eats. The raccoon on the *Moona Waa Togue* travels around the deck with the men. At night we shut him up so nobody will grab him and eat him, because he's good eating as well as good company.

Because of all that life on the boat, but mostly the fish smell,

65

birds follow us. Pelican, kingfisher, gannet, ducks, geese; and sometimes land birds will swoop way out from the hill, curve by us, and go back to the shore.

We like to see them. A bird means something over the water even when it may mean nothing. It can be going as hungry as us. The bird thinks the boat is over fish, and we think the bird is over fish. Many a time a kingfisher dives down and comes up with nothing but a drink of salt water; more often with that than with a fish. Plenty kingfishers by this coast line this time of year; little black body, kind of bluish-looking, a white breast and white ring around his neck. Stays close to shore, goes for small fish.

The seacoast, it has its own bird troops. The pelican, he's the king of birds that follow menhaden boats hereabouts. There's brown and white ones; both with long bills big enough to hold a kettle of water—or fish. The white ones spread six-seven feet sometimes. Pelican make a big splash when they hit the water; don't go in smooth like the gannet or the king-fisher, but they get the fish. They'll fly low, very patient, a long stretch over the coast waters, hide behind rollers, come up behind the fish when the roller breaks, let the sea foam act like a curtain to go before them, then strike down smart and pick up a whiting or a perch.

On the Florida and Georgia beaches you'll see little fast-moving birds we call maggot eaters; call them sandpipers, call them phalarope. They move on spindly legs so fast that the first time you see them they may look like big spiders walking. They eat the skim that floats into shore, like the menhaden eats the skim offshore. Ducks will get close to our nets, tangle in the webbing. Duck is good eating, and if there is time the captain will shoot him and bring him to the Cooking Devil. Sometimes we steer the big boat into the marshes and sounds; in there see big, pretty white swans, long necks all a-curve. If you get in that close you're apt to see a hundred kinds of birds. Most of these won't get out of the sounds into the open sea.

The pelican, gannet, gull, and kingfisher watch us make a set, take just as much interest in it as the captain. When they see the net come up and thousands of fish flip all over the surface, they get all excited, make a lot of noise. They'll settle on the cork line, bob up and down, whistle, sing, and hawk till they can dive in and get a little something. Sometimes the birds fly around the nets more like an insect swarm. You can hear them jabbering, screeching, maybe thinking, "Look what the big bird that sits on the water going to take home."

What those sea birds like is when we foul up a set. If we have to let fish loose, or they get out somehow after they been packed in close, thousands of them die very fast. Then the birds whop down on them, pick them off; that's when you learn so many birds are first cousins to vultures.

The last use of the birds, they become a name for the captain when the crew is below and beefing. "Old Pelican Crothers done this or that," or, "Captain Gannet think he's taking us out thirty miles today, but we ain't going to let him."

A lone gannet went around us now forty or fifty yards away, circled the crow's-nest.

Captain Crother had a .22-caliber automatic pistol that would shoot sixteen times. A German-make gun with a barrel eight inches long. Captain, he was a crack shot and he liked to shoot sea gulls from his perch in the hawk's-nest. Or a shark if he saw one trapped in the menhaden net. He could knock off a half dozen gulls flying in a column fifty or sixty yards away and never miss. The men don't like to hear the captain doing all that shooting. They don't like it that there's a rifle in a rack in the captain's quarters either, but there is one on most or all menhaden ships.

The captain was bored looking for a red line that didn't show. "How far you think that gannet is from here?" he asked.

I guessed fifty yards.

The bird went in a steady circle round and round the mast, lassoing the captain's nerves.

If a gannet come down out of the sky fast and hard, it looks like a long white bullet when he hits the water. Goes down ten or fifteen feet, comes up with a fish. You can hear his b-r-r—r—r-p when he shoots past the boat. The gannet is one of our pilots. Sometimes you'll see a fleet of a hundred gannet spinning down at the water. Head there then because they may be working on a school of menhaden.

"That bird looking for trouble," the captain said.

The bird was looking for fish; it knew that fish and pogy boats go together. The bird dipped down and looked into the fish hole.

"He's a big one, ain't he?" the captain said. "Bet I couldn't miss him if I shot him by looking over my shoulder."

"You couldn't do that," the striker-boat man said. He wanted to see the captain use his gun once that way.

Captain worked himself up. "I can't see the sea for that damned bird!" He nudged the pistol in his holster. Very anxious to do business with the gannet.

The gannet came in close and looked straight at the captain. That's where he made a mistake.

Captain Crother said, "I catch this fellow right in the head." And aimed his gun.

A gannet's head flying forty yards away is a small target, but the captain, he just traced his gun in a curve along the gannet's trail and hit the bird right as he said he would.

The fowl behaved like a slow-going helicopter; kind of stopped in the air and flopped over. Then fell in a glide down toward the deck, landed on top of the pilothouse.

The crewmen ran up by the dead bird. It looked much bigger laying out there in its full wingspread than flying around; about six feet from tip to tip. A long pointed beak, yellowish head and neck, white underneath, and white and brown feathers; webbed feet like a duck.

"Call the Cooking Devil," somebody yelled. "Captain got us a real fine gannet!"

The cook came out to see the catch. McNally said, "I cook him for the noon meal if you say so, but he's tough meat and you men got to pluck out all his feathers."

Two or three bunt pullers plucked the gannet till it looked white-skinned like some fowl you might buy in a poultry store. They gave it to the cook to cut up and boil down; and old gannet went to pot.

The cook clanged his iron at noon to come get lunch. We in the crow's-nest just about fell down the mast to get to the dinner table first. As I got on deck I saw Mister Grass come up out of the forepeak. He been laying down in his bunk in all that dark and swelter, trying to get himself straight. Maybe he wasn't too sick to come eat; anyway, somebody called him, and when he stuck his head out the hatch he said to me quiet, like a schoolboy that raise his hand to ask the teacher can he go, "Mister Mate, where is the toilet?"

I didn't want to tell him the whole story. Let him find out for himself; a mate can't take care of everything. "It's stern-wise."

"Mister Mate, which way is sternwise?"

I pointed aft. "Right straight down deck. You go straight to the end. That's the toilet."

The crew hadn't gone into the galley yet. Blu said, "This going to be good. He wants the toilet. I'm following right down behind to see whether he finds it."

Blu trailed about ten feet behind Mister Grass. Went on tiptoe and carried a coil of rope to look busy.

At the stern Grass looked around for the toilet. He peeked down the staircase of the engine room. He yelled at Stovely,

"Is the toilet down there?" That's what he called it, the toilet; had good upbringing.

The engineer hollered back, "Hell no! What's the matter with you?" He was real mad about it.

Mister Grass looked like a lost kitten. Which he was.

The ring setter kept very busy right nearby, made out he was knotting a rope, and looked over on the water. In fact, everybody was watching, and didn't nobody go in even when the cook clanged his iron a second time and began cussing.

Three or four edged down by Blu to see the fun.

Most of the crew worked down aft, whistling, eyeballing at the sea, and closing around.

Mister Grass turned to Blu, who was making a very important knot in a rope connected with nothing, and said, "Mister Blu, can you-all tell me where is the toilet?"

"Right there," Blu said. But he pointed over *behind* the boat.

"That's the *water!*" Mister Grass said. His hands were on the rail and he looked down at the sea foaming up by the buttock of the ship.

"*That's* the toilet too," Blu said.

"What you mean *that's* the toilet?"

"On a pogy boat *that's* the toilet!"

Mister Grass looked over the water very uncertain. It could have been eight fathoms there. "How am I going to do it?"

"Like you always do. Here, let me show you."

In a second Blu swung over the backboard of the boat. There is a rope line which you stand inside, like a window cleaner that has a leather strap around him while he leans out over the street, cleaning the outside of a window. Blu slipped right into that line. He put both his fists over the toprail, hung on sharp, and rested his feet on the guardrail. The guardrail is about even with the deck on the outside of the stern.

Then Blu leaned back in that position, the position of driving a chariot, and he said to Grass, who was staring at him in the mightiest of surprise, "Get it?"

"Oh, Mister Blu. That's *dangerous!* I can't do that!"

"Well, the rules of menhaden fishing don't allow you to do it on deck, in the fish hole, in the forepeak, or anyplace else. You got to do it *over the stern*—in this *line!*"

"Why didn't they tell me they don't have a men's room on the boat?"

"And no ladies' room neither," Blu told him.

Blu was smiling like a satisfied pelican. He jumped back on deck and said, "Now let's see you do it."

Mister Grass hesitated. Something he wanted to know. "Do the captain do it this way too?"

"Sure! He got the same ass you and I got even if he is white." The captain was in the galley waiting for the crew so he could eat.

Mister Grass had big eyes to begin with. Now they was round and even bigger. "Ain't the captain got no private men's toilet bowl in his quarters? I thought the captain was well take care of."

Blu told him the one where if you want to keep a man down in the gutter you got to get down there with him. "So the captain, he's down in this gutter with us. Only he makes fifteen or twenty thousand dollars a year and us bunt pullers don't."

Mister Grass wasn't too green and wasn't too seasick. "For twenty thousand a year I'd do it from the hawk's-nest!"

Mister Grass looked around modest, like he didn't want the crew to see him. He been used to going to a two-holer in private all his life and didn't want to be a spectacle. Some turned their heads away. A few started for the galley.

Mister Grass climbed over the stern and put his feet on the guardrail. He held onto the gunwale for dear life.

He was using the line like an old-timer, like they do on most pogy boats.

71

I know just what he was feeling. The water from that propeller whupped up a regular white foam on his bottom and made him as clean as his mother made him when he was a baby.

A few years ago it looked like the *Moona Waa Togue* was catching up with the twentieth century. The ship fell into the hands of a Delaware captain for one season. He didn't like to hang out over the stern in a line and agreed to take the boat if they put in a modern toilet. The company spent six hundred dollars on it, set up a nice clean toilet right behind my mate quarters, and that whole season the men used it.

But the next year Captain Crother took over this ship. He looked at that toilet as if he was looking at a space ship, and it was all so new and different this world might be coming to an end and he might be going to another. He told the shipowners, "This the only menhaden boat in De Leon with an enamel seat on board. This going to give them damn crews bad ideas. Next thing you know they'll want toilet paper in different colors." He wouldn't take the ship 'less they took out that toilet, which they did; so we all sitting over the line again these days like they did way back in the olden time.

Saw one man get drowned falling off the back of a boat from using that line. Before he got inside the rope some men in the purse boat had tossed a food fish toward the deck and it fell on the guardrail, where they will land sometimes. This fisherman put his foot on that fish, slipped off the stern, went under. Vibration of the propeller, or the sucking of it, probably shocked the air out of him. He never came up.

Rev said grace. He sat near the head of the table, his head bowed over macaroni and fresh pork. The smell came into his nose, everybody's nose. Because the Cooking Devil sure knew how to make up pork. Plenty of boiled potatoes steamed up from a big tin bowl in the middle of the table. All had itchy elbows, couldn't hardly keep their arms quiet waiting for Rev to finish. "Kind Lord, make us thankful for what we are about to receive. . . ."

Just then a couple of the bunt pullers raised their heads, got ready to pitch into the food. Rev looked at them from underneath his bowed head, and they stopped.

"Thanks to Thee, Lord, for this fine food, though we . . ."

More of that tinware tinkled somewhere else down the board, and Rev raised his voice like the boat raises up on a wave, *"Though we not getting any fish out of Your bountiful ocean."*

Rev looked down to where that last sound came from.

The cook, he stood beside the mast. He held a platter of vegetables in his hands, waited for Rev to finish. The mast, more than a foot thick, it ran through the galley; it was between the table and the stove; and the cook was always bumping into it. He was facing us. The stove that burned with fuel oil was behind him. The whole kitchen was about twenty feet long and ten feet across. The table we sat at, it ran about fifteen feet, with a wooden bench on each side. Port windows on both sides let in light. Life preservers, ten of them for the whole crew, were stacked into racks in the rear of the galley at the ceiling. Tin drinking cups hung in a line on hooks centered in the roof just over the table, and three overhead lights were spaced along the galley but weren't on now. It was all kind of gray in there, but the Rev, he was busy shedding light.

"Thanks, Lord, to him who work so hard all morning in the galley for us crew. . . ."

"Come on, Rev, that's enough!"

Not that the crew lacked religion and appreciation, but they was hungry. They don't like it when a sheep get out of the pasture. Rev needed to be fenced in. Besides, the potato smell was even better than the pork smell because the cook got a special way of steaming potatoes so that the steam comes out in the open at the very last minute before they're ready to be eaten.

Could be Rev was inspired thinking how good that boiled gannet was going to be, he talked sharp: "Now I ain't finished grace. And I don't want nobody to get started before I finish giving the Lord thanks. Because we catching no fish, *that's* the time to be grateful we got food!"

He started again, "So, Lord Jesus, whose spirit is above this ship, we thank Thee ever so much from our . . ."

"Aw hell!" Somebody said that and went right at his plate with more strength than he pulled bunt.

Somebody else took up for Rev. *"Give the man the chance to say what he got to say!"*

"I ain't got much more," Rev said, trying to hang onto his glory as long as he could. "Not much more."

"We hungry! We believe you. We know the Lord's good!"

Rev picked up from that. "I just want to say, Lord, Thy bounty is above all . . ."

The dishes clattered almost as bad as if they'd fallen to the floor. The potatoes were almost gone from the big bowl in the middle of the table, and the Rev himself was reaching.

Cooking Devil didn't wait no more for Rev's holy words. He was busy talking, like always, about his good cooking. "Now I got good hot biscuits coming," and they would be good, too. "Anybody wants their coffee now, I might could pour up some here and there."

But the cook, he got out of his tether when he said that. Captain Crother said no, don't serve it now, let the coffee kettle stay on the floor where it usually rested till the end of the meal, because we was rolling a little and somebody might get scalded if coffee was by their plates.

Captain Crother, when he first got here and saw there was

no partition in the galley for white, he built a wooden panel in the galley to hide himself behind when mealtime come. The bunt pullers got word to Merrick Thorpe that the new captain was building himself a white wall. Thorpe called in the captain and said, "What's this I hear you building up a wall there in the galley?" The captain passed a bad remark, said he didn't eat with such. Thorpe said, "You tear down that partition or we tear up your contract. You works for *me*, you eats with *them!* That's the way we do it here!" Captain Crother wanted to know why. Thorpe told him that colored crews had walked out on him before because of Virginia captains wanting to eat separate, and he was finished with that. "I got to catch *fish*, that's my business, *fish*," Thorpe said. Crother went from the owner's office straight out on the floating property and tore down that partition himself. He must have sure needed the job. He been eating with us since. I don't know what he thinks, but he's got a mighty appetite.

The cook bragged about some "damn fine sweet-potato pie coming." He said, "Rev, you best get busy on that nice piece of meat there." He helped Rev to get his plate full because he felt good that Rev had praised him in his prayer. While the cook moved around he kept promising the gannet would be served at the last. "You can just let your mouths start to water for that gannet," the cook said. "I never had so much success in my life with any bird."

When somebody praised him for the macaroni he spoke right up. "I know it's a good macaroni. I know it as good as one-two-three. My mom, I used to see her make a macaroni. She put just certain flavorings in it and showed me when to take it off and how long to cool it before you best eat it. I don't dread nobody making a macaroni!"

Somebody backed up the cook. "Yessir, he don't have to be afraid of nobody making a macaroni! We got us a cook this season!"

The reason for all that excitement over Cooking Devil, it was because sometimes you can get a bad cook and be stuck with him a whole season. In some parts of the fishery the poor eating is a fighting matter.

You can get a cook so poor you think he's deliberately evil and he's in there trying to figure out new ways of putting up good food bad.

Just last season we had such a cook and all had to go to Captain Crother together and tell him he either get us a new cook or get himself a new crew. The captain had to ask that cook how it happen he served us beans twice in a day. That cook answered that his beans had special flavor to them; it was a good strong food and it would keep a crew strong. The captain had to pay him off. He went and hired McNally, and we had McNally for cook the late part of last season and all this season so far.

Sometimes when we made a set and had some fish in the hold Cooking Devil would come take a look in there and say to the crew, "Now you keep your eye out for a good drum. I bake a fine drum." Or some other fish he'd talk about. If the men found a few food fish in there among the menhaden, they'd bring it in to the cook and we'd have us a fine fish plate on top of anything else he planned. In fact, that eating problem is so serious on menhaden boats that I have known crews to sit and talk for two hours about the cooking they had, good and bad, all up and down the coast.

The men can afford to be a little particular about their food because they buy it themselves and bring it on board. The cook will go to the store with some of the men, grub up the boat. Each man puts up about twelve dollars every two weeks. That comes out of his earnings. You go to any store at De Leon Beach, tell them you work on a menhaden boat. Grocer gives *you* a ticket, and *he* keeps a ticket for a record, and sends the bill to the company. The company watch that very close, take it out of your pay. If you ain't catching fish, that bill will pile up. That way we got debt fishing, like sharecropping. You can be eating on the boat and your family on the hill be going meager. Takes about three hundred dollars to feed the whole crew for two weeks. That's why, with food money coming out of the crew's own pocket, they will get impatient sometimes and say at the captain, "Captain, can't you guess better where them fish hiding?"

Cooking Devil, he was serving up corn bread, two pans of it, thirty-six muffins to a pan, and everybody was drinking their coffee and saying, "We want that gannet for dessert." They talked about the fine coffee the cook made. He boiled water in a big two-gallon kettle and put the coffee right into the boiling water. The grounds simmered to the bottom; you get a good strong cup that way. Cook held up his hands—they was very big—and he said, "There's the secret of my coffee. Them hands hold big handfuls of coffee. It takes *lots* of coffee to make *good* coffee."

"How about that piece of gannet for dessert?"

"Now I'm going to bring you the gannet," the cook said. "They ain't going to be but a small piece for each one of you. Just a tongue's bit so you know what a gannet taste like."

Then the cook started to laugh. He was such a wonderful-nature man anyway that when he start to laugh you got to laugh with him no matter what he's laughing at. Besides, a cook may be more important on a menhaden boat than even the mate.

He carried this boiled bird over his shoulder like he would a sack of potatoes. The fowl looked like a long white arm with a big round bunch in the middle. Cooking Devil must have known it wasn't going to be easy making this gannet taste like something, and he just tossed it in his kettle and let her boil. He whammed the bird down on the table so her balled-up middle made a noise powerful enough to split the boards.

"I got you-all a new tom weight," he said.

Everybody just jumped from the concussion on the table. Cooking Devil said, "Captain Crother done caught a bird most as tough as himself!"

He looked at the captain, gave out with a laugh that vibrated the galley like the engine vibrated the stern; made the captain wrinkle a half laugh.

And in fact it wasn't a soul that didn't have himself a split gut over the Cooking Devil's fouled-up fowl and the odd way he preached the gannet's funeral.

On deck we knew the time of day by the white cap of the sun setting straight on our heads. Temperature might have been about ninety-five degrees right then. Had been around a hundred and five yesterday at this same time.

Captain Crother and me headed for his quarters to use the radio. A plane flew over the ship, had been flying about for a half hour.

The captain cussed out "them damned Beaufort fishermen." Reports been coming to De Leon all year that they was using planes to spot menhaden up around the Beaufort-Morehead fishery in North Carolina. The captain honked out a very disgusted pheu-f-f-f and said, "Hawk's-nest ain't good enough for Henley no more. Henley won't be satisfied till he finds the thromping horn." Henley was the big man in the menhaden business, always looking for new and faster ways to catch fish. He had bought up more than a hundred menhaden ships and owned a dozen fish factories along the coast. He was the first man to have his captains use fathometers to spot fish under water when you couldn't see them near the surface. Now he had planes going over coast waters, with the pilots radioing the captains on the ships right where the fish were. At least in smooth weather the planes could spot them.

So the boss of our plant at De Leon, he thought we best try

it since the fishing was so poor lately. He hired out this local man that had a tissue-winged one-motor plane. Today this pilot was running up and down the Florida coast looking at the water from five hundred feet up. He had been in our hawk's-nest a couple of times, long enough to get an idea what a menhaden smear looked like on the surface.

Till now the radio been used just for ship to shore. The radio was on a stand next to the captain's bunk, in his quarters.

The man in the plane said, "It's fish or something a half mile to your lee."

Captain Crother: "Fish or a sand bar? How you know it's fish?"

The aviator: "A sand bar don't move."

The captain: "What shape is it?"

Aviator: "Like a bird's wings, but it stretches a hundred yards across, seem to be going inshore."

Captain: "If that was pogy it ought to be round, or bunched like a diamond. Bird-wing shape don't sound right to me."

Aviator: "All I know it's big, it's moving, and it's changing shape too."

Captain: "You could be seeing the reflection of a cloud."

Aviator: "You see any cloud above me?"

There wasn't a cloud in the sky. Captain Crother said, "I'll tell my striker-boat man. Let's see what he say."

Captain Crother went out on the bridge and yelled at Carib up in the nest. *"Plane say it's fish a half mile to lee. You see something?"*

Carib saw nothing. He called down, "I think you wasting your time if you go there."

Back at the radio the captain said, "My striker-boat man up there, he don't see nothing."

Man in the plane, he swooped right over the boat. "Why don't you send your dry-boat man out? I'll fly over the spot."

Captain answered, "I think you crazy, I think they ain't no

fish, and I think they's crazy up in Beaufort, but I'm steering the big boat over where you say and putting out the dry-boat man."

Captain Crother gave orders. Fitch turned shoreward and pulled the trip at his side that signaled the engineer to step up the governor.

Man in the plane, he flew over the bird-wing-shaped patch in the water, went up a thousand feet high. Circled a few times till we came up close. Still we didn't see nothing.

What it was, the aviator could see *below* the water, from five to sixty feet under the surface. He could spot movement down there that we *never* could see from the hawk's-nest. When we was right over the school he said, "Now you right on it."

Captain at the radio said, "I don't see a goddamn thing from here. My dry-boat man don't see nothing from the nest either. No color, no whupping, nothing!" He let out with his disgusted pheuffings.

We didn't see nothing because the fish were down deep.

But by our big boat being over this mass of fish, our engine must have frightened them. Some came to the top and flipped around like thousands of drumsticks on a bubbling drum.

It nearly drove the captain wild.

He had learned something. We all learned something. That was the first time we ever got help from a plane, and there wasn't no question about it. Matter of fact, it was remarkable the plane pilot saw them, because the surface was a little rough and when it's rough plane-spotting isn't much help in menhaden fishing. But by it being broad noonlight and clean, deep water, he had brought us over fish that sprawled lazyish all around.

Captain Crother ordered the Diesel shut so as not to shock off the menhaden. That engine action can lose you a catch of fish. You can control that but can't control what's going on

below water. All day, all night long, all up and down the
Atlantic coast and in the Gulf, each summer, it's a war that
goes on under water. While the menhaden move in swarms
and eat the skim, or plankton, and grow each instant, the
shark, whale, bluefish, tarpon, and even smaller fish like
pompano, mullet, and flounder, they all smash into those
moving fish cities, feed and forage. Menhaden, they call it the
natural feed of all other fish, natural fodder. Menhaden grinds
up the plankton; the other fish grind up the menhaden. Deal
of the sea.

The crew manned the purse boats. While the small boats
separated and the mesh sank in about thirty-five feet of water,
the big fish were down there tearing holes in that solid pack
of pogy. No way to tell from the top just what kind of fish may
be working on the menhaden. Sometimes it's shark, sometimes
bluefish, sometimes all kinds of fish be gnawing at the menhaden. Practically always that's going on, mostly bluefish
cutting up the menhaden mass, using it like people cut up
herds of cows, like cows cut up fields of alfalfa.

They never took a moving picture of that war on the menhaden, but if they did, it would show hundreds, maybe thousands, of bluefish flashing in like swords on the menhaden
school. Coming in with their mouths open and tack-pointed
teeth tearing the small fish apart. Bluefish, that's the big
enemy of the menhaden. The bluefish is all tooth and knife
when he shoots into the pogy. Kills and eats some, kills others
just for killing. Eats on them and eats on them; moves out of
the school long enough to rest; then knifes back in again. The
bluefish is a long, sleek fish, dagger of the sea; if he was as
big as a shark he would *be* the shark of the sea, not the shark.

Bluefish, all knife and tooth, when he's full he acts like a cat,
wants fun with the menhaden. Kills just to see blood and oil
flow, just to smash up the school, to drive the fish this way and
that, addle them. Bluefish a real bully, bully and cannibal,

looks for the big feast, menhaden, because the menhaden has no way to defend itself, and it's a banquet on that soft, oily, bloody little fish full of life and taste. A school of bluefish will chase an acreage of menhaden a hundred, maybe five hundred, miles north till the bluefish has eaten so much and got so big they may just get lazy and let the menhaden school get away from them.

Then lay out and wait for another armada of menhaden to come along.

Porpoise, tarpon, shark, they'll tear in there with mouths wide open, take a dozen small pogy into their throats in one gulp.

A shark may run through them, double back, and run through that mass of fish meat again.

In our world a man breathes the oxygen out of the air, and the air is all about and you got to breathe it to live. Still you pay most of your mind to people, working for or with them, or worked by them. That's the way of the menhaden's world too. He lives, breathes, and eats out of the water all about, like it's his air, his world—yet his truest life may not be the water itself, but the fish all around. He got to worry about the fish warring on him each minute. His fear and his life and death is from the drum, the tarpon, Jack Crevalle. The fish don't live by ideas, like man do, and it's no control over who eats who. Right or wrong for land—and it's wrong—it's true for the sea that the big fish eat the small. Even the menhaden eat what's smaller, and plenty of it too. The pogy goes through the water all the time with his mouth open. His head is a sieve that takes in water and plankton. The water goes out and the skim, the streaks of small animal and plant life that you can't see with the undressed eye, that stays in the pogy's body and he grows on it. That small life for the microscope digests in the menhaden's body; he gets bigger on it, bigger and oilier.

In the ocean, under it, it ain't going to do no fish no good to be a Christian.

When all these fish have eat their fill of the pogy and they slide out of the school and sound, one of the menhaden's biggest enemies is still up there on top. They sense us in the big ship, run from us as fast as they will from a whale. They'll feel the vibration of the engines. They'll surface in a rush, splash water all over for acres, and be gone.

Whale may fill up on a few hogshead of menhaden, then go on his way, but man gulps down menhaden a quarter of a million or a half million at a swallow, and he's never satisfied.

Why the menhaden is the big grazing ground of all the other fish and man is because they got nothing but their numbers. Nothing but the mystery of their spawning: how they spawn in millions; multiply, not one fish at a time, but schools multiplying by schools. A million pogy in one school may be eating that skim, growing a little each day; and grow just enough and maybe more than enough to make up for what has been lost to the other fish—and to us. Fast as that skim gets changed into fatter menhaden, that fast the shark, whale, and bluefish eat them up.

The menhaden go close to each other, maybe in a school that runs two or three acres wide and fifteen or twenty feet deep. All that's solid meat and oil. And the menhaden must do two things, move forward to pick up that skim and screen it through its gills—and get away from all that's after it.

In fact, the menhaden may could give man a better battle than he does the fish. Fish attacking menhaden always eat. But a pogy mass often gets away from our nets. That's the kind of trouble we had yesterday. Sometimes you'll make ten or twelve sets a day and not catch them. There's only a few things the pogy can do, and they can do them with *us*, not the fish. They can sound (that's go under) so that we can't reach down for them; or go out to sea, or go inshore. They fight for

83

their lives with nothing much to fight with. The menhaden got no teeth; his body is smooth as oil and can't hurt nobody; his fins don't have sharp points; you can grab him up, he won't hurt you; no poison in him to hurt any other fish; and he's got no speed. Only thing that he can outrun is a shrimp. Everything else goes faster. The small mullet, faster. Crab can beat him running. Just food, that's all he is, a big bin floating along the coast for everything to banquet on. Alfalfa of the sea, hay of the bluefish, grain of the shark, main dish and side dish of everything that got fins and teeth, or flies like the gull, pelican, and gannet.

No wonder man wants him too.

Maybe the pogy could hear us now, the chantey we sang to help raise them:

> Oh, I can stand here and look
> In the barbershop in Georgia.

It was wavy and the purse boats went up and down. The ten bunt pullers, the purse-boat engineers, seine and ring setters— sixteen men—yanked in the linen. A bad sea makes the pogy wild. We call them "hard workers" then. They worked hard and so did we.

> Oh, I can stand here and look
> In the barbershop in Georgia
>
> > (Pull)
>
> And see my brown,
> O Lord, see my brown.
>
> > (Pull)
>
> I'm going to ask her
> If I can lay my head in her window
>
> > (Pull)
>
> If it's all night long,
> O Lord, all night long.
>
> > (Pull)

Pulling web, you never know what's coming in besides the pogy, but you can just about always count on getting some fish other than what you after; those that are in there eating on the menhaden.

We weren't near the bunt yet. A great plenty more wing webbing to haul in. Water was choppy and that didn't help. One o'clock, an ovenish hour to have to pull mesh. The sky hot, like over a factory. That helped the menhaden, not us.

Somebody yelled, *"Shovelnose!"*

This shark had been below, maybe a few fathoms, chewing the pogy from underneath, and found he was caught in something. Came up, whished past the captain boat, shot to the middle of the cork line, plowed back through fish toward our mate boat.

Little shovelnose shark four or five feet long, his fins cut the water on top like a rudder upside down. Back and forth like a knife, and just as dangerous to the webbing. He's addled and he's addling the menhaden; they're easy scared; and you got to get rid of this big fish because he may rip the net. If you shoot him, that may make the whole school of fish wild and powerful, and they may get away.

Mister Grass, in my boat, he got excited. He had heard about shark all his life, thought maybe the fish would come into the boat and take a man away with him. Maybe take *him.*

But most menhaden fishermen are right handy with sharks, have no particular fear of them. Deal with them all the time, and know how.

Shovelnose kept hitting the net, looking for a way out. He never stopped moving an instant. I never saw a shark still, only in the movies. In the water shark always moves. Each time shovelnose hit the net he turned, dived back into the menhaden, very thick at the surface now, and wormed toward another part of the web.

He came toward our purse boat. As he did, half of him

85

lopped up on the taut webbing that stretched between the boat and the water. Bob, the Louisiana bunt puller, grabbed the shark's tail, laid both his hands on it. The tail is rough and stringy, not smooth, and it can be held. The shark ain't slippery, his skin is like sandpaper. At the same instant two other bunt pullers wrapped their arms around his middle. Then they slipped a rope, with a slipknot, around the shark's middle.

The more the shark pulled against the slipknot, the tighter the rope drew around his center. He flopped, twisted, splashed, but he was griped, and dragging behind the purse boat. All in about twenty seconds.

The *Moona Waa Togue* came alongside. That's when we had to watch it, that our steel boats wouldn't crash against the ship's hull.

Two bunt pullers from the captain boat jumped from their stern onto the big ship, and I made the jump from my mate boat.

We had to set up a small hoist, we call it a fish fall, so as to pull this shark up on deck.

This is a weather-change belt. Right over us clouds beat their way eastward fast, and way up above that some other wind took a cloud mass westward. Seemed the water surface was whipped from the southeast. That's poison to the fish off the Florida coast. Gives them more weight in the water; they pull harder on the net.

While we worked from the deck, the men hung onto the web of fish that took on more heaviness from this southeast push.

I dropped a steel hook overside. Somebody put the hook through the rope around the shark's tail.

Mister Grass hopped around in the small boat.

The shark, as we hoisted it, swung toward where the green man was. Mister Grass, he may have thought the fish was going to bust loose, come for him and take him down. He let out a great commotion. Stood up in the boat and made like he was going to jump or fall into the water. Which, one or the other, he was.

Somebody jumped on him and pulled him down.

I tried to calm Mister Grass, told him this shark couldn't bite because his nose was in the way. This kind of shark got to turn bottom side up if he's going to bite.

Mister Grass had me an answer. "He looked bottom side up when you swung him toward me!"

Mister Grass, he was just about crazy.

The Louisiana bunt puller told Mister Grass that if there was one thing those sharks were afraid of it's a man. Louisiana said, "Next time a couple sharks get in that net you watch me jump in there and swim around with them!"

"Don't tell me you ever swim where there's sharks!"

"I tell you and I do it too! Half the men on this boat ain't afraid to swim in a net with sharks in it." There was some little truth in that, because when a shark is trying to escape a net and save his life he's not looking for trouble with something else. Louisiana told Mister Grass that a shovelnose wasn't half the problem a whiptail was. "You get you a whiptail shark, you got something. I won't go swimming with him. He hit you with his tail just once and you be saying, 'Hello, Pete.'"

Soon as the shovelnose laid on deck I pulled the dirk out of my belt and cut his throat and belly. We had to let him bleed to death on the boards, because if you throw a shark back into the water before he's dead, he'll show a lot of life sometimes, go right back in the net and start eating the meshes again.

It may could have taken seven or eight minutes, and we thought the shark problem was settled, so we made our jumps back into the purse boats. Drew bunt again.

> *If it's all night long,*
> *O Lord, if it's all night long . . .*

"O Lord!" That was Mister Grass. He gone and done it. They hadn't told him never to pull bunt when you wearing a ring. The worst thing you can do.

Grass's hand, it was all tangled in mesh. Oh, his finger. Oh, his finger. Over and over he yelled that.

My boat had to stop pulling web. The web, it laid out in the water with this great haul of fish inside, and we had to once more just try to hold.

Because we always put a couple of experienced men around a new man, Blu and Fort were on each side of Mister Grass. They uncovered the webbing around the green man's fingers and saw that his ring finger was caught, and cut and bleeding so you couldn't easy take away the hand from the linen bars.

"Captain! Captain! Mate!" Blu called out. "We got to cut the webbing from this man's hand. No other way."

Captain Crother, here he was with fish almost in the hold and a net worth more than a man's finger, he yelled, "What the sonofabitch wearing a ring for? Didn't none of you tell him not to wear no ring when he pull bunt?" That detail, it got lost somewhere.

I drew my net knife, still blood on it from the shark. Very sharp-bladed, it can slit that linen fast as cutting through paper.

I cut away a foot of netting from around this man's hand.

His ring finger was twisted at the knuckle. The hand bled like a pig with its throat cut, his other fingers were strained and stiff, and poor Mister Grass, he been through so much today, he was no more any good.

Mister Grass, a young fellow of twenty-five, he been all through the South Pacific for Uncle Sam, been through battles, but menhaden fishing, that's what thrown him.

He laid down in the bottom of the purse boat. His dark face looked very gray. He didn't let out no sound.

We moved Mister Grass over onto the big boat. Fitch and

Stovely, they had come on deck to see us pull in the fish, and they helped carry the hurt man into the galley.

Almost anything that happens, the men got a chantey to cover it, to start over again from whatever happened, something to help them on their way, a thought that's been thought before in a hundred and forty years of menhaden fishing along this coast. For a green man something too. Always a green man gives you trouble on the water. What they going to do with a man that get hurt? Will he stay? They let him go?

> *Captain, if you fire me,*
> *Oh captain, if you fire me, fire me, fire me,*

They started pulling.

> *Oh, captain, if you fire me,*
> *You got to fire my buddy too.*
> > (Pull)
> *So we can catch a local,*
> *Local, local,*
> > (Closing the circle)
> *So we can catch a local*
> *And get on down the road.*
> > (Packing the fish in closer)

You can't just stop menhaden fishing unless it's real bad serious. Less it just monkey-wrenches the whole set. Otherwise you try to keep going. You don't give up easy for a bloody finger and a smashed hand, and a nuisance shark. The men are used to the things that can happen with a green man. New men always get things wrong and there's always something more to teach them that you ain't yet taught them. You don't know how dangerous this kind of fishing is till you see the wrong things a new man can do. A green man can take a line, handle it wrong, and wrap that 580-pound tom weight around your neck. I saw that happen and a man barely live through it. Another time I heard a captain say to a new man, "Cut that line through the rings," and this new man pulled out his knife and started cutting up the purse line with it. Heard a captain once say to a new man, "Throw that tom weight overboard." And this new man said, "Captain, I threw that overboard when we was leaving port because you told me then my job was to throw that thing overboard." Green men, sometimes they'll come on board, stay a week, go back to the farm, never look at water again. Farmers don't always make the grade on the furrows of the ocean.

> So I'm going back to Weldon,
> Weldon, Weldon,
> > (Maybe Mister Grass go back to the hill?)
> So I'm going back to Weldon
> To get me a job in the Weldon yard.

By this being a new kind of set for us, fish that been spotted by plane, we never knew how big the school was. They could have spread a city block wide and long down below. No way of knowing just how much shark, bluefish, and other fish was down there sucking up pogy. Fish do most of their living, fighting, and eating *under* water. Just the outer edges of their wars that's going to go on at the surface. In fact, the worst jungling of all may be at the very bottom, in the clay, sand, rock, and mud, where the fish hide from one another and jump out at one another. But the menhaden don't do that. It moves in the water, and it's between the surface and the bottom—and it's eaten between the surface and the bottom.

Maybe our net had dropped through just part of that school, the way a net sometimes will. Could be other pods of fish had come in right while we was working. No way of knowing. But the mesh always crushes some menhaden, squeezes their heads

in the linen bars, and blood and oil spread through the water.
Shark and other fish going to get that scent and come up on
you right while you making your set.

Baby sharks surfaced.

Hundreds of them. Could have just come along, or could
have been there.

Spread out for acres inside our net and outside of it. Maybe
they had been on the underside of the pogy, busy eating from
below, so busy feeding they didn't feel they was being drawn
together in a net—till now. They got up close to our boats and
smacked big dollops of water at us; very sassy, no fear in them.

The sharks inside the net threw themselves at the cork, tried
to get over the line; tearing at the corks, eating them.

The menhaden, they stampeded.

Hundreds of tons of the small fish surfaced, jammed against
the cork line, sponged out the netting full. Made the whole
web taut as bow strings in the bunt pullers' hands.

Some menhaden seemed to swim against the wind, straight
into that southeast breeze, as if that might help them. They'll
always head into the breeze, the breeze or the sun. And the
rest moiled and whupped all ways from fear and panic of the
sharks. Because the sharks just about gone mad.

A sober shark is hell, even a sober baby one, but a gone-mad
school of young shark ain't been writ about yet. Those babies,
two and three feet long, some four feet, just sassy fish, seemed
to want everything. A few swallowed pogy, like all this excitement was part of the meal. Some rushed the netting and
made to break through it; others tangled with the corks and
tried swallowing them. Blamed the corks. And most punished
the pogy pitiless. Slapped their tails at them fierce to get them
out of the way, chopped them in their jaws three and four fish
at a time, like surprised and mad that the little fish had this
net trick left to pull.

That's in just a few seconds: like a squall will sometimes suddenly fall without warning. Till Captain Crother yelled loud enough to be heard inshore: "SAVE THE NET!"

Ordinarily you make the mistake of putting your net out where an acre of baby shark is nursing on a pod of menhaden, you won't ever do it a second time if you know it. Baby sharks love to chew it right up. Take it as food. They'll eat up every mesh in the net till they get to the corks. Then try to eat the corks too. Tear at the corks bobbing up and down there like children will bob their heads at a hanging Halloween apple. The cork is hard for the sharks to get at, bobs out of their mouths, but they'll stay with it till the cork is a shred like the core of an eaten apple. They'll eat five thousand dollars' worth of net in a few minutes if they happen to school up on one of them and you ain't lucky enough to get free of them or scare them away with a dozen bullet shots.

We let out all the netting till it got slack and the pogy and the sharks had a way out over the lines. The bagging got big and loose.

Shark, wild pig of the sea, he ran through those menhaden, knocked them out of his way.

Pogy and shark, now they both rushed over the cork so fast, in one place you couldn't see the cork line for fifty yards wide and around. Flowed out with a rush, like water going over a falls.

Gulls, gannet, and pelicans down on them now by the hundred, hopping from one cork to another, screaming, grabbing the dead and dying pogy, keeping away from the slap and flash of the sharks.

We all sat back. Held the boats down hard so the stampede wouldn't school up under us in all that rough water and tip us over.

In a few minutes the fish was gone, headed offshore and under; but thousands of dead menhaden turned over on their backs and floated white around the mesh and the cork line and scattered over the water. The gulls and pelicans sang, dived, and splashed down at those small white bellies like raindrops. But drops that rose and fell again.

We brought into the purse boats in the next half hour this big battered net, with corks missing, a half dozen big holes in it. Yet it was saved. It could be patched and sewed back at the seine house at De Leon port. In a couple davs this net be ready to catch pogy again.

The southeaster got heavier. The purse boats lifted and fell beside the mother ship, so one minute you be up above the deck rail of the *Moona Waa Togue* and the next minute be looking up ten-fifteen feet at that same rail. Bad weather for menhaden fishing.

Because working with that net in these slippery purse boats is rough as birth. On a boat, whether it's the small one or the big one, it ain't nothing between you and death but the rail of your ship. In these small boats, when you have net gear, lines, webbing, weights, machinery to help mess you up with the fish and the sea, you are always getting a little closer to your Lord.

Nothing to do now but get off this sea, get home! Get before the rollers take us into the beach. Beach your boat, it's like lifting the manhole cover that lets you peek down into whatever future they got for you below sand bottom.

We hustled to raise the purse boats into the kleafs of the davits on the *Moona Waa Togue*. The men was making their jumps from the small boats to the big ship. Very hard to do in a good sea. You are moving around on slippery steel all the time, digging your knees into the steel gunwale, the metal bottom, priming and holding yourself against the iron seats, working in sea brine and slipperiness from the pogy oil brought in with the net. Iron hardness mingled with the skim of the sea, and the only thing you got to save yourself with is your balance. Don't have no ramp between you and the big boat, nothing but water to drown in.

You got to be faster than a wave.

Faster than two boats can pull apart or rush together.

Got to have stretch in your legs.

An eye like a measure.

And nerve to make the jump at the right second.

Morris, the New Mexico seine setter, he was in the stern of the captain boat measuring his jump to the mother ship. The small boat went up and down on a hill of water, pulled close to the big ship, then away.

He was jockeying for a position like he was on horseback and going over a hurdle, a high one; got to take it and make it, watch everything, the horse under you, the fence and what's on the other side. Everything bobbing, waving, like you a ball bearing inside a socket and no control over the socket.

If he makes his jump and the small boat happens to slide back on a wave while he's in the air and he don't stretch far enough, he lands in the water. In a sea like this that might drown him.

But that mistake has another mistake right behind it.

Morris made this other mistake.

The wave brought the purse boat up high, even with the deck. Then he made his leap, tried not to leave one foot behind in the purse boat.

But a sea came up under the big boat and threw it toward the small one. The small boat, on its wave, slapped bullet-fast toward the big one.

Morris's right foot got up as high as the deck rail, but his left dragged a little for the speed of the sandwich that the two boats made and they closed on him up to his ankle.

That's four thousand pounds of steel purse boat sandwiching a human foot against the big boat, both coming together with the sea's blink of its eye.

Even if his foot hadn't been in the way, that meeting might have dented both boats. Instead the dent was in Morris's foot. The steel and wood hit so hard you never heard the crunch of his foot.

He screamed, fell back into the purse boat. Went out with no fuss. He laid in the bottom of the small boat, his smashed foot straight up over the gunwale like a stick.

Maybe we shouldn't have tried to board the boat over the starboard side. Maybe we should have gone stern for mounting the ship; that's safest. Now we worked the purse boat around aft of the mother ship, backed the stern of both boats together.

Three men, including Captain Crother, lifted Morris aboard. He was still out.

Morris was a man that fished eight or ten years. You can be careful that long, have the best luck, no bad accidents—then one day you going to get it.

Captain Crother had me to go see Stovely down by the Diesel. I told Stovely what the captain wanted; get this man back to De Leon Hospital as fast as the ship could make it.

We had three hours to go upcoast to get to St. Ann's Entrance, into Alta River Bar, and home.

The crew laid out in the galley, smoked, coffeed up, talked over Grass's bad hand and Morris's bashed foot. Cussed the sea and the sharks, took a hard on against the boat itself.

While the men laid around you could see their chests still going up and down from what they been through. Some heaved like that halfway back to De Leon.

The captain and me, we stayed in the pilothouse and helped Fitch with the wheel. By the sea hitting us on the windward side, and we rolled, it was work for three on the bridge.

Two-three times Captain Crother had just one thing to say.

95

Each time I had just one answer to it. He'd say, "What I tell you, Bix? This my week, hey?"

If I didn't answer quick he'd say it again, "This *my* week, hey?" Like he owned the week. Like he bought the week, he carried it with him on this floating property, and the week only belong to him.

"Everybody's week, Captain Crother. *Everybody's.*"

Third Day

JULY 13, 1949

THOUSANDS OF TIMES I turned out of bed in the middle of the night to go fishing, but this time my bones ached. At fifty-eight you can do with more sleep. That and the heat hit we been having. I barely got out of the house at three o'clock. My job, it's to go wake up the crew. While I get the men out of bed in my part of the town, the captain, he's supposed to be over on his side waking up the engineer, the pilot, and one or two bunt pullers that live closer to him. But sometimes I have to wake up Captain Crother too.

Next door to me, that's where Carib lived. While I knocked on his window, his alarm clock went off. I told him to hustle, we wanted to be in the channel at four o'clock, please help me to wake some of the crew.

I went through the colored side of De Leon Beach. That's the south side of town: dirt roads, small one-story cottages, a few nice two-story houses among them. About two thousand colored live in through here, a region a few blocks deep, a half mile long, goes to Center Street. Some got their property fixed up as well as they can afford; a few live poorer, glad to have a roof over their head, and in winter a coal or an oil stove in their living rooms. These houses, most are plain board, a few of them painted, most just one big room, some two or three rooms. The streets in this section, they're not paved, but they're broad roads, grass and paths along the sides, fern and palmetto trees along some of the streets. The dirt roads all over the town are so soft and comfortable the dogs sleep in the middle of them.

The white, there's about two thousand of them too, they live scattered. Mostly their houses are bigger, nice-painted, gardens in their yards. They live along the beach too, that's a mile from the center of the town. That beach, five miles long, it's all built up. Colored can work there but can't live there. In the town colored and white live separate, but the people get along. Better than twenty-five years ago, when they had some sharp trouble. Now white and colored buy at all the stores; they stand in the same line at the post office (some Florida post offices have Jim Crow lines), and colored and white each have a new school. The white is a brick school and the colored is wood, but the wood school is clean and modern, better than in many colored neighborhoods in the big cities. On any weekday you'll find as many colored on the main street as white, and if they don't howdy one another to death, they still show one another reasonable respect. Because in this town the colored working in the menhaden and shrimping industries and at the paper mill, they help keep the white side going, and there's got to be peace if the work is to be done. Now and then when it's some serious matter, the colored and white church leaders and a few people in politics on both sides will get together, see out for things. We got a few nice churches, some good preachers, one or two NAACP people. There's colored meeting halls, a few juke joints.

In a half hour I went from one street to the other, woke fifteen or sixteen of the crew. Whammed at their doors, called out in the streets, walked into their houses, knocked on the windows where they slept, opened a screen window, and touched a bunt puller. "Get up, Westley, we starting at four!"

Walk down Eighth Street, you can go straight through the town, past the Container Corporation, two miles on, to where the menhaden plants sit along Alta River. The men all walk that distance through town to the *Moona Waa Togue*.

A right nice town, cool in the winter because it's so far north in Florida (just at the border of Georgia), and in the summer, like now, tropic. I grew up in the Carolinas, but settled here ten years ago because we're five hundred miles below North Carolina, and it makes a heap of difference in the climate and the fishing too. You get a smaller fish here, but a longer season to hunt.

Going along the train line now, waking up the last of the crew, those that live by the tracks. The line runs along the waterfront, carries away menhaden and paper-mill products. A few beer halls and restaurants by the tracks, and streets that lead from the Alta River across the tracks, straight over the town.

I wasn't the only mate making these rounds, waking up crews. Mates on all the other menhaden boats running through the streets doing the same. The fishermen all getting up now. Each morning been the same way for a long time back, the menhadeners hustling to the docks for the long trip out the channel so as to catch fish early in the day and get back before the heat of noon—if there's fish around.

A steady stream of fishermen going down Eighth Street now

toward the menhaden ships. Maybe two or three hundred. Mostly married men; many with little cottages in this part of town; some fishermen from other places just boarding here in the colored section. All filing through the streets in the middle of the night while the insects and a few night birds whistle and hawk and hiss and make whatever sound the Lord give them to blow their horns with and find mates with.

With the fishing season poor, the men making no money, their families not too happy, the men went through the streets with no more in their pockets than the hope of a good day. Some of their wives, they'd be getting up in a few hours and go over on the white side and do housework and washing to help out.

I sneaked up by Fort's house, whispered into the window, "Fort, you up yet?" No answer from him. Louder, "Fort, you up yet? Time to go!"

Fort twisted on his bed. I said, "Don't wake Noah."

Noah, he's an old menhaden fisherman, maybe seventy, he lived in the same house. Lord knows how he kept alive. Had been staying there for years. Noah loved to fish, but no captain wanted him any more. His bones cracked like wheat being threshed. Tell you the truth, I didn't want him on the *Moona Waa Togue* myself. But he snuck aboard one or another menhaden ship every day or two, and each time they had to carry him or put him off.

My captain, he lives just over the other side of Center Street where all the captains live, in a seven-room house, wonderful-fixed inside. Modern rugs from over there, and pure, refined water with no sulphur in it. Us colored and most of the white about town have sulphur water all the time unless you can afford to refine it. The captain has this refined water and a stout, refined wife. Excepting what I heard, that she nagged him all the time and she was the captain of that place.

Sometimes Mrs. Crother made a small breakfast for her husband before she sent him out on the water. She'd be up early with him, like now. At the door I asked was he up. She said, "Yes, but very upset about the fishing. He's afraid Thorpe going to send the ship to North Carolina soon if the fishing stays bad."

"We catch fish today, Mrs. Crother."

Captain Crother, he was shaving. He came out, shaving cream all over his face, no shirt on. Upper part of his body very white, white hairs on his chest; just red arms, red from the sun, and his mouth going with chewing tobacco this early in the morning.

"Bix, you got them all up?"

"They be there by four, Captain Crother. Shall I go across the road and wake the engineer?"

The captain said he would wake the engineer by phone, bells always made him jump to attention.

I went out the captain's yard, down a side street toward Front Street, along the river front. There's a road by the railroad track takes you straight down to the Merrick Thorpe Menhaden Company. I went on down in the dark toward the factory yard and the docks.

The lights on the river, the buoys, the beacons, the black and red cans, I could see them in the channel going straight out toward St. Ann's Entrance. The moon made everything on the water clear and shiny.

All the roads leading toward the docks had men going along them now. The men just a parade crossing the railroad tracks, cutting along the dirt roads, side-stepping the ruts, moving in the lanes that led to the plants and the menhaden ships.

Everything and everybody going toward Alta River, the waterway that carries you out of Brunswick Sound into the ocean.

The river, a few hundred yards wide, it runs along the west

side of the town, the whole length of it. All along the water the buoys showed up strong, some occulting, some flashing long and short. The moon, it was full enough to show the red cans and the black cans angled, flopping and waving along the channel sides to keep the boats from going afoul. Along the town side of the river you could see twenty or thirty menhaden ships, with their crow's-nests running high, against the lighted dark. Hundreds of shrimp boats too, with all their rope rigging, docked like a line of fence all along the river for a half mile. Twice as many shrimpers as menhadeners, because shrimp is the biggest fish business in the South, after menhaden.

I walked into the Merrick Thorpe yards, first man there, like so often. Jubilee, he was up and came stuck out his wet tongue at me.

At the dock our ship waited on us. Looked like a piece of carved wood, a used-up antique, very black and sleepy against the channel electric and moonlight.

In a few minutes men jumped from the docks onto the decks of those menhadeners. You could hear one thump after another in the dark as the fishermen got over the deck rails.

Some menhaden boats break down more often than a dollar watch. Going out the channel, I had to yell all up and down deck, "Check that ratline rope, she looks about to bust!" . . . "Tighten them purse-boat lines, they slack too much, that small boat going to swing out of the davits!" . . . Sun, water, wind always working, rotting the timbers, shredding the ropes. "Hey, Texas, go help pickle that net. Throw the salt in, man, that net going to rot before your eyes!" . . . Everybody jolly, jiving, anxious to go; from that minute on you got to start fixing. "Carib, *you*, dry-boat man, get out your hose, wet up the deck there. Look at them flies. They having a fish banquet on them planks. Clean it up!" . . . Keep repairing all day.

The pumps may wear out, the Diesel bearings jam up. "Latch that rubber tubing to the head of your purse boat, ring setter, else you smash your prow when you hit the ship out on the set!" . . . Every minute it's something to be hammered, tightened. These are not the best-built boats to begin with, so you watch the ship's condition each minute like the gulls watch the fish hole for scraps. A wind can give a twist to each cord and cable on the ship, put a new strain on them, something happen in a second. "Watch them lines on your feet, Mister Pumpkins" (a name we may give to a new man) "else you lose a leg at the hip!" . . . A loose coiled line on a boat, that's a ship's snake, you keep out of its curls, and you're out of its fangs. A line may be hooked to anything, a purse boat, the brailer, part of the rigging; the ship gives a lurch, and that line will straighten out like a stick. If it sideswipes you, you can burn an inch deep or lose a limb. Old rope and cables, they're always under strain, break regular. And a menhaden boat is about held together with these ropes and cables. You just about walking in rope like a farmer walk in wheat.

Each time a pogy crew goes out of the bar, takes off in the open sea, it's a question in their mind, Which way will the captain go?

In my mind too. I won't even know.

Sometimes the captain, he don't even know. The captain is like the Lord. When he places one foot on the deck us crew can't tell which way in the world he's going. The captain, he may look at the sky and say, "There's a southwester breeze, maybe it'll bring the fish over that way. I think I'll go there." This is about all that tells a captain where to go, what he guesses about the wind and the current . . . and maybe where he's caught fish before. Captains keep going back to spots where they caught fish before.

After we got beyond St. Ann's Entrance, Genty, the Arizona bunt puller, a great beefer and worrier, always keeping the men a little uncertain, he walked past the captain, he said: "Captain, which way we going today? You going south, you going north?"

A crewman don't usually ask a captain that. Captain Crother gave Genty a sharp look and stopped chewing. I think the captain hadn't made up his mind where he might find fish this day. He said, "I'm captain around here! When we *there* you see where we *went!*"

"Yes sir, Captain Crother. Just thought I ask."

"If the mate himself don't ask, why *you* ask?"

"Didn't mean nothing, Captain. Just I like to get a good set feeling whether I am going upwind or downwind."

They was by the icebox on the bow side of the galley. The captain stood squat, his feet apart, solid, and started his jaws chewing again on his Half and Half. "Sure you ain't telling *me* which way to go?"

"Oh no, Captain. You the captain of the ship!" Genty, he was a slim fellow, he shied around like a willow, knew he'd made a little mistake.

"You think *you* know where those fish going to be?"

"Oh no, Captain. No idea, except they will be in the water."

"You right! And while we all on this water together *I* find the fish. *Me, myself, I.*"

Genty stood like a different kind of a tree now, all straight. Seemed sorry he popped his mouth at the captain.

"Yes *sir*, Captain Crother!"

Captain Crother, he put more tobacco into his mouth, kept plugging it in, like he was filling a fish hole full of fish, till his mouth wouldn't hold no more; and he went up to the crow's-nest and sat by Carib.

We went out St. Ann's Entrance four miles along the government-built jetties; that's stones piled in a fence thirty feet down and twenty-five or thirty feet across, to give us boats a straight pass into the sea through the shoals.

Outside the jetties, Captain Crother ordered the pilot to turn north, then due west, back toward Cumberland Island, into the shallow waters of the Georgia coast.

You get in there, the water is just a few feet deep, but in these waters the menhaden will sometimes be. Passed up the coast, by the village of Greyfield, but you couldn't see it from shore; a few miles more up to Long Point.

By now the sun watched us poke north. The day warming, and it was half-past seven.

Many years on these close-in waters, you get to smell what's on the bottom: clay, sand, mud. The smell comes to the surface, you can tell just as you get over it, "That's clay," "That's mud," or "That's sand." You can't smell rock or shell bottom, but if your ship graze over it, you know what it is. If you're in mud and your boat scrapes over that, soft mud will come up on all sides; you can feel the hull sliding through it. Sometimes you'll go over mud bars that ain't even shown on the charts the pilot may use. Mostly, in through here, you go without charts, because the captain, me, and the pilot know the waters so well.

Sometimes in that shallow water the chart will say one thing, you'll sense another. Maybe there's been an underwater change in the last six months or a year. You put down a lead line, a hollow piece of lead on the end of a cord, and take a measurement in feet or fathoms. That way you'll find out just what's underneath, whether you better get away from it or you can get through it. Deep-sea pilots don't know about this kind of navigation, don't know how dangerous it can be. When we going over these shallows the crew will sometimes look over the rails down below to see if they can make out the bottom.

With the sun up, and us by the beachhead, you could see through the water to the floor, like you see the white of a cup bottom through water you are drinking from it.

We got to the edge of St. Andrew's Sound, but the captain

ordered us away from it. We used to fish a-plenty in the sounds till the law stopped us, made us go farther out, said we were interfering with shrimping and food fishing. It's good fishing in those sounds, and we still sneak in once in a while. It's marshy in the sounds. Marsh means you're inland, that's the safest way to keep out of danger. In some places where it's wooded they've made channels so boats can pass through. We've gone through when we was desperate for fish and just went in anywhere for them. This marshland, it goes all the way from Florida up along the Georgia coast into South Carolina. Many inlets into the marshes from the ocean; bars sometimes two-three miles long that take you from the sea inside the coast line.

The fish will come in there, spawn, move around in big schools. Sometimes, if you get into one of those sounds early in the morning, you can catch a load of pogy and get out in a hurry.

Get inside these coastal areas, then you're neither in the sea nor on land. Lost between the two on salt marshes. Got to know how to maneuver a ship when you get in there, or even in as close to shore as we been going the past few hours.

Shore all about, you'll see the plant life up close, sedge, barilla, rushes, and shoving up out of swamp water, bay and gum trees, oak, magnolia, palmettos. Under the boat you'll have fish—bass, whiting, flounder, maybe a pod of menhaden. Go in close and back out into the bay, you'll be passing over crab, shrimp, clams. The big stingray comes in there too, porpoise, drum, and shark get inside sometimes—and early in the day you'll see fishermen with special kinds of gear going for the different kinds of fish. All along this coast it's small islands, and the big ones that run fifty miles north and south. The ocean fronts them, and when you are out a mile or two, like we were now, you know that behind these islands always there's that salt marsh and land jungle.

Close in, some of the men worried about grounding. They meant for the *captain* to hear, but they hollered up to *me* in the nest, so it rang over the whole rigging, "*Mate,* where *you* taking us?" I am the man in between, catch it from both sides, maybe the hardest-put man in the menhaden fishing business.

But all of a sudden Captain Crother ordered, "Fitch, take us east. Due east!"

Due east. That could be a mile or two out, or, the way we found out in the next hour, ten miles out in about seventy feet of dark water. Go offshore, the water gets darker, because it gets deeper, like a man's mind. Mostly the ocean's look depends on the depth of the water, but wind will change the color. Wind may be the most important on the water. The ocean don't flash back the same look and color and cloud formations as the sky shows. You see it, feel it from all angles; even your own eyesight may be different than the next man's. Red in the sky may make the water light. Sometimes clouds darken the surface, make you think you're sailing through clouds themselves; that's when the sky comes down close and shows its face to the surface.

It was a little like that now, heavy clouds rolling around, but no rain in them, just moving over us fast, darkening the water, making some of the men worried. You got to remember, most of these fellows are farmers, some feel closer to soil than the sea.

But land, it's no more in sight. Just the line of sky and water all around. And some grumbling among the men.

Going in a ship built maybe eighty-five years before, water always in the bilge, slivery wood that gets in your feet if you're going barefoot, or slivers in your fingers if you slide your hand along the rail; that worries some fishermen, and it should. As I get older I worry more myself, find that when I'm way out I think more of the hill.

I pointed inland, in a line that fingered Sea Island Beach, a small strip of coast in southern Georgia. I asked the captain, did he remember what happened there a week ago? Never should have mentioned it. The captain spit his tobacco juice up in the air till it rained back in our faces. Wasn't a chance for him to forget what happened there the rest of his life.

We had seen this big school of menhaden near the beach, first fish we spotted in days. "Don't go for them, Captain," I warned, "we'll get sanded. Them fish are in five and seven feet of water." Even the crew cautioned the captain not to get too greedy. But he ignored everybody; the sight of fish just filled his soul with wonderful ideas. He started down the rigging. "We'll go for them anyway." He said if they got the fish in the net we could pull the purse boats and the net out of the shallow water with the horses. The horses are ropes, strong ropes you tie from the stem or stern of the big ship to the small boats. A dangerous game.

We made the set. The fish were webbed in, and we pulled the meshing into the purse boats. Then we called the big boat to come in close alongside so we could brail the fish into the fish hole. The *Moona Waa Togue* came as near as she could, poked into the shallow water slow, like a blind man with a cane finding his way over a busy street. Pretty soon the pilot yelled to us in the small boats that the bow touched bottom, he couldn't come closer without grounding.

The dry-boat man, he rowed to the mother ship and hitched the ropes onto her stem bitts. Then, we hoped, the ship could back up and pull the purse boats, the net, and the fish into deep water. Once we got the haul out in deep water, we could get the fish on ship.

But while the horses were being hooked onto the small boats that net settled into the sand. The men holding the web could feel trouble below in that shallow water. The bunt didn't move when they pulled it. Sand had sifted through the bars of the webbing. The net settled into hard, sucky sand. It kept spreading over the sand and the sand kept covering the mesh till a hundred bunt pullers couldn't get it up—and the *Moona Waa Togue* couldn't do any more than pull the ropes and bust the net.

"Cut the net! Cut the net!" the captain yelled.

The men got out their dirks and slashed away at the net, tried to save a few hundred yards of the linen meshing.

The fish got away, except for thousands that floated off dead. Turned over on their backs and made the top of the water white, like a field of cotton blossoms.

We stowed onto the mother ship what we saved of the web and went back to port.

On the way home the crew jumped on the captain. "We told you not to make a set so close to the beach!"

The captain, he was up on the pilot deck, looking down at the men and yelling, "I'm captain from stem to stern! If I want I can cross the ocean, and you going to do what I say when you fishing with me!"

Captain Crother stayed in his quarters till we reached port. Before we docked I said to him, "When we go to the company with this sanded net I want to share the blame for making this set. I could have stopped you if I hollered loud enough."

Captain Crother, he said, "Can't let you do it that way, Bix. God Almighty couldn't have stopped me."

When Merrick Thorpe heard about the sanded net he could have busted through one himself.

We carried what was left of the net into the seine house near the processing plant. That's a big barn given over just to housing and taking care of nets, keeping them salted and mended. The company has reserve nets in there in case of accidents like this sanding. The nets are rolled up on spools thirty feet high inside this wood building. Webbing is all over, on the floor, in the corners, hanging from lines and hooks, till the place looks like the work of some great spiders. A few of the bunt pullers helped the seine and ring setters to throw in a corner what was left of the torn-up netting.

It could have been with that net sanding that our troubles began.

The sea was quiet. Ten miles off Georgia, opposite Egg Island. About eleven o'clock noon and the men began to whip sweat off their bodies with the thumb and forefinger.

I spotted menhaden a quarter mile off our starboard.

Captain Crother, he jumped like a young boy. He had a good strong voice, you could hear him in a bad wind. He stood up, his orders breezed over the whole ship, *steady to starboard, lower boats, help off the striker boat.*

He started down the port ratline, you'd think he never saw fish before. I followed down the starboard ladder. I went slower; could feel the crew moving, hear that rumpus by the davits where the seine and ring setters were lowering the purse boats.

Carib, he was already in his oar-powered rowboat and shoving off from the big boat toward the pogy school.

Many captains excite when they spot the pogy and many a captain "falls out the mast." Like Captain Crother did. That means go down the ladder in such a hurry you can't barely see him do it. And the captain wasn't no young man neither. In his fifties, big, fat in the belly a little, heavy thighs, still he went like a shot.

The captain got on deck, he raced aft to see was the purse boats lowered quick enough. It wasn't till that instant that the pilot sent his signal to the engineer to cut the motor and drift.

The boat kind of bumped to a sudden slowdown. The captain, because he was so big-weighted and moving to stern so fast, he couldn't stop.

Went right over the rail like a plane off a carrier's deck.

Kind of flew, with his arms all out too. Landed in the water
B-A-S-H-O-O-M.

"Man overboard! CAPTAIN overboard! Captain B-A-
S-H-O-O-M!"

From halfway up the rigging I saw the captain. Funny how
you will laugh in the first instant of something that may turn
out misfortunate. I hustled down the stairway of the engine
room, yelled to Engineer Stovely to start his governor and back
up slow.

Captain was fifty or seventy yards behind, splashing around
and having a good cool-off. We could have been in sixty-five
feet of water.

The ring and seine setters, they been lowering the purse
boats, but they put them back in the kleafs, and they and the
whole crew ran to the stern rail to see the show.

We backed till someone threw the captain a cork belt.

He grabbed onto it, wrapped it around his body. But that's
when it looked like he got into the most trouble. That belt
around him, he started floundering, got his mouth full of water.
His head went under.

Captain Crother socked at the water very desperate and tore
off that belt. His mouth rolled. "Goddamn cork's carrying me
under," he yelled. Which it could be. By these life belts being
on pogy boats so long, eaten up by the wet and damp, hanging there in racks in the galley right over the table where the
steam from every kettle of potatoes smokes up those belts, they
will get heavy as lead and carry a man down under quicker
than a wave. "Throw me a rope!"

They tossed rope to the captain. He wrapped his hands and
arms all around it.

They pulled him up on deck.

Water dropped from him like he was a fresh fish, rained off
the white hair on his chest, dripped off his shorts. But he
looked cool.

That was the first time in weeks the captain done anything the crew liked, and they wanted to enjoy it but wasn't sure should they laugh or take it serious.

The captain, he knew what should be done. He looked over his black crew and the white pilot and white engineer, and he cussed out a permission. "Laugh, goddamn you-all. I'd laugh if you-alls went bashoom!"

The crew of the *Moona Waa Togue* just about split their gut.

"Captain went bashoom!"

"Captain got himself a cool!"

They sang it and whacked their hips.

By that delay, the fish got away.

Carib came back in his rowboat and said the menhaden had moved out, gone northways. "A big play too." He and the captain and Booker, the purse-boat engineer, went aloft. I stayed on deck with the crew.

The crew, they'll hang over the fish hole while they're waiting for the fish cry to come from the hawk's-nest. The fish hole is a magnet for the men, for the fish, even for the birds. There is so little extra space on a menhaden boat that the men are drawn around that square space toward the stern where you can look ten feet down on a floor twelve feet across.

When the men look down into the fish hole, see fish there or nothing there, they look into life.

Most of the time the men are ready to be good-natured, laugh at most anything. The time has to go, they figure, and it may just as well go pleasant when they're not making a set. Whether they're around the fish hole or pacing up and down the decks, they'll jive, gossip, rest, read, play cards, whittle, play a guitar, make a toy boat, play a phonograph record, dance a few turns. They may gather in three or four groups, about the fish hole, up at the bow, in the galley. Sometimes all will be together if a good bull session is on.

While we hunt fish there is sometimes hours when the crew has nothing to do but wait; then they're fishermen, not seamen. The engineer and the pilot run the ship, three men in the lookout watch for fish, and you'll hear the crew from one end to the other. A man might just catch his foot on a planking, the fellow next to him will make a joke of it, say, "What you kicking the ship for, getting even?" That little matter might pass swift as it came, and a few feet away somebody else might just say, "You see that damn pelican go by my face? He liked to have washed it, he left so much spray." Talk about each little thing, anything, in a steady stream.

Lift, he tried a riddle on Lawyer, the Tennessee fisherman. "You hear what the pogy said to the bluefish?" Lawyer asked what the pogy said. Lift answered, "The pogy said to the bluefish, 'What makes the bluefish blue?' And the bluefish answered, ''Cause I ain't had no pogy today, that's why I'm blue.'"

A story like that calls for one back, like one drink calls for another, though they won't be drinking.

The fishermen always looking for something to be jolly about, to keep up their spirit.

They will even have fun with each other if there's nothing else to laugh at. Sometimes that kind of joking will get serious. That's where it's my job to keep the peace on ship.

The men have to be kept on an even keel, like the ship. I talk to them all the time, say, "Well, fellows, we're in six fathoms now. The chart say it's coral bottom around here." Some men always looking over the rail trying to see bottom in the shallower waters, watch what's in the water, study nature, remark about every bird that flies over. Talk, it goes on each instant. "What's that off there, a freighter?" One man may want to test out the knowledge of the other. They'll argue over it, whether it's a freighter or something else, talk about the rigging of that ship or the shape of it, and have that between them till this ship comes close and they see what it is and it's settled. A few cents may change hands.

It's best when the men shoot the breeze. And it shoots all day long. One man digging another, making friends, sometimes building up a mad against someone. The men get to know one another's family life. Sometimes, if a man feels like talking, the whole crew will get his life story. He may tell it in a nutshell in a few minutes or he may spend hours telling it. On board a boat men get to know each other. Few secrets there. A man soon shows what he's made of by what he does, and what he thinks he's made of by what he says. They'll know about one another's women. "You figuring on marrying Helen?" "Hell no. On what we making this year I do well if I can keep in fishskins."

They'll talk about money a good deal of the time. The whole world does. Where they got less of it they may talk more of it. The married men always sound much more sensible about money than the single. If they be gambling they'll set a two-cent limit. They may borrow something to read that a single man bought and paid for. They're going to have better account of their money. A single fellow is going to spend his not so careful, but at that many of the single men will send a few dollars every two weeks, on payday, to their families back in some inland state. Somebody may ask for a smoke:

"Give me a cigarette, huh?"

"You mean you can't buy a cigarette? What you buy with your money?"

"Whiskey."

"Well, smoke the whiskey."

A game, if you can call it that, it's a little more serious. It's called "the dozens." I have seen a few bad fights come out of "the dozens." Some man may start talking about another man's relatives, his wife, or his mother, or his sweetheart, or all of them. If his words get out a little too far, the other fellow may get in his licks too. A dozen insults may pass back and forth, with the crew listening. There may be a fight in the fish hole over that, or it may settle down to some bad feeling that will just stay between the two men, or it may pass quick. That will happen when there's too much leisure at sea, we not catching fish, or things going bad.

A joke even about a word can go along for a whole day, like the time Fort didn't handle a rope right and the purse boat fell out of the davit and came down kerplunk hard on the deck. Fort jumped back and said, "Jesus, that's a catastrophe."

The word struck the fellows funny.

One bunt puller said, "Fort got himself a catastrophe."

Everybody picked up on the word, kept shoving it back and forth, up and down deck, up the ratline and down to the engine room. Anything that happened or didn't happen, like a gull flew over the stern, let a dropping fall, Blu said, "That's a catastrophe." The cook dropped a tin plate out of his hand, it rolled out the door, and he yelled, "One catastrophe, coming out!"

Some of the fellows spit out the word casastrophy, castrophy, catascoopic. They just tore that word apart for the next three hours, till finally it became cat's-ass-trophy.

Then they called the captain a captastrophe.

Till if there was a real catastrophe on board there wouldn't have been no word left to describe it.

Most of the men read pretty steady. Wish I had the money they spend on funny books, true stories, detective stories, and like that. Especially comic books. Most of the men will buy one or two of them before they come on board. They read it and pass it on. There may be ten new comic books on board every day. Sometimes a man will be reading a newspaper that's put

117

out in De Leon, or a Jacksonville paper, or a colored paper. It can be quiet among them for a half hour while they all sit around reading one another's papers. Most know how to read, and if a man don't and wants to learn, he can learn from someone. Each swap his general experience with the others. That's what makes some fishermen and seamen pretty smart. Many men's knowledge becomes one man's knowing.

Kirwan, the purse-boat engineer, and Westley, the Alabama bunt puller, were talking about some moving pictures they saw at the De Leon Beach theater. The colored sit in the balcony and sometimes they will laugh at something that strikes them funny which the white downstairs don't appreciate. These men were talking about that and finding out one another's tastes.

Kirwan asked, "You like the musicals?"

"Better than all those murder pictures," Westley said. "Them white folks sure can murder and put on murder pictures."

Kirwan: "You know that. You know they good at that."

Westley: "I seen a picture a few weeks ago, it showed some people living up on top of one of those tall buildings in New York. Big thick furniture all around, chandeliers up a mile high in the ceiling, and the women all running around with more off than on. Fellow and girl chasing each other all over New York, Chicago, and San Francisco, then back to that room with the high chandelier."

Kirwan: "Did they do it on the chandelier?"

Westley: "No, that was the whole trouble. First she couldn't get him to do it—anywhere—then he couldn't get her to do it at all. Then they was flying in the air again back to Chicago and from there down to New Orleans."

Kirwan: "Did they do it in New Orleans?"

Westley: "I wouldn't be sure. There was one shot, it closed out very quick and it could have happened then, but I don't think they was kissing hard enough for it to have happened then. You couldn't rightly tell."

"Then what?"

"Then they on a ship to France. They get in Paris. He gets there first and she gets there second. They bump into each other in the hotel lobby."

"Did they bump hard enough?"

"No, didn't bump hard enough. Them white folks sure stay with it when they going to do something or they *ain't* going to do it."

"Then what?" Kirwan still giving this story a chance.

"Well," said Westley, "I never once seen one of them do a lick of work or even go to the bank. Seem like they have plenty of pocket money. Just the question is, Will they or won't they?"

"Did they?"

"I'm getting to that, Kirwan."

"It seems like each one been keeping a skeleton in the closet. He had a nice sleek, well-hipped skeleton in his closet, and in her closet she had an old man she didn't love. Only loved his high chandelier."

Kirwan: "Same old picture they making out there all the time, ain't it?"

Westley: "Yeah. I could figure out a better one."

Kirwan: "You wouldn't know from going to them musicals and high-white-living pictures they was ever a pogy master like the *Moona Waa Togue*."

Westley: "No, you wouldn't. Just the same, I would like one of those flying trips from De Leon Beach to Venice for no better reason than to get a little of it. Good a reason as any to travel."

Kirwan: "Hell, you don't have to travel for that."

Two or three other crewmen came by while the talk went to pirate pictures.

Westley asked, "You see that pirate picture a week ago?"

They all hopped in on that, Lawyer, Blu, Carters, Lift. "Yeah, I like that," or, "That pirate was worse than Captain Kidd," "Oh, you can't beat a good pirate picture." And like that.

Westley: "Did they ever have black pirates? All it ever show in the movies is white pirates."

Lawyer: "Man, don't you know all pirates is white?"

Lift: "And all white is pirates."

Carters: "I sure like them pictures since they put them in colors. Them pirate captains was mean dressers."

Kirwan: "Yeah, all those fancy pants and all. You'd think they'd cut themselves up with all them swords and knives banging around their belts and necks."

Westley: "You suppose that pirate stuff was real?"

Lawyer: "Sure it was. This Florida coast was full of pirate stuff. Buccaneers. They say there's plenty money right over there on Amelia Island if you could find it."

Kirwan: "Amelia Island is damn big. Where you going to start?"

Lawyer: "You better stick to pogy, man, you may be able to bring home a couple loaves of bread and a pound of coffee tonight."

Lift finished off the pirate talk: "You suppose we could raise the halyards, kick the boom, heave down the marlinspike, smack open the forward deck hatch, fire the sixteen-pound shot, and knock off Captain Crother's grouch?"

The men all laughed like hell.

How some of the white folks live—at least in the movies— made the new seine setter, Mohr, wish he was rich, white, and handsome, like Clark Gable, and not have to work.

Lawyer, he got his nickname from what he knew or claimed to know, he said, "You getting yourself some damn bad ideas, you want to be white."

120

"Well, why I can't be rich, *black,* and handsome? You like that better?"

Lawyer didn't like that any better, asked Mohr why he didn't want to work. Mohr asked why should he want to work?

Lawyer: "When the captain be pushing us to make eight or nine sets a day I go with you, I don't like that none either. But I'm talking about you said, 'Wish I was rich, white, and handsome.' You really want to be a sonofabitch like that? Even the captain, he's working. Some days, right hard. Everything works. Even them pogies are hard workers when the wind is blowing right."

"I ain't no pogy. Not being no pogy, I just wish I could have fifty thousand bucks and retire to my country home."

Lawyer told Mohr he better just forget about that because he wasn't going to get it. "You and me don't own the menhaden industry, and nothing much else. You might just as well pull that bunt, sing that chantey, and get your ten and a half cents on a measure of fish. If you want to get more money, we get us up and go to the captain and tell him to get us more. But you might just as well come down off that dream about you being rich, white, and handsome—because you *poor,* you *black,* and you the *ugliest* sonofabitch on the *Moona Waa Togue.*"

"Say here, Lawyer, you want to go down in the hole with me?"

Lawyer: "No, I don't want to go down in the hole with you."

Mohr: "You don't want to go down in the hole with me because you know if you do you just might not come up on deck!"

Lawyer: "Got lots of confidence in your hands, ain't you?"

Mohr: "I got confidence I can take you. I can make it with you." Mohr said that, he looked over the men and said to them like they had been hearing the most impossible thing in the world, "Lawyer thinks he can make it with me."

"Yes, I can make it with you."

"Well, you going to have the chance to make it with me. Now I'm leading the way to the fish hole!"

The whole crew gathered for that. Just when they don't catch no fish things ain't normal. The men talk a little hotter about anything that's on their minds. And they might just get relieved by having a fight down in the fish hole. It might be more of a test of strength than a real fight, because if, on a pogy boat, they was to be doing any real fighting among themselves, the crew would break up, they'd catch no fish, make no money, and some would be looking for another ship or another job. But a fight in the fish hole over a half-good reason is about like medicine for the crew when they're worried, making no money, and their nerves spilling over a little. Sometimes after a plain strength contest, like bending the elbow, if a man didn't want to take the decision that came that way and believed he could best a man with his punches even if he hadn't won with his elbow, he might invite the winner to come settle it in the fish hole. Everything that goes on in the fish hole ain't pogy.

The fish hole ain't slippery when there's no fish in it. It's kept flushed out. The square bottom of the hole is just about the size of a prize ring. Maybe a little smaller. But big enough to settle a fuss.

When the two crewmen got down in there all the others stood around by the fish-hole rail and looked down. The fishermen were calling out to whichever one they wanted to win, "Give it to him, Mohr," or "Let him have it, Lawyer," or "Knock him cold." Or someone might say to both of them, "Now make it good or I go down there afterward and take you both on!"

Below Mohr posed like a champ. "Okay, Lawyer, put up them baby fingers!" Lawyer's baby fingers were hard-knotted bunt puller's hands.

Lawyer put up his fists. He started to move around Mohr in a circle, and Mohr followed him around.

Lawyer got in a terrible smash on Mohr's face. All of a sudden like that. Just boom-bam, and Mohr didn't know whether the boat capsized or not. He just went down flat as the boards he laid on.

In a half minute or so Mohr came to. He sat up and stared about. All the fellows were looking down at him, waiting for him to stand. Mohr looked around, but he didn't see anybody in the hole with him. He thought he may have killed Lawyer. He just didn't know he been hit. He said, "Did I hurt Lawyer bad? Where is he? What you do with him?"

The crew gave him one helluva time then. They said, "Man, come out of the hole, you can't fight. Lawyer almost had you crucified with one nail."

Once I saw two men go down in the hole and have a knock-down fight over how you pronounce Beaufort, North Carolina, and Beaufort, South Carolina.

This bunt puller said: "Up here in North Carolina we call it *Bo*fort."

This other bunt puller: "Hell no, we call it *Bu*fort down in South Carolina. That's what you ought to call it in North Carolina."

The first bunt man: "I'm telling you it's *Bo*fort in both places."

The second: "*Bu*fort!"

The first: "*Bo*fort!"

"Come on, fellow, you going down in the hole with me, I'll show you it's *Bu*fort!"

"Okay, mister, I'll show you it's *Bo*fort!"

They bufed and bofed, just about knocked each other out. When it was all done, both places still said it the same.

No warning at all, the whole *Moona Waa Togue* suddenly went up, zo-o-O-O-M, and dropped on her starboard. The hull slap on the sea shook everybody. Water whooshed up over the rail.

A whale maybe ninety to a hundred feet long turned over in the water and slid off away from us.

The big fish had come up from below and gave us that sharp swipe.

From the nest I could see the whale roll off and slip behind. On the sea you always ready for the unexpected, but when it happens you still don't expect it. As soon as the ship got righted some of the crew set up a holler: "Sea serpent!" "Killer whale!" "We gone, men!"

As this whale sideswiped I had a cigarette in my hands. When the whole rigging had been thrown way off angle over the water, while the boat rolled, I could have dropped that cigarette straight down and it would have taken a path way to the side of the ship.

Captain tried to make his voice go above all the others. "Get the pumps going in that fish hole!" A couple tons of water had swept down in there. That's dangerous. Water in the fish hole can capsize the boat if she's rolling.

The crew was giving orders to Captain Crother, the pilot, and the engineer: "Head toward shore!" "Full steam to the beach!" "Get away from that thing." The men feared the big beast would come at us again and stove us.

We had Exeter, a new man on board taking Mister Grass's place, he yelled out, "Where the safest place to be at a time like this?" The safest place was the hill, but it wasn't a chance.

Those in the galley, they ran out. Cooking Devil came out, and he yelled at the mess boy, who was right at his side, "Roger, tend to the biscuits in the oven!" That was the cook's job, but this time McNally dreaded something that wasn't in the cookbook.

The captain, he wasn't bothered by it, kept looking for menhaden as soon as the ship straightened out.

But it looked like the whale *was* out to get us. He settled right behind the boat. The top of him showed, like a gray hump, his head stayed under water.

"He gaining on us, Captain!"

The captain gave orders to ring up the ship; that's send her full speed.

We raced northwest toward shore.

The whale just swished his tail a few times and slid right up behind us. If you was at the stern you could see his head, right up out of the water now, and his mouth open. It looked like a cavern in there, and the men shouted, "He going to bite the stern!"

But he closed his mouth right away, ducked his head under again, and settled about fifty feet behind.

He stayed right there and followed.

By the whale staying with us like that, I went down deck. I stood midships, told the new men and some of the older hands all that the whale meant was we might be in the neighborhood of menhaden. Whale love that little fish.

The cook was really scared. Cooks on menhaden boats are cooks, not fishermen and not seamen. Some don't even like to look out the port windows of the galley at the sea. Just keep their eyes and their minds on the sink, the stove, and the cooking. McNally said to Roger, "I thought I told you to tend them biscuits."

"Mister Cook, sir, I couldn't keep my mind on those biscuits for the whale," the boy said.

That gave the crew the only laugh since the whale showed.

A few minutes later the captain and Carib called out, "Red line on the le-e-e-e-e-e!"

"Fish, fish!"

125

We heard the bell ring in the engine room. The engineer got the signal to halt.

As the ship slowed, the whale slowed, drifted along on our starboard about a hundred yards away and waited to see what we was going to do.

Lift said, "He want to see us make a set. Everybody like to see menhadeners make a set."

Nobody heard that, and nobody heard it when the captain, he stepped off the rigging on deck and ordered, "In the purse boats—hustle!"

Nobody acted as though the boat had a captain.

Nobody moved.

All stood by the rail and just looked out where that gray hump floated.

The captain, he turned to Fort and asked him why he didn't get going. The seine setter said, "Captain, if you want that fish out yonder you can sure go get it."

That meant the captain could lower the purse boats, unroll the webbing, drop the tom weight, pull in the purse line, haul web, and brail the fish into the boat—all by himself.

His mouth turned on, like the Diesel down below had been turned on before. "I ordered, 'Lower the purse boats!'"

Nobody moved. They just watched the captain perform and stared at the big blob of whale convoying us out in eighty feet of water. Shallow for the whale. Deep for us.

I couldn't understand why the captain, he wanted to risk laying out a net for those fish and putting men in those small boats while that monster was out there. The crew wasn't exactly scared, I don't believe. Most had seen bad storms, sharks, big fish and small—they just thought it was a bad time to put out the small boats. If that whale could push over a big boat like ours, which he could, those purse boats would be just toothpicks for the whale to pick his teeth with. And he could rip a net apart like it was a slip of silk thread.

Besides, the whale had something to say now about whether we was going to make a set. He suddenly moved in closer. Just a few yards off port. He seemed to be just as long as the boat. The wash from him slapped against our hull.

The men grabbed onto bitts, ventilators, rails, anything handy.

Captain Crother, he hung onto the galley door just as hard as anyone else. No more yelling from him about lowering the small boats.

The ship tipped to port like it had done at first.

We could see the water up close by our faces, just even with the deck. The men jumped the opposite way. Because if you jump the way a boat is capsizing, you won't have a chance. You might be swept right overboard.

The big coffee kettle, it been on the floor in the kitchen, now it skimmed right out of the galley, hit up against the rail. Biscuits came out behind the coffeepot. The purse boats, they swung and creaked in their davits, like to have gone overboard. Everything croaked and screamed.

The boat righted.

The whale came up about a hundred feet away, squirted a stream of water straight up, floundered around, and went away from us and under.

The last wave from the whale shuddered our ship. And it lost us Ready Yet.

The wash tossed the pig up against her pen. She smashed through the boards. She squealed in the air. Still she was chewing on something at the same time. She hit the sea, went under.

That made the men feel bad. Ready Yet was going to make some nice eating when the autumn cool would come in, and a few men had got attached to her in a friendly way.

The deck was drenched. The men stood around with soaked skins, looked at one another.

127

The whale had followed us about seven miles before we parted company. We were eight or nine miles off Altamaha Sound in forty feet of water.

"Mate, what you suppose that whale wanted?" someone asked me.

How you going to answer that?

For a few men it was the first time they had seen such a whale. One or two said it was the first big one they saw in two or three years. Mostly we see small red whales in these waters.

Another said it was the biggest he ever saw, and that was me.

The captain, he put on a great show of guts as he started up the rigging again. "Should have made that set," he complained. "Should have made that set." Kept going up the rope ladder, kept saying it. When you fishing, whether you are the captain, the mate, or the crew, you can't admit anything got you beat for very long.

I stayed on deck.

What happened got the crew into whale talk, real excited talk. I was glad they had what to occupy themselves with till we found pogy. Whale talk led them right to Jonah. Jonah took them to the Bible. So for a few minutes that made Rev the big man on deck again.

Lift, he must have had it in mind to have some fun with Rev. Lift was very serious. No laughing lines at the sides of his mouth like he usually had. He made out he was very interested in something in the Bible. From what he said it appeared he may not have been raised deep in the Testaments like some of us.

"Rev, did you read that part about the whale swallowing Jonah?"

"Yes, I read it."

"When he puked him up on the beach?"

"Yes, I did."

"After he been in the whale three whole days?"

"Yes, I know, I read it. I know the whole chapter and verse. What was you going to say?"

"I bet you couldn't have got that sonofabitch with a motorcycle going down that beach."

When they stopped laughing Rev lectured Lift about blaspheming around the Bible. He quoted from Timothy about how a man ought to shun profane and vain babblings because that was going to lead to more blasphemy and transgressing against the Lord.

Lift apologized and said he didn't mean nothing against Jonah nor nobody. Especially not the Lord. "I just couldn't help myself, Rev. That was too good a one to pass up because that one is hard to believe anyway. That's like a man may be bending over in front of you picking up something and you got all you can do to keep both feet on the ground."

Fishermen don't like Jonah too well. They don't like talk of being in a fish's belly for so long. It don't sound like good seamanship nor the best kind of fishing.

This brush with the whale, it set me thinking how the piddling little menhaden fish has chased the mighty whale out of the country's life.

Around the time I started as a mess boy on my first menhaden ship, a sailboat, in 1904, that was the time big changes was coming over the country. Factories, railroads, automobiles, all that changed things—killed off the whale fishery, made way for the coming up of menhaden.

The country was looking for more oil and new ways of getting it. About that time the railroads stopped buying whale oil. That was the last big market of the whale fishery. Electricity and petroleum oil came in, cut the last props out of whaling. Besides, the whalers had killed off the pickings of the whales. On top of that, American whale men didn't keep pace with the Norwegians. In Norway they worked up better fishing methods, made more use of all the different parts of the whale. Whaling companies here went bankrupt, switched businesses, or entered the menhaden fishery.

Even as far back as 1875, menhaden oil was giving whale oil a run. Maine fishermen, they found the oil wells of the seas that's in menhaden. They were mixing pogy oil into whale oil or selling it outright as whale oil.

In New England the whaling men saw menhaden sailboats and steamboats go offshore a few miles, come back with twenty-five or fifty tons of fish, grind it up, squeeze out the oil, and the crews spend the night at home. By 1910 whaling men said, "Menhaden is the big fish now." The great whale was sounding.

A few years back menhaden got scarce along the New England coast.

The fish appeared to school farther south in warmer waters.

Nantucket and New Bedford are nothing no more, as far as whaling goes, just graveyards of the whale fishery's past.

Today the life of the sea that passes on into the life of folks on the hill, it comes mostly from other towns, other places: Amagansett, Long Island, in New York; Wildwood, Tuckerton, and Port Monmouth in New Jersey; Lewes, Delaware; Reedville and Fair Port in Virginia; Beaufort, Morehead City, and Southport in North Carolina; Fernandina Beach, Apalachicola, and De Leon Beach in Florida; Empire and Cameron in Louisiana; Pascagoula and Moss Point in Mississippi; and Port Arthur in Texas.

Mostly, menhaden, the biggest fishery in America, it's moved South.

By this whale chasing us, the cook's noon meal just about fed the walls of the galley and nothing more. He and Roger had to start cooking all over again, and it was two o'clock before we ate.

All through the meal Captain Crother, he chewed on his rough luck as well as his food. He had more to say about luck than all the prophets. He believed in it, like some in God. Talked of Luck, the sea, and the seasons, like some talk of God and heaven and hell. He rankled how one set after another been lost. Something must be the causing of it and he just wished he knew. "You can settle bad luck sometimes, once you know what's causing it."

About luck, there is probably a law behind everything in nature, but it's when you don't know what the law is, you have to trust in luck. I told him, "Captain, if we just keep our boat shipshape, everything hammered down, leaks calked, ropes spliced, decks clean, keep her just so, we make our luck and less going to go wrong."

After we ate, Captain Crother, he moved up and down deck trying to think. When the captain cruises around like that the men don't want him to hear what they're saying. They'll switch their talk so he can't make anything out of it, "Look here, old Jim Crouse, he took us down ship today." Another man may answer with some foolishment like, "Is that so? I hear he is doing pretty well these days."

The captain can't make any sense out of that. When they see his back they may drift back to whatever they was talking about.

Captain Crother foghorned it from stem to stern: "Somebody on this ship bringing me bad times! If I knew who I would just take him straight to the hill!"

The Louisiana bunt puller, he was close to the captain, and the captain was looking at him when he said that, so Louisiana said, "Yessir, Captain Crother, somebody got to go."

The captain liked that. He repeated it. "*Somebody got to go!*"

When the fishing is bad a crew may be just as quick as a captain to look for someone or something to blame.

Captain Crother gave a suspicious look at the hatch. He moved over by it and looked at it, like it was a hot firecracker that might go off. He bawled out, "Anybody on board we don't know about?"

"No, sir!" Quite a few spoke up. "Nobody that ain't booked." "No, nobody like that!"

Captain Crother, he wasn't so sure. He walked around the hatch. He said, "You know, more than once we found old Noah on board when we thought we left him behind. He's stowing away on one ship or the other every day, *and I just wouldn't want him to show up around here!*"

Captain Crother whupped around like a bad wind. "Here you, Blu! Bob! Westley! I want you-all to go down in the forepeak. See into each bunk *good*. Go through the forepeak with a piece of netting if you have to. If Noah is down there, hyst him up."

One by one the bunt pullers squirmed down into the forepeak.

That hatch is small, square, and very black to look down into. You can't even see the ladder as you go down. That forepeak is a narrow dark hole in the front of the ship under the deck. It takes the shape of the ship's bow. Bunks laid out in tiers of four on each hull side and along a partition that separates the forepeak from the bulkhead. Sixteen bunks are stacked in there, close, like candy bars, one atop the other. Only sixteen supposed to be carried in the forepeak by law, but they laid in boards and mattresses for more besides. No escape hatch. The sleeping quarters is supposed to have a companionway to leave out of in case of trouble, but if there ever was one on this ship it was blocked up long ago. Lights supposed to be on in there day and night, it's so dark, but the one little electric bulb we had, it was burned out. In the dark, if something jammed and you were in there, you couldn't see nothing. It's blacker than black shoes worn in the dark. The hatch is usually open in weather like this, but it was closed when the fishermen went down.

They could have had their flashlights on down there for a minute or two, and then we heard a great commotion and joking coming out of the hatchway.

Sure enough, old Noah, he stowed away.

Old Noah been a bunt puller maybe forty-five to fifty years, from way back in the sailing days. He helped pull up millions of fish, may have emptied the ocean of more fish than any other man that ever pulled bunt. Now he was old, his joints cracked like burning leaves, and no captain wanted him on board. He would get his feet mixed in the lines and he wasn't pretty to look at no more. His hands was knotted like some ropes you seen. Noah's hair was white, and a lots of it, and his white head crowned his sad black features. There was furrows in his face like the waves he been riding all his life. And he no more smiled. But he just had to be on a pogy boat. Didn't have no other home. No close kin back on shore. Didn't know nothing any more but to pull bunt and live with a crew down in a forepeak and up in the galley and out in a purse boat. Like an old prisoner that's been let out of jail, but he's alone and lost and don't know how to make his way. So he goes back to the prison door and he says, "Captain, I come back home."

That was old Noah.

Old Noah, he had the rheum. Had it bad and had had it for many years. A great many pogy fishermen get that. That's our disease. You stay out on that water, you sweat pulling bunt, you sleep in one of them forepeak cells for long enough, get in all that wet and sweat, you get fevers. These fevers come and go, and you may work along with them. But one day you wake up in the morning, an arm or a leg is burning, and it burns for weeks. When it stops burning you're left with crinks in the elbows and knees, and your muscles feel hard as wood. Then you got something to carry to your grave. You ship out after that, your bones and elbows will tell you more about the weather than the clouds or the radio reports. You'll see men going to the medicine chest in the pilothouse where they got tape, gauze, alcohol, iodine. Men be rubbing themselves and trying to get spry again.

Old Noah, because of that rheum, he walks like he's on stilts. You can see one foot thinking of taking the other along if it so decide.

So the pogy boats, they can't easy use him.

Nobody pensions off an old pogy fisherman. They just fade away on shore somewhere, maybe with relatives. The government don't take care of them no way, and neither does the fishing companies. So old Noah, he just went stowing away on one pogy ship after another, sneaking on during the night and going along just about for the ride and for what they would give him for being on board and doing what little he could. He might mend some netting or help the mess boy in the galley. They said, "He sure getting to look like the colored Davy Jones." And if they was having bad luck Noah was a handier thing to blame than their own mistakes.

As the old man's shock of white hair showed up over the hatch the crew gathered about to have themselves a time and see what the captain would do. Cooking Devil McNally and young Roger, they came out from the galley. And Carib, ordinarily he'd shove right back up into the nest as soon as he ate, but he hung around too.

Captain Crother, he stood up stiff, like he had predicted the end of the world and the end had come. "There! You see what I told you? I *knew* it was a jinx on board!"

He got wrathful with the old fisherman. "Don't you-all know when to lay down?"

134

Noah, he said nothing, but he kept looking at the cook. Him and Cooking Devil, they was old friends.

"You picked *my* boat to lay down on!"

Noah said nothing.

"Now just supposing you was to die down there. I would have to go back *twenty* miles to port with you."

Noah still quiet.

His clothes was real far gone. Shabby old fellow, but he held himself square.

"Ain't you got nothing to say for yourself?"

Then Noah said what he always said, what he told all the captains and all the crews every time they found him stowed away. "I bring in many a fish in my time, Mister Captain. When I was a young man it wasn't nobody called me a jinx. I webbed them in by the thousands of measures on the *Patsy Warner*—"

"*I know, I know,*" the captain interrupted him.

"—on the *J. S. Marquart,* the *Lawrence Queet,* the *L. S. Simmons . . .*"

"You been on them *all!* It's time you quit! That don't cut no ice on *my* ship!"

"When the *Parkins* went down there off Cape Hatteras in 1942 and seventeen men got drowned I lived through that to fish another day. . . ."

"I don't care what you done in your time. You the causing of all my run of bad luck. I just think I best order Fitch to take us to the beach and put you off on the first sand we come to!"

I spoke up. I said to the captain, suppose he let me be responsible for Noah just this trip. I said I didn't think he was bad luck. I fished with him many years and I known him to be a good hand.

Captain Crother cussed me hard. "*You don't look no better to me than Noah when you stand up for a jinx like him!*"

135

I started to say something, but he was doing all the saying. "Did you look in the forepeak to see whether he was on when we came away? You know you always supposed to do that."

I told him I had one of the men to do it. The captain asked me who it was, and I said I didn't rightly remember.

It was an instant's quiet. The captain stared at Noah like Noah was some trash fish that needed to be thrown out of a net. "We got to feed *you* too," he said. Seemed he couldn't make up his mind what to do.

That's when the cook spoke up. He came by the forepeak where the captain and most of us stood around Noah. "Oh, it's plenty of food in there. Noah must be hungry. I think he better come have some biscuits and coffee. I saved out a few that didn't get washed overboard."

The cook put his right hand under Noah's arm. He had a wet left hand on his hip. Looked like a mom taking proper care of a growing son. Besides, it would be the crew to pay for Noah's food, not the captain, and not the company. "You must be hungry, ain't you, old man?"

Noah nodded his head. Just the smallest nod, you could hardly see it. Maybe he nodded only with his eyes.

Even the captain got quiet.

The crew scattered. They dusted out aft like a bunch of flies that been swatted.

Captain Crother, he wheeled about, jumped into the rigging, and pedaled for the crow's-nest as fast as he could climb.

In the nest the captain gave some fresh signals to the pilot. The engines appeared to pick up. We headed in a little closer to the beach. We were ten miles out and still northerning it up the Georgia coast.

Upcoast, steady. Toward St. Catherine's and Ossabaw islands, big islands practically tacked onto the mainland. Mid-afternoon, the sea is wide awake. Fish, fish everywhere, but

136

not one for the net. About two miles in, a long sand bar. Teeth of the ocean, breakers, eating at that hill in the water.

Like the land with its crawling, growing, and flying, so it's in the ocean, especially coastwise where we catch our ocean oil. If you could see the bottom in water five, ten, and twenty fathoms deep you'd see more life there than you would walking on the wildest part of the hill. Maybe every square inch of the bottom, it's life. Flounder, brim, croakers, starfish, yellowtail, they use every ditch on the bottom for a street. Crabs and lobsters crawl from bank to bank like on land tame and wild game over the fields. Most fish stay at the bottom. Maybe it's warm there, maybe they can jump on each other, feed better there, maybe they can hide in the coral, sand, and clay down there. Maybe all those things. I only know what there is to see and feel. Let down a menhaden net, you'll bring up in it all those kinds of fish, sometimes a barrel of shrimp. All that fine skim gets over the meshes, the skim the pogy eat, and you get some idea what a food barrel it is down there.

All day the sun beats down on that water, churns it, warms it. It's a fool that only looks at the top and the foam and says, "That's the ocean and she runs down for miles." It's the *life* that runs down for miles. When I first took to the sea all I saw was the big flat top. Just that, and the feeling how deep it was beneath the ship. Now I look at the sea, it's not the water I notice so much, but the life in it, living off the sea and on itself. See it like you would look at the ocean through a glass-bottom boat. Except I don't use glass. My mind's eye, and all I've seen of the ocean along the coast from Maine to Texas, *that's* my glass. I wouldn't know how far back it was I found out that the real dimension of the sea, it's not the depth or the weight of the water, but the life in it.

Travel the coast from Long Island to Daytona Beach, let your ship go in and out of those inlets, bays, harbors, rivers, jetties, see and feel all that water, know all the life that's in it, and you can easy see the Lord's everywhere. He don't leave no empty space nowhere. Right where you think it's just wet, there it's life. Where you think it's space, there it's full. Where you think it's calm, it's spinning.

A thousand times I seen before me the charts of the coast. They're about four feet square, tell you the depths of the water where the slews and the shoals and the coral reefs are, where you can bring a ship of a hundred-feet length, and where you better stay away. The Coast Guard, they got it all charted, the length, the depth, the wash, the mud, the clay, the white earth and the dark earth under the water.

They got plenty charted, but ain't no man yet and no fisherman and no boat charted the amount of life. From that skim plankton that you *can't* see all the way up to the big whale you may not *want* to see, *there's* the Lord's creation. Keep looking at that and lay your net down into it, you learn to respect nature and God and the bigness and smallness of things more than anything else.

The sun is in the ocean and the moon's in there too. The wind's in there and the clouds may come from there. Man and ships are down there, all up and down the coast, like any chart will show you.

You talk about your Mississippi, and you think it's a big river. I hear tell that's a big river, but there's a river down in the ocean and she's the biggest in the world. She's the Gulf Stream and she goes up the coast to the cold northern parts. A real river, broad and deep, fast and big, and she carries the blood of the oceans over the world.

You see and feel the way that river flows, like blood, through the ocean and you can easy get the feeling the earth is a big round ball of a man, *alive*, and moving around in a family of live balls, the moon, the sun, and all the stars. Makes you think the world of stars is a live family, like human beings are alive. You feel that ocean moving under you, and it's like your boat is moving in the blood stream of something *alive,* a big round man or woman. That's the way the world feels to you under a menhaden boat sometimes. Man, he's just a barnacle on the bottom of some *live* thing we call the Earth. Volcanoes erupt like boils on a man's body. A tide sweeps over the land, like a rush of blood to a man's face. The ocean swells sometimes, like the whole earth making love. Makes you think a man's body is in a way in the image of the ocean, that you live and move like the sea; makes you feel part of the whole thing, and that's when a man feels best.

Out here you see each wavelet has its will and its way. And nothing ever's quiet even when it seem to be quiet. Just when the surface is like glass, that's when the fish on the bottom may be moving at each other.

You might think a starfish a pretty thing. And they are, to us. They're all over the bottom of certain waters, especially along the Southeast coast. But ask an oyster what he thinks of a starfish, he'll run. Starfish go for the oyster like bluefish for pogy.

I seen plenty fish that look in the head like toad frogs, like cows, like chicken hanks. Only head I never seen matched on a fish is the human head, but many fish heads have reminded me of people I didn't like. Wouldn't know their names, there's too much in the sea to give a name to it all. Saw a fish off Texas, about a foot long, color of a frog, but it was a fish, and its eyes were red as blood.

Hundreds of sea cows, a foot or so long, each with two horns, a tail like a fish, and a head like a cow. Spied them in bunches farming the ocean surface. Devilfish as large as a small house. The stingaree with his long tail and the eyes on top of his head. He's wide in front, comes to a point in the back, and there his tail begins. You'll get him once in a while in the net, then you got to get him out, throw him back in the sea, or if he's small, grind him up for meal.

Plenty in the sea unknown yet. Plenty not been seen by man

or his cameras. I once saw a fish bigger than the boat we was on, it came up by the stern so close that it sprayed us with as much water as a high sea would do, drenched the ship. None of us knew what it was. Came high as a roof out of the water. Had a long head with worried-looking bumps on it, just small eyes you couldn't hardly see, something like horns behind its head. But that could have been fins. When she heaved out alongside us she looked like a leopard, had white spots on her. She saw us, got scared, and went under. We argued whether it was a whale, a shark, or something sent by the Lord to warn us to go in closer to the beach. "Stay in, Captain," we said, "this deep water's not for us." The captain rung up the ship. We told folks about it when we came to the hill, but nobody believed it.

From time to time they get something on this Southeast coast, they call it the red tide. It's fish, millions of them. The fish die and high water carries them in to the coast. Low water strands them on the beach. She blows in, red, on the shores, by the hundreds of thousands. Once when a Florida beach was flooded with them they sent the factory workers from the De Leon menhaden plants to clean up the fish, yard-rake them off the beaches, carry them back to the plant, make meal and fertilizer out of them.

Some kinds of fish, they're so plentiful in these coastal waters, from Florida to North Carolina, that you don't need nets. Just go out with clubs and beat about in the shallows and club your kill to death. You can take a yard rake and pull it through shallow water and rake up scallops in some places.

There's big hills in the water off North Carolina, canyons that go down a mile or two. Different kinds of fish live down there, find their way up top into the shore, then into the nets. Maybe you've never heard of the pen fish, fins sharp as pens, thorns on his bottom, we used to catch them in schools, make machine oil of them, he's good eating too. Catch him schooling with menhaden. And the hairback fish, comes late in fall, we call them kyaks. The kyak, he's got one long hair on his back, nothing but solid oil in him, all oil, so into the grinder with him. Sometimes in the pogy net you'll catch up the croaker, he's good eating, or the cigar fish, you grind him up for meal, and he makes a fine grade of oil too. Old heron hog, a long fish, he plays around the boat as we move, gets his scrap and waste.

Close in to shore you'll see the hump-backed porpoise chase the menhaden up into the sand. They and bluefish, they'll shepherd the pogy into shallow water, then the shepherd swallows the sheep. That's what we were looking for now, some big fish to be herding the menhaden in toward the beach where we could get at them. They say it's bad luck to bring a porpoise to the hill. Saw that with my own eyes. Helped get one on deck, we winched him up onto the rigging. Maybe it was too much weight on the mast. The next day this wooden mast broke in two, caved over onto the deck, and the porpoise slipped back into the water. The porpoise gets hurt easy, tangles with a net, he dies quick. Heard tell of a porpoise pushing a corpse into the coast. They say old porpoise don't want nothing nasty in the water, but maybe he was just playing that way.

Mussel, it's a white sea fan, something alive in it; hard and sharp, wide as your hand, it will stick out of the mud, tear up your net. Coral bottom will tear your web. The bottom of some bays, they're hard as cement road. Shore waters, there's treason on the bottom. The bottom is waiting there all the time with tricks and traps to catch us.

The human dead in the seas happens mostly along shores and coasts, not way out.

The whale man, he went down in two miles of water. The rest of us sink in ten and twenty feet of it, in breakers, on rocks.

Dragging for menhaden in these shallow waters, you'll come up sometimes with oysters and clams in among your oil fish. You take them out or grind them up for oil and meal. Seems as if those pressure cookers at the factory, they'll about turn a rock into oil and meal. Most any kind of fish, shell or bone, will go through them, become food for the hogs and turkeys, or fertilizer for the country's fields.

But sometimes . . . when you not catching fish . . . the coast is a weary place, like it is tired of carrying its whole load, water, fish, and on its shoulders the weight of the sky. I seen it like that a hundred times. You can be sitting hunched in the crow's-nest, feeling the same way. Down below the crew be just lolling like that too, just a-wearying.

It was like that now.

"Ain't nothing doing," you say to the captain.

The striker-boat man, he been staring straight ahead till his eyes hurt like there's sand in them and he says, "No, everything on the sea look dead. Don't see not even a gull."

"Sure pretty quiet," the captain say.

The boat rolls along like the engine's tired. You can hear the seams of the boat crying for their hurt and not wanting to go and not wanting to fish no more.

You look down between the engine room and the galley to where the big square fish hole is empty, like nothing in its stomach and it feels bad.

You can see a ring setter leaning against the port rail down below or somebody else just drag into the galley for a cup of coffee. Nothing for the fishermen to do now but wait for the menhaden to show. And they're weary too. Not much talk among them. No fun, no cuss words. Cigarettes just barely hanging out of their mouths, and they look out across the water, lonely and wondering.

Then you see each man is a world to himself. Maybe they

not even standing in a group nowhere now, but each off to himself, one on the bow staring forward, another wandering by the bridge to see what's doing with the pilot. The pilot seem like a dead man staring straight fore and his hands on the wheel, spread out like Christ's, waiting for a strike, and just going on. To starboard maybe a man leaning on the rail seeing the hill, maybe seeing his Lulu, someone, just staring, waiting for the fish that just not showing. A few feet from him the seine setter reading out of a funny book in a half kind of a way, as if the paper may fall out of his hands. A few yards beyond him a bunt puller just staring at the water, maybe wondering why it's not a ripple there and all so quiet.

Down aft two or three men laying flat on the deck, staring up at the blue. One be saying, "Hell." Man next to him mutter, "Some stuff." No telling what he mean, what he be thinking of.

Just nothing on board the whole boat, only the pilot up front and the engineer below doing anything much. Us in the crow's-nest half asleep.

That's when the ocean can seem a tired thing, and life run slow. The big weariness of the water fetch up inside each of us. The ocean will do that to you. Take your strength away sometimes even when there's no high wave, no wind, no hot sun, nothing. Just the big weight of the sea all around, like it's a magnet, draw you into yourself, and you and the whole crew just stand and sit where you are, ghostly, half dead, weary. Life and fish and making money, all just about come to a stop.

I say to the captain, "Sleepy, Captain?"

He answer, with all the weight of the sea, so you can hardly hear it, "Yeah."

Yes, the ocean seem to sleep sometimes and the things in it and on it seem to sleep. A weary kind of sleep. Then in a way you well off, nothing happening, nobody getting their

143

hands hurt, the lines not meshing in your feet, the engine behaving okay. Then you're out of pain. Everybody out of pain. The ocean itself seem to feel no pain.

At four o'clock I was on the bridge by Fitch. On the boat, all that weariness and quiet.

We were in thirty-five feet, gray sand and shell bottom, and traveling about eight miles an hour. Could have been sixty-five miles from port. A long way to go for fish, but other menhaden ships were up this far too. Four miles off St. Catherine's Sound. The sea was smooth, the sky clear. You couldn't hardly see a streak of white up there. Water so clear you could spot whiting, perch, shiners, moving between us and the sand base. A porpoise came up by the bow and coughed water at us, went under. Seemed to be plenty of birds all of a sudden flapping around.

A spray, thin as a fog, fizzed over the whole ship.

Everybody stopped what little they was doing, wondered about that. Maybe a wave had slapped up on us. Maybe the porpoise did it.

All on deck looked up, straight into the clearest sky, just sun and blue, sun and blue. Just a streak or two of gray cotton a long way off, a speck, like the moon will show sometimes during the day.

For the wonder of the sea, it's not the bigness of it, it's the thinness and smallness; a drop of water, the plankton, a shark's fin, a few-inch pogy of blood and oil, the heat in light you can't even see. Big as the ocean is, it's all that delicate smallness, all those parts together that makes the big life-and-death, blood-and-oil sea.

And yet we all knew just what this was. It was a thin, misty shower, thin and hard to see, like a Portuguese man-of-war is hard to see, but we were washed with it, and where was it coming from?

The men, they been too much weighed down for days with the coast's whims, and maybe they weren't able to take any more of its trickery. They sounded bedeviled.

"Where this rain coming from?"

"That rain appear to be coming from the sun!"

"Lord God, what's going to happen now?"

The top of the ocean is like a human's face; sometimes full of wrath, sometimes angelic, devilish, smiling, anything.

It was more like a few tears crying for all we been through. Right while the mist washed our bodies, the sun burned hotter and the sky's blue color, it seemed to lighten. The sea is a strange place. Ain't no man ever writ the history of the sea yet. Wasn't enough wet in the air to cool us or wash us, just enough to worry us with wondering, "What's next?" But Luck has a curved arm, she may bend it your way any time.

We were silent, like a minute's prayer.

Then you could hear the music that went up, from hawk's-nest to the bridge, from stern to bow, starboard and port, even from the cook and Roger in the galley.

All my years at the sea I never before saw a whole crew, behold menhaden at the same instant.

Everyone sang it out in one long word:

"*P-O-O-O-O-O-G-Y-Y-Y-Y!*"

Pogy a hundred yards to lee! Pogy straight ahead! All around!

Blood-red menhaden, they came up from all sides to meet that little bit of crying from the sky. They surfaced, they flipped their tails, sparkled, they about jumped out of the water. Flew over the sea for acres. Millions of them. Enough for a half dozen ships to work on for hours.

We looked nestward to Captain Crother. He pointed down the sky maybe a quarter mile away. A thin breeze blew toward us from there. His words fell down among us like stones. "That *damned* rain, it came from *there!*"

145

He pointed to a shadow in the sky. You wouldn't think it had anything in it. But it had that spray and gave out with it, and it fell, more like a veil over the *Moona Waa Togue* than a rain. You could just barely see it settle on the water a few acres around us. Then it ended, gone, like a tear that's been wiped away and won't never fall again.

These menhaden, they have strong sensibility to everything going on over the water and under it. Fish that live off that skim that a man can't even see, they can feel what we can't. Maybe they felt the tears that fell from the sky and came up to see who was crying.

Seeing the fish, the first in some time, the men got a little excited. Old captain kept yelling, "Get to it! Get to it! They may move!"

The bunt pullers hurried up the seine setters and the ring setters to lower the boats.

We put out the small boats and the men just about fell into them.

Some men have a wild look when they're bringing in the fish. Like they're doing the greatest job. Look fierce, brave, awful. Pull with great motions of their muscles. Others that go about it quietly and sing a little at the task, they may be doing the real work.

> *Captain, don't you see*
> *That dark cloud rising over yonder?*
>   (Pull)
>
> *Captain, don't you see*
> *That dark cloud rising over yonder?*
>   (Pull)
>
> *Lord, Lord, it's a sign of rain,*
>   (Pull)
>
> *Lord, Lord, it's a sign of rain.*
>   (Pull)

That time it was a sign of fish.

Takes a whole crew working together to bring up a few hundred thousand pogy. No one man ever did it alone yet. Till one does it alone you can bet, "Many men make one barrel of oil."

You pull web, you work with all your senses. You smell the water and fish; you feel the spray and the wet; you taste the splash; you feel the fish against you; and the captain roar; and you think you're getting rich—but you ain't.

We had such a mighty number of fish in the meshing that once, when they sensed they were trapped, they moiled and tried to strike the net. They swung the tom weight back up to the top, just about knocked it out of the water.

Some of the men, their hands were raw from pulling. Then they used the beckets. The beckets are small pieces of rope on the gunwales of the purse boats. You make a twist in the net and tie it to the beckets. That will hold the meshing in the purse boat while you rest your hands, crack your knuckles, straighten out your fingers. After a minute, untie the beckets and pull web again.

For the first time in days we got the fish into the bunt.

The *Moona Waa Togue* had moved out and got behind the cork line. The purse boats drew the net right up to the side of the mother ship. Cables were hooked from the big boat to four rings on the cork side of the net so as to hold it close to the ship. The small boats were at angles to the big boat, so that the fish were jammed in the triangular center.

For a while the bunt pullers just tugged at the net, made that triangle center tighter and tighter, got the water out of it, packed in the fish closer, till the pogy made a solid mass in the bunt.

Carib and me, we jumped onto the big boat to brail the fish from the bunt over the deck rail into the fish hole. The bailer is worked from an overhead boom that hangs from the

147

mast. You steer the bailer with a long pole we call the triptail. The bailing net, we call it the scap net, that's a basket-shaped iron ring five feet in diameter. The net bag drops about five feet, it's big enough to hold a ton of fish. The bottom of that basket is closed by a series of twenty-two rings, with a chain running through them. When the net hangs over the fish hole, you release those rings, the bottom of the net opens, the fish drop into the hole. Jerk that chain, close the bottom again, and the net is steered by the triptail back overside to scoop up through that iron ring another load of fish from the bunt.

The bunt pullers stayed in the purse boats, held the webbing till all the fish were taken from it and dropped into the fish hole. Two hatch plates on the deck were opened, and a few fish that landed on the deck were swept into holes that led into the fish hole.

We scooped fish for a half hour. Live and dead ones went into the hole a ton at a time. Till a third of the hole was filled with maybe 150,000–200,000 fish. Fifty-sixty tons. A fair-sized haul for one set.

When the hole is full there's fish in there we call trash fish. They may be poor in oil or meal. Some we throw to the birds, but others will go through the same suction rig and pressure cookers as the menhaden.

We threw scrap fish overboard. Sickle-winged gulls and the hawks came toward us, thick as flies around the rigging, trailed behind us like banners with teeth, banners with geeking sounds. Gulls, real air pirates, they planed around us, blatted, ate the trash fish we threw them, the swept-off leavings of salt and slime that we brushed off the deck.

There is a time when the ocean sings. Then the water is not smooth, but she ripples. The wind is not hard, but there's a breeze. The sun is warm, but not too hot, for evening is coming on. The gulls and pelicans behind us, *they're* chanting *now*, for the scent of the menhaden. The crew busy at their sweeping, pumping, and net-salting tasks, gay. The boat drifting, while the captain make up his mind what to do next. You're not inshore, but not out too far either.

And the captain, he's even got a smile, thin as a caul, around his mouth.

That's when everything is singing—that and when the fish hole has something in its belly.

Blood and oil, guts and gore, right there in the fish hole. Life stuff, death stuff, waste no sympathy on it, it's money in the pocket, a man got to make a dollar. "And see thou hurt not the oil and the wine." Some like them big, eighteen inches long, and some like them short and fat and oily like they come in the Gulf. Me, I am an old fisherman and I like them in the hold, the way they were now, six to eight inches apiece.

Once I stopped to look at all that white-bellied meat laying there in the hole. Life was in there a few minutes ago. Life *still* in thousands of those fish, life of the sea, of man, animal, plant. All that life moving in a big school a few minutes ago, and it had God's breath in it—as much as you or me have God's breath in us—or as little—and now it was all in there dying and hardening. No wonder it raised such a great stink, almost at once. That's the holler it put up for being caught.

The sun was an orange just over the rail of the sea. Threw a red line over everything—the coast, the boat, the fish, the crew—everything.

"We'll lay the anchor," Captain Crother said. "It's still plenty of fish in through here. We'll make another set or two in the morning, deck-load her, and bring her in tomorrow."

Ordinarily it's best to get a haul of fish into port as soon as you can, within ten or eleven hours anyway, so they won't spoil too much, but with fishing poor like we been having it, you'll stretch a point. Everybody was glad to stay out, and the Danfort anchor went over the stern.

Carib, he opened the deck plates, swept the loose pogy into the hold. The bunt puller, Billy Ritchie, he had the job to go down the ladder into the fish hole and pick up whatever eating fish was there. Two or three yelled into the galley door for McNally and Roger to hurry up with the supper, they was plain devittled.

Plenty of water still in the fish hole. A pump, worked from the deck, leading down into the hole, sent a big blurp of water overside every few seconds.

Blu and Lawyer walked up and down together on the port side of the fish hole, just for something to do. Blu stopped all of a sudden because he saw two bare feet and legs sticking up out of the top of the fish where the fish was about five feet deep. He saw this man's bare black soles, his ankles, and maybe an inch or two more of his legs kicking out the top of the fish.

A man with his head buried under many tons of fish, he's going to be very quiet. From that minute on he needs help; he can only talk with his flapping heels.

Blu pointed. "Christ sakes!"

Lawyer yelled for the crew.

The fish were sucking down Billy Ritchie like he was in quicksand. He had tromped around on those fish a little too free, he must have been drawn under. Which is what the menhaden will do sometimes if a man is misfortunate enough to get in among the fish before they have hardened.

The whole crew, captain and me, even the engineer, we swarmed around the hole.

Fort yelled, "Hang onto my legs. I get him!"

The seine setter almost dived into the hole. Blu and Lawyer grabbed onto his legs, and two other men held onto Fort's thighs.

They lowered him right over that pair of ankles.

Fort grabbed onto one ankle, and the other foot slipped under fish.

That suction of the wet fish, the oil and water, it's like mud or thick glue, it brings you right down.

Fort held onto Ritchie's ankle with one hand and threw fish out of the way with his other, till he could get both his hands around and under one of Ritchie's knees. He pulled Ritchie, and four men pulled Fort. No sound, nothing from Ritchie, he might be suffocated by now.

The five men pulling on Ritchie, that forced him upward.

Plenty hands reached down to pull him out; then they put Fort on his feet.

Ritchie was so wet, smooth, oily from the fish that he slid a few inches on the planking when they laid him down, but he wasn't breathing.

He couldn't have been under those fish for long because old Noah, he said he been looking in the hole just a few seconds before.

I straddled Ritchie, pushed his chest up and down, worked his arms so as to get him breathing again and start his heart going. Somebody held a looking glass by his mouth to see was he breathing, but no sign of it.

That went on five or ten minutes. Some began to moan over it, some got excited. They thought the Texas fisherman sure been sucked to death by the fish.

Captain Crother, he was serious upset; buzzed around, talked, and ordered.

Old Noah, he stepped in. "Here," he said, "try this." He rubbed his fingers under Billy Ritchie's center piece. He said, "Sometimes that may start the nerves working and get something going in the brain. It will do it for a live man and it may do it for someone that ain't yet dead."

Noah kept rubbing that underneath part and sometimes

151

tickling the man under the arms. I kept raising and lowering Ritchie's chest.

Maybe Noah helped out best.

All of a sudden Ritchie sucked in a real deep swallow of air. His chest went up like a filled-out burlap bag.

Noah stopped what he was doing. The captain, he said, "All of you get back off and let this man get some of that air."

Someone washed Ritchie's face with water. I kept working that top part of his body, filling his lungs with what air there was.

Ritchie hadn't swallowed much water, but he been suffocated by the pressure of the menhaden. If his lungs had filled up with water, we might never have brought him around—because there was still plenty of water in between the fish.

When the bunt puller came to, he looked at us with the popeyes of a dead fish. He closed them, started to breathe regular.

Captain Crother, it seemed like a big weight was off him, he said, "Bix, don't let that man stop breathing!"

Ritchie got stronger. He looked from one to the other, asked what happened.

Nobody said nothing to him yet because he didn't seem in shape to hear anything anyway.

"Was I fighting somebody in the fish hole?"

The fellows laughed. They laughed with joy that he was going to live and laughed at what he said. "You sure was fighting something in the fish hole!"

Accidents on the ship, around the docks, no way to total up all that. No way to tell how many men been hurt and lost their lives in this kind of fishing. They keep track of the fish they catch, but not the fishermen that are caught.

You got about two hundred and fifty ships out each day, all summer, from New York to Texas. Many are old floaters like ours. That means about five thousand men on the water in all kinds of weather, and new men among them all the time. Multiply what may happen on one ship in a season by two hundred and fifty, you'll get the idea.

Wouldn't know how many hands and legs been crushed, how many men caught the rheum in the forepeak of these ships—but it's a bigger measure than what the men get paid. Somebody gets killed on a ship off Texas, nobody up in Reedville, Virginia, may hear of it. The local paper where it happened may not even print it. A ship off Long Island may have a fire, nobody going to know of it in the Florida ports. They may just learn about each other when they get into one another's ports, weeks, months, years later. "You hear about this? That?" "You hear what happened to the *Moona Waa Togue?*"

Falls in that fish hole, freakish twists like what happened to Billy Ritchie. Once I saw a man fall into the hole from the mast and break a leg; he was lucky, most would be killed in a drop from that height. Another time a lady came on board to see her husband while the ship was at dock, wanted to bring him something before we went out. She passed by the hole, the ship rolled, she toppled in, landed on the floor, never came out alive.

Death be all about you some weeks, some seasons. I knew two cooks to get washed overboard from different ships. Seen two mess boys killed, one blown overboard in a bad wind, the other in a fall at the dock. Sometimes fires in the forepeak, from lamps and stoves that tip over, fires in the engine room. Stovely, the engineer on this boat, he was blown up on deck once from an explosion in his engine room, but he lived through it. And bunt pullers, they're always in trouble around the net and the small boats.

A man loses his life in this work, his family gets nothing. Not unless they carry their own insurance. If a man dies on the job, the company will send him home and pay the cost of his burial, nothing more. The fishermen get no pension from the companies when they get old, wind up like old Noah. Off season, the local factories won't hire menhaden men because they know as soon as spring and fish arrive the menhadener, he'll be gone, because the men love the wide, wide sea. They go with the sailor poet who say, "Some people like the mountain, Some people like the sky, Some people like the desert, But the ocean is for I."

Some menhaden ships been condemned in the past, but the government ain't inspected them much since World War II. A ship got to be in mighty poor condition to be put on the hill. So many ships like ours around, bilges filled with water, planking waterlogged, hulls weakened; ships that creak like old farm sheds in the wind.

The *Moona Waa Togue*, she's been drunk with salt water and fish rot for half a generation. But she'll go out on a blind trip like the one we're on now, and sometimes come back with a half million fish anyway!

When the moon came up, she seemed to give off as much heat as the sun. Evening didn't cool the air the way it sometimes would. We saw menhaden flipping all around the boat. They'll glisten in strong moonlight and starlight. You'll see little lights on top of the water.

The moonlight splotched over the ship like yellow oil showed us the skippering of the fish beside the hull. Fishermen and scientists, they don't know too much about menhaden, neither by day or night. When you got a banquet before you, you don't stop to figure out how each vegetable grew, or what each piece of pig or beef felt and knew and lived through before it was cooked. It's like that in this industry. There's so much fish, they just catch it and grind it. But the fish don't sleep at night, like the fishermen do. They run and play and move and eat at

night. Maybe because the big fish forage on them after sun-
down as much as during the day. Maybe the fish sleep when
they move. I don't know. But you can see them sparkle at the
surface like we saw them tonight, flipping like diamonds, holding the starlight and the moonlight right in their scales.

We have even put out nets at night, by moonlight, and let
the fish stay inside the big loose webbing all night, and pulled
them in in the morning. Carib would go out there in his rowboat, have a lantern with him, wave the lantern "Come on"
when he got among the fish. Then the crew slip into their purse
boats, glad to get the night light and the night air, and put
the big linen spider over them. It was that kind of a night tonight, full of light on the water, full of fish living all around us,
a night for us to slip a shroud over the living oil of the sea—
but we didn't do it. Nobody felt like a night set. Too uncertain,
too dangerous.

The fish in the hold, they was pretty hard now, all dead,
and blood and oil spread over them like a film. When the fish
harden, their blood and oil forms a reddish liquid that gives
up ammonia fumes. Pulling Ritchie out of there had busted up
more fish, broken their heads, squashed them. The day's heat
was still in every plank. Decks still hot under our feet. Those
fish had sunlight and energy in them before we got them. Now
they was giving that to us along with their lives.

We had to go up in front of the boat so as not to catch the
full blast of the gas coming off the fish. If you was down by the
stern or had to hit the line, where the fumes were worse, you
liked to have died. If you don't have the fish off the ship by
nighttime, you can hardly sleep in the forepeak. Your eyes
begin to pour, same as from wood smoke.

The men laid about the boat, smoking and talking. Somebody had them a bottle of wine, a few men each had a swallow
or two, and the evening dragged till ten o'clock.

The captain, he had a pint of bourbon in his belly. That's

how he fought off the ammonia fumes and the smell. But he wouldn't stand for any serious drinking from the crew.

Liquor talks loud when it gets loose from the jug. Just before the captain went to his quarters and fell into a pickled sleep, he said to the crew, "I don't want to hear no beefing about the gas. It's no way for pogy to smell like orange blossoms, lest you leave them in the sea." He made more sense in bourbon than he did sober.

But nothing going to stop the crew from talking about the fish stink and the gas. Like people in the public street talk about weather, that's the way a menhaden crew going to speak of what they got to live with till they reach port. "When the pogy stinks in the fish hole it's because he's away from home." Another fellow say, "One menhaden fish on a plate, it tastes like a herring and it's bony, the smell can be cut with some marjoram. But a fish hole full of menhaden ain't found its marjoram yet." (At home my wife will tell a stranger, "When the pogy smell floats over town from the factory we know Bix is making money." Plenty cracking about that odor in the menhaden ports.)

We could hear the captain's snores all over ship. The men talked of it. "Snoring right through that smell!" "Got the jump on the fumes!" "He must have known what was coming!"

The men got a story to prove that what Lucifer has down in hell, it's not sulphur at all but ammonia gas. They tell it, "When the devil didn't have nothing better to do he said, 'I'll give them fellows upstairs the idea of catching menhaden in a net. I'll make them put it in a fish hole on a hot boat, and then let's see what happens.'"

Lucifer, he done succeeded.

You could hear the men slip the password from one to the other. Wasn't much else they could think of. "Mellow, eh, fellow?"

"Real mellow, fellow."

By midnight those fish so far gone that the gas flew up out of the hole like smoke exhausts from the back of an auto. Wasn't much breeze to carry the fumes away. They raised over the ship and stayed over and on the waters all around like an umbrella. Your eyes smart, get bloodshot, close up. The ammonia fumes get on your face, irritate your skin, make a misery. You living with the odor of death.

The fellows tried sleeping. Some went down into the forepeak, left the hatch open, but had to come out. Four went into the galley, laid on the benches beside the table, stretched out on the long eating table. Others stayed up front by the bow, put blankets on the deck, and tried to sleep. One man, he went up to the crow's-nest, stretched out on the floor board up there to catch some shut-eye. Old Noah, he couldn't sleep either, but then, he been sleeping a good part of the day anyhow. He told how once in a hot spell he rode all night on a gassed-up menhaden ship, and when the men made port in the morning they were so beat out they didn't even stay to watch the fish measured out, but went on down the roads home.

Two or three fellows tried the forepeak again, and in all those fumes fell asleep. You could hear them calling hogs. When the others heard the snores, they climbed down the ladder. Best bet was to try to close the eyes, get through the night the fastest way. In the dark their chests pumped up and down; they tried to catch some air that wasn't full of heat and chemical smell.

Topside, lights were on in the rigging, one on the port, another on the starboard side, a light on in the pilothouse and one up in the hawk's-nest so no plane come down low and clip the top of the ship.

On these old boats the bilge will have water in them most of the time. The water flows off the fish in the hole, spreads to the bilge, and it will go up through the cracks of the bilge into the forepeak. Water in the sleeping quarters, it was a few inches deep.

You get a new mattress each year, but it gets moist right away. The air makes it givey, and in the summer, when you sweat, then lay on that moist mattress that the salt air been working on, it will soon get rotten and hard and be the same as sleeping on wood boards. You can just about feel the water next to the soaked-up wood hull. Feel the boat rise and fall in the light sea while she swings at anchor. The bilge water smells, the rats squeak, and the little electric bulb that's supposed to work still ain't been fixed.

Sleeping in there at night, a few miles off coast in an old oxcart like the *Moona Waa Togue,* that's one reason why the men don't want to stay out on long trips. Not safe and not pleasant. They'd rather go out each morning, come back each night.

There's a special dream that menhaden fishermen get. It's from being in the forepeak. A man will wake up in the morning and say, "That's funny, I dreamed of alfalfa last night, just wandered in alfalfa all night long." Another will come out of the hatch, say, "Seemed to me I was smelling magnolia in my dream. What that mean?" They'll smell hay, cornfields, sweet pasture, flower beds, dream of their truck gardens. "Smelled fresh like a radish bed," a man will say. They'll breathe the fish smell and the ammonia fumes deep into their lungs, and it will come out in the dream like the rich smells of the farms they have worked on, the sweet smells of the hill. That's how nature makes a turn, makes it so a man can fit himself into anything, takes a stinking forepeak and turns it into a dream of honey and wild flower. The inside of a man is a mysterious thing.

That's when the fishermen got their real thoughts. What's really in their hearts will come out in their minds, more even than what they'll say to one another during the day. That's when a fisherman dreams of the hill, his shack back there, his people in it. In the middle of the night there's women galore on that boat, women and children. There may be the faces of a hundred kinfolk riding there in the forepeak, on the deck, in the mast, hanging onto the rails. The men got their people right on board with them then, and the talk of some twenty houses is going on in the men's minds.

I know what the crewmen think because I know them, their families, see them at church, at weddings and funerals, sit and talk with them on their porches. Some come to my house and I go to theirs. In a small town where it's only a few hundred menhaden men we know about each other's lives and ways. They're seeing about what I see when I lay in my mate's quarters, maybe a woman at work in the kitchen back there, the truck garden with too many weeds in it, and the vegetables how they're coming along.

Stare straight in the dark for a half hour, see the collards, watermelon, peas, beans in the garden, see myself back on the hill taking care of the vegetable rows. Or see my house. My house, it's two stories high, just a few rooms in it, but a good kitchen, a living room, and a bedroom downstairs and two rooms upstairs for my three children. We been building and fixing the house for ten years; always something to do, a door to be hinged, a screen to be put in, and the grass out front to be fixed neat.

Sometimes you do what the Book say, "Let thy eyes look right forward, and let thy eyelids see straight out before thee." Stare in the dark while the ship is anchored off Ossabaw Island and not be on ship at all but back home arguing with them, or feeding the dog under the back stoop, or just see myself in the living room resting while the family be going back and forth. Sit in my comfortable chair, better for comfort than the board I sit on in the hawk's-nest, and from that chair look out the front window to the dirt road that goes by.

159

There's no sidewalk along that road, but the neighbors have made a smooth path, calling on us, and we on them.

Each wave that come in the night toward the boat, it can bring me a talk with my wife, a sight of that house, the living room with the picture of the Last Supper on one wall, Jesus Himself alone in a brown frame on another wall, and the wall with the calendar put out by the local bank. The table with the Bible and newspapers on it, the coal stove in the center of the room for the cold winter days, the sofa with the cloth cover over it so the dog won't get on the good cover. A man don't go through the wind of menhaden fishing for nothing. You do it for a woman, a family, a house, a living in a land.

Have my eyes wide open there in the dark and see my wife, just about figure what she be doing. A house without a woman in it, it ain't nothing. Mine, when she's finished her work, she'll sit and sew or read the Bible and wait for me to come in, or be bothering with the children. She knows her Bible, got the parts about fish and nets carefully marked up with a pencil. If I'm out overnight, like tonight, I know she got the Good Book right by and may be reading of it:

> But Jesus said unto them, They need not depart; give ye them to eat. And they say unto him, We have here but five loaves, and two fishes. He said, Bring them hither to me. And he commanded the multitude to sit down on the grass, and took the five loaves, and the two fishes, and looking up to heaven, he blessed, and brake, and gave the loaves to his disciples, and the disciples to the multitude.

I don't ever tell her what happens on the boat. No use to upset her. Once, way back, I used to tell her what, but she'd get scared if I told her I climbed out on the boom, or dived under the purse boat to cut away the net from the propeller. Now I still do all that but keep quiet at home.

I never saw danger in the early days. Now I see it on all sides. When I was a boy I didn't have sense enough to see it. Now I'm older, fifty-eight—and all I got is sense. Once it was all wonderful to me; fresh salt water in my nose, each lift of the ship over a peak of water and down, it was a great wonder and a pleasure—but now it's just hard, hard work.

But if you been at sea as long as me you'll get salt in the grain of your face, spray in your blood stream, a ship in the middle of your guts. And I got to go, like old Noah got to go, till they drive me off the ship, or till the crabs get me, or the pogy all been eaten by the bluefish. Got to go menhadening over the curve of the South Atlantic coast till it's no curve no more.

Fourth Day

JULY 14, 1949

EARLY IN THE MORNING the moon left out of the sky. You could see the sky changing color then, but the arms of the sun showed before the face. At first just tremors of light over us, then all of a sudden streaks, like arms that pointed to the top of the sky reaching for a cap to tip. Then the silver cap of the sun coming right up out of the bottom of the sea—and man, we got busy. For all around the menhaden whupped and threshed and it was hay we had to harvest.

Some of the crew was up, waiting for the morning catch. Carib, he was out on the water in his striker boat when I got on deck. Captain Crother, he was up like a bride, ready to do something.

On deck we could hear the fish thumping against Carib's

rowboat, patting it, hitting it, fussing with it, never knowing they was touching death.

Rev, in my purse boat, said, "I prayed for this school of fish. I prayed for it." I said, "Rev, prayer won't get these fish out of the water, let's get to work."

The sea laid out straight with its eye wide open, but still in a calm sleep. It was cool and a fine time for making sets. Captain Crother, he yelled over the deck, "I told you I was going to find you fish!" Like he had led us to this school with his knowledge, instead of it just being so much good fortune. Because unless all menhaden schools have gone upcoast or haven't showed at all the whole season, sooner or later you going to find fish. Like tacks that find their way to sidewalks, point up, sooner or later they'll be there.

> *Oh, captain got a Luger,*
> *Luger, Luger.*
>
> > (Pull)
>
> *Oh, captain got a Luger,*
> *And the mate got a .45.*
>
> > (Pull)

"Boy, we laying it this time!"

"We going to deck-load her, men!"

It's times when the sea is generous, gives us fishermen bounty, maybe more than we deserve, because we're always quick to cuss out the whims of the sea, the bad luck, the misfortunes. The sea is not really cruel to itself, it is just a big life unto itself, with the many ways and currents and moods all life has got; but it is hard on them that try to take a living from her. She is anxious to take us into her belly and turn us into oil with the rest of the fish. And she is never in any hurry to give up to men the life that is in her, even with a net a quarter of a mile around.

We laid in a big buntful of fish, filled the waist of the hole right up to deck level. I ordered, "Everybody in your places, we making another set right now, men."

The crew was in a happy frame, the men filled with singing and pulling strength:

> *My gal's got a fever,*
> *I declare she won't lay down.*
> (Pull web)

The men felt wild and good over how the pogy rippled all around.

> *I got a woman, I got a woman,*
> *Got legs just as big as my boat.*
> (Pull web)
> *Go bring her here,*
> *O Lord, Lord, bring her here.*
> (Pull web)
> *I can show you,*
> *I can rub 'em just as long as I want to.*
> (Pull bunt)
> *Just bring her here,*
> *O Lord, Lord, bring her here.*
> (Pull bunt)

They was going to lay their head in her window, They was going to ask her (Pull), Let them lay their head in her window (Pull), If it's all night long, O Lord, all night long (Harden the fish).

On the sea you find out what a wonderful thing a man is. For rightly speaking, a man's place is on the hill where his legs intended him to be, yet he is out here in the midst of all this, the fierce life of the big sea, the winds that cuss down out of the sky like the Lord's bad moments. The men may cuss as all seamen do, or drink from time to time as all seamen do, but the right thing and the big thing is that they stand together when the time comes to fight the fish, the captain or the company itself—or a man that does wrong among themselves. When the signal comes, "Hey, play!" or "Strike to leeward!" then the men close in a way that fish may not know how to do, and no school of birds by air or wolf pack by land. Man, he builds and works, plays and fights, but he's got in himself the danger of the squid's ink, the sawfish's teeth, the shark's mouth, the whale's weight, the man-o'-war's cunning—all that in man. All in his boats, his skills, his figuring out, and his working together when the set is made. That's why the Lord's right and man *is* the earth's real master.

On our second set of the morning we deck-loaded the ship, filled a big part of the deck itself with the fish that before long was going to be oil and meal, vitamins and solubles.

The upper part of the fish hole is built up with boarding that we call the hatch coaming. There's a few deck posts that stick up from the fish hole as high as the ship's rail. These posts can be boarded up so that many tons more fish can be placed between these boards and the rail. That's deck-loading the ship, loading it with fish way up above the fish hole itself, turning the deck space into pens to hold fish. It's dangerous, and you take on far more weight than the ship supposed to carry, but all the menhadeners do it.

By six o'clock we had about a half million menhaden aboard. The harvest lay in the hold and on the deck, threshed, bound by the walls of the fish hole and the pen of the deck.

We hoisted the purse boats back in the davits—and started to port.

During the night ammonia fumes had painted the whole ship a silvery galvanized color. A menhadener will take on that rust pretty quick, like the skin surface gathers blood when you rough it a few seconds.

168

The hull, the deck, the rigging, galley, and bridge, even the lighted electric bulbs—an aluminum cast settled on it all.

A pail, no matter what color it was before, now it was grayish. The anchor laid up in a corner of the stern, it looked sick with the sheen over it.

Two or three of us with gold teeth, now our teeth looked changed to a silvery prima coat color. Any metal you be wearing got that blood-and-oil-gas tarnish over it. A coin in your pocket turned greenish, a penny got to look like a dime.

You wore shoes, they became grayish-black if they been plain black before.

The ferment, it spread over everything till even the skin of you had a film of fish fumes sensed into it.

When those fumes and the color changes come over the ship some of the men get a slow kind of a headache that stays with them till they get home. Others, the white part of their eyes gets red-streaked and their eyes tear. If you had ten eyes apiece you'd be crying from each of them. I knew one man to go blind from it.

Ordinarily, if you catching fish right near your port, you may be able to get the catch into the factory before that odor and gas gets too bad. Usually it will blow up while you're at port waiting for your ship to get unloaded. But last evening's catch, the night's heat, the staying anchored in the one spot, and the morning light beating down on that menhaden, all that put the last touch of ferment on the pogy, and the fumes coated us all a ghosty gray.

When a bride has a child in her before the preacher starts asking questions, that's trouble already. That's how we were early this morning with this load of fish, pregnant with ammonia gas before it was time, maybe ten-twelve hours from port.

The fresh fish we just caught, that crowded out some of the smell, it seemed, but we couldn't expect it to last too long. The worst part was ahead because we could only make six or

169

seven miles an hour. By afternoon that sun sure going to cook us a kettle of fish there in the hold.

After breakfast the captain took off alone for the lookout. Sometimes he wanted aloft by himself. That would be when we had a full load and it wouldn't do no good to spot the red line anyway. He'd say to Carib and me, "Handle the deck. My turn in the nest." That meant for us to stay below, let him be to himself sixty feet above deck, away from the crew. Look at him then, he seemed really alone—unless he was up there arguing with his wife or maybe Merrick Thorpe. Then the sun didn't touch him, maybe the sea and the ship wasn't under him, and maybe he was even separate from the air. Just a man on a mast going south, and now and then taking a nip from his hip flask.

He shouldn't ought to have been drinking way up there, he could fall and land on the bridge—and have no more bridges to cross. But the bad week been bothering him, and the crew, he never wanted to be with them any more than he had to. "I think they mighty fine boys," he'd say to white folks. "The only one I can't take, it's the one born down here, he goes north and then come back south. He ain't the same. Comes back here like he owns it all. That's the fellow, we got him to kill."

The captain liked a bird's-eye view of everything. "This colored man is right where he want to be," he'd tell you. "All he wants is to be treated right. I got to look out for him. If one of my men gets in jail I just goes over to the chief of police and say, 'This here is my man, let me take him home.' I pay his fine, sign a slip of paper, get him out. Then I take the fine out on payday. That's all they is to it. This fellow is right where he wants to be. Everything in this world got its place. Just that fellow that go north and come back, he bears killing."

Our captain thought that was the whole story. Lots of people think that's the whole story.

Down-coast slow, like a glutton loaded with food. Just two or three miles off the beach. With a load like ours, a ship like this, you not going to be too far from the hill if the engine and the rudder can keep you in close. We could see the blond line of the beach, see breakers spit at the hill like a man that hits over and over from revenge. A shark fin might seam the water close by. A breeze will sweep past and the sea will answer with a little roll, like the two go together, a song and its chorus.

Most of the crew stayed by the bow because the fish odor tended to slip off the stern, leave the air up at the front end a little cleaner. They leaned over the rail, tried to see the future of themselves in the deep glass of the ocean.

Woman talk just about came down to this: Them that didn't have women, they did the most talking about it. Those that had women regular, the married men and some of the single, they didn't say so much, but thought a lot. The others talked about the mystery of women.

One said, "It say in the Bible, 'The Lord put man on the earth to be the master of all he see,' and that mean He put man here to master *women* too!" Some damn foolishness like that, though many men believe such as that, till someone else said, "Any time you damn fool enough to think you the master of women, you still got to grow up. Don't forget, 'The hand that rock the cradle rule the world.'" Back and forth like that, and get nowhere finally.

Politics, that's when it get hot.

The men *always* talking politics. For a colored fisherman, politics is the race question, anything to do with a man's rights. You going to find every idea among them, conservative, radical, Bigger Thomas, nationalist, Uncle Tom, race man, "I'm an

171

American too," left, right, dead center, sound views, senseless views, businessman's, union man's, everybody's, anybody's. Just as much difference of opinion on a menhaden ship as you will find in the whole country; religious, not religious, democratic and not so democratic. *For the stone which the builders rejected is become the chief cornerstone.*

Mohr claimed he knew how to handle white folks. "You got to get them *coming* and *going*," he said. He forgot how Lawyer chopped him down, and they was at it again.

Lawyer: "What you mean?"

Mohr: "Like this: If the white man come to you and he say, 'I got to hand it to the colored man, he has made more progress in a hundred years than any other people in the world,' you got to hit him over the head this way: 'That's a damn lie, mister, we still second-class citizens, ain't got this and ain't got that. So many lynchings and such.' Hit him hard. That way you'll get more."

Lawyer: "All right, now you got him *coming*, how you get him *going*?"

Mohr: "Like this: If the white man come to you and say, 'Colored people got it mighty hard, they are second-class citizens, they ain't got this and they ain't got that and they getting lynched,' you got to fight that because it's a streak among people they don't want to be connected with what's poor and what's been put down, so you say this: 'That's a *damn* lie, mister. We own such-and-such property, we in such-and-such unions, we equal in defense production, and the Supreme Court done so-and-so.' That way you got them going."

Lawyer: "Any chance we get *ourselves* mixed up by this *coming-and-going* tactic?"

Mohr: "Not a chance. Because the whole world's *coming* and *going* in that very same way!"

When the men talked on color you would mostly hear them say they believed in free and equal, they want what others

172

have, according to law, and what anybody is by rights supposed to get. Brotherhood and like that. Do for me as I would for you, and such. Plain equality.

But this new man Exeter, the fellows called him Ex, he showed a stronger feeling than that. He been thinking it through, to hear him tell it, and he said, "Hell with that free-and-equal way, I want better than that!"

Three men, Rev, Westley, and Carters, jumped on Ex and I felt like getting in on it myself.

Rev said, "What you want better than that?" Westley asked, "What's better than free and equal?" Carters asked it too, and a few others looked at Ex very sharp.

Ex said, "White don't believe in free and equal. The laws don't even say free and equal. The way it is, white is on top and the law say he is supposed to be on top."

Westley: "You wrong. The Constitution say it's for all of us the same."

Ex: "That's still paper. It ain't worked out yet."

Rev: "It seem to me you want the world to be made in six days. You want better, you got to work at it, and I takes my stand that the whole country *is* working at it! 'Our feet are now standing within thy gates, O Jerusalem.'"

I asked Ex just what he meant, that he wanted better than free and equal.

Yes, yes, everybody said, what *is* better than free and equal?

"I want to be where the white is," Ex said. "I want to be on top! And let the white man get below and stay below so *he* find out what it is!"

That just about blew up a gale. One or two others said Ex had the right idea, but the most of us took up against it. Captain Crother, he was aloft, nipping his bourbon pretty regular, and I don't guess he could make out what we was hassling over.

Billy Ritchie, he pitched in on Ex: "The best thing would be if the world was set up so it's the same between man and man!"

Ex: "Bunk! Crap! Nobody believe that. White man don't even believe it. Just *talk* it. I want *my* rights with old white man *on my terms!*"

I asked him, "Ex, what you mean, *on my terms?*"

Ex: "I want to say what it's going to be! I want to be the boss! I want the white man to humble himself like I been humbled! You got to get strong enough to make white eat humble pie! I want *them* terms!"

Ritchie: "You asking for trouble. You do that and black themselves will set you down and tell you it's wrong, tell you you going too far!"

Westley: "Free and equal, that's what it should be!"

Lawyer: "Any time anybody is on top, and working it too hard, somebody below going to throw him off—and find friends on top to do it with!"

Exeter, he been sitting down. Now he stood up, right at the stem, pointed his finger hard at one man and the other along the forward rails. "You thinking white man's thoughts! *Think* black, *see* black, *be* black! We be safe only when we're on top and white on the bottom! That's my terms!"

One or two still stood by Exeter, but most of the men, they jumped hard on this let's-get-on-top. I didn't like it. I said, "Ex, that way you get nowhere fast in this country. Top is bad, bottom is bad. Free and equal, that's for me!"

Lawyer: "Yessir, first-class citizens, that's where we got to go! It's a fool to look beyond that!"

"First-class citizens, that's where we bound!"

"Yessir, that's it, man!"

The loud talk at the poker game in the galley, that broke up the gum-beating by the bow. I went aft to see about it.

Kirwan and Booker, Genty and Louisiana Bob, they was hot on the trail of straight flushes, four of a kind, and other big kills, to hear the way they raised their voices. Blu, he was right behind me, he said, "That sound like somebody got a royal flush."

Not much money passes around in one of these games because the men don't have much. They may play two-three hours, each man starting out with fifteen or twenty cents, maybe borrow from one another along the way, and finish up with one man winning seventy-five cents or a dollar. Play for pennies. But they will get serious about it.

Genty: "Okay, I raise you two pennies."

Kirwan: "You got to make it *two!* Can't you raise *one* penny? You must have a full house."

Genty: "Put up or shut up. Two cents!"

Kirwan: "There's my two, now I raise *you* two!"

Genty: "Oh, you raising *me!* You just must have *four aces.*"

Maybe they both bluffing on deuces and treys.

We got into the galley, we heard Booker say he pass. He folded his cards, leaned back, and tried to look out of his right ear at the cards in Genty's hand.

The cards been passed out and the talk got hot. Genty said, "I want to bet a *nickel.* You want to see my hand you got to start putting up *nickels!*"

Kirwan said they agreed on a two-cent limit. Genty said he hadn't heard no limit set. Kirwan said it's always a two-cent limit. But Genty got hard: "Not *this* time. I'm raising *your* two cents a *nickel.* You want to see my hand it's *five* cents!"

Louisiana Bob got in on that. "Aw no! No nickel! We got to have *some* law about this. It's always two cents high even if nobody mentioned it before this game begin. Stick to the rule!"

Genty handled himself like his pockets was full of money. "How you ever going to amount to anything if you afraid to bet a nickel?"

Kirwan, he held his cards up against his neck, tight, so nobody see what he had. He still held out for a two-cent limit. "I

175

only got seven cents left. I can't play no nickel high. I got you beat anyway. No use you raising me any more!"

"I raise you as long as I raise fish!"

"You be raising fish *forever* and you ain't going to raise me *that* long!"

Voices very high. I didn't want to see no serious argument. I told them all if they hollered any more they would wake up the dead fish. "You guys quieten down or I make you get out the checkerboard." Card players would rather lay down and die than play checkers.

The men settled on a two-cent betting limit. Kirwan called. Genty put down his cards, a pair of kings and a pair of eights. Kirwan laid down his hand, a pair of aces and the other pair of eights. He won about thirty-six cents.

Everybody jumped on Genty. "Trying to get Kirwan to pull out by scaring *nickels* out of him when he had higher than you!"

Louisiana Bob low-rated Genty for several minutes. "It's things like that that's ruining poker on board this ship. Hereafter we going to play *stud* poker so no one can bluff *that* bad!"

Bluffing is one of the most important parts of poker playing, but all poker players hate it except when they're doing it themselves.

We'd have that kind of an argument on board ship, maybe sometimes bad enough for the men to go into the hole and slug it out, but nothing much more than that—or a menhaden crew couldn't stay together.

All season the crew been after Ronay to lift the tom weight. The tom weighs a quarter of a ton. All that weight is jammed into a piece of lead the size of a pail. There's a round eye hook on top a man can get his fingers into.

Back at the bow Lawyer was needling Ronay to lift the

weight, kept saying, "You big but you can't lift the tom."

Ronay, he stood nearly seven feet high, the biggest man on the ship and maybe the biggest in the menhaden fishery. In our work smaller men is the rule, medium-size fellows, men that can get in and out of boats fast. Big fellows in the small boats can be clumsy, they puff a lot at bunt pulling, lose their footing easier. But Ronay, he didn't get in his own way or anybody else's. A good bunt puller, a very quiet fellow, he stayed to himself a lot. "Don't bother me none with that, Lawyer. The tom is for fishing, not for busting a gut."

This bunt puller was so big he could pick up children on each finger of each hand, hold four children on each side of him. I seen him do it. The people took him for a show. Most folks never saw anyone so big. He had big hands. Either hand would reach around a gallon jug so that he could drink without having to touch the handle.

Lawyer stayed with it. "Ronay, you lift the tom and I take a collection for you right here. Get you a couple dollars."

Ronay, he wasn't interested. "I collect from the company on Saturday. You let the tom be and let me be." But he egged the men on by saying, "Besides, you know and I know and everybody know I can get that tom off the deck."

The men didn't want to hear him say that unless he was to do something about it.

I was against it. It could rupture or kill a man to get that lead off the deck. A senseless kind of a test, but something like that be going on when the men not fishing, just headed for port and trying to find what to do. Bouts of strength and skill all the time.

Lawyer got very busy. He fished out a quarter and put it in his cap. He went from one to the other, and they raised about two and a half dollars.

"You get this whether you lift the weight or not. You get this if you just try."

177

Ronay said it was too hot and he didn't feel like it. But the whole crew started down the port deck to the purse boat that had the tom weight in it. They winched the tom down on the deck. And there was the lead at Ronay's feet, him standing over it, wondering how so much weight could be packed into such a small block.

The men began to mutter he couldn't do it anyway and he knew he couldn't, till all of a sudden Ronay, he was taking off his shoes so his feet would get a better feel of the deck.

He was in shorts. He took a couple breaths to catch some air in his lungs, but there wasn't much that was fresh. It was midmorning and hot.

He was sweating before he began, maybe sweating to think of it, and the water ran down him plain for all to see.

The crew, they started placing bets. That held up Ronay a minute. The bettors started to wonder about the rules. How far he had to get the tom off the deck and how long he had to hold it up. They agreed if he just got it up even a half inch and let it right down he had lifted the weight.

"Come on, Ronay! Come on!" The men started to stamp their feet in a light kind of way and clap their hands a little.

Ronay, he leaned over the tom, put the big first finger of his right hand in the eye of the weight. Pressed the finger tight around the eye till the finger came around and dug into his palm.

He was crouched over the lead, his legs apart and his left hand on his left hip.

A few seconds it seemed he wasn't trying to lift it. Just feeling how heavy it was and getting himself solid. Shifted his feet an inch or two, bent his back lower.

You could see the muscles in his arms—both arms—tense up. The muscle spread moved up to his shoulders and rolled down his back. The tendons hardened up on his hips and thighs. The strain got into the calves of his legs.

178

His soles seemed to spread out flatter on the deck. He had big toes.

Soon his face trembled like a treetop when the wind blows hard.

Up went the tom weight, the whole 580 pounds—one inch, two inches, four inches, six inches . . .

He held it there one second, two seconds, four seconds, six seconds . . .

The weight went down, a little faster than how he brought it up, but it seemed he couldn't put it down too fast.

And then for a minute Ronay couldn't get his finger out of the eyehole.

But he did and he stood up. He worked the fingers of his right hand into the palm of his left, round and round like you knead bread.

They started collecting bets, that small money they could afford to put up. The money they collected for Ronay, he put it in the pocket of his shorts.

The crew moved around all excited, full of talk.

I had never seen that before, and never seen it since. Ordinarily it takes three men to lift the tom weight. The crew knew they had done seen something.

Seemed to me we moved unnaturally slow. Till all of a sudden I found why.

Old Noah, he been down in the forepeak, resting his bones. He came out the hatch, walked over to me easy, like not to get in my way, and he said, "Mate, something to tell you."

"Yes?"

"Down in the peak. Too much water coming through the port hull. It could get real bad."

"How much water is in?"

"Could be two feet on the floor of the peak."

"Two feet!"

I asked Carib to come with me down in the forepeak.

We went below. Touched water before we got to the bottom of the ladder. It looked to me three feet of water was in there. The whole bottom of the sleeping quarters well drowned out, and each time the boat rolled a little the water drifted from one side to the other.

The flashlight showed seepage coming through four or five strips of hull planking. The calking washed out. The heavy load of fish must have put a great strain on the whole keel and on every timber.

I went topside, aft to the engine room where we kept a tool-box, got out some gray paint and plenty of canvas.

The crew saw me go back down the hatch with that canvas and paint. They knew right away it was leaking down there. They got hold of Noah, asked what he had done told me.

In the forepeak I stretched canvas over the leaky boards, painted all over the canvas and around the edges to hold it against the wood. The wood was rotten. When I finished, it still didn't look too good, but it should help keep the sea out till we got home.

We put a pump to work.

A few of the men climbed below to see how serious it was.

"We shouldn't ought to have deck-loaded," some of them said.

"This ship can't take it."

"Hell, we won't get in till midnight."

I went aloft, told Captain Crother.

"You fix it?"

I told him what we done.

He kept staring down-coast. Said to tell Fitch to keep close to the hill.

I came back down deck, hunted out Noah. "Noah, you done earned your keep this trip. If any of them fleck an eyelid at you, you let me know."

180

The crewmen, they was about the bow again, and Noah was among them. "This boat ain't safe," the old man said. "It ain't safe. She should go into dry dock when we get in—if we get in."

"What you mean?"

"This ship need to be wormed. Barnacles got the whole hull. She need to be scraped, calked, plenty copper paint slapped on her before she fit to go again."

That set the men serious, got them into ship talk.

Westley said he wasn't going to ship out on the *Moona Waa Togue* after this year. Next year he was going on the *Captain Lewitts*. "It's a faster boat and it's safer." Our ship was just 350 horsepower, one of the weakest pullers around. Because of that we often got into port last, even when we caught fish before other ships, and we had to wait at the dock to get unloaded. Had to live in all that gas while other ships got emptied of their catch.

Lift said the fish deliberately stayed away from our ship. I told him how wrong that was, that last year this same *Moona Waa Togue* caught nineteen million menhaden.

Genty talked of a race a year before out of a Gulf port between the *Rapid Heron* and the *Captain Packer*. (Many menhaden ships are named after the captains.) "They was both converted sub chasers made into pogy boats," Genty said. "They was coming side and side toward port. I was on the *Heron*. The *Packer*, it got right behind us. I stood at the stern and held out a five-dollar bill to the man in the bow of the *Packer*. I said, 'Catch me and you can have this bill.' That fisherman, he reached and he almost touched that bill, but not quite, and we just got docked about two ship lengths ahead of them. Man, that was some race!" Another bunt puller, he liked Genty's story, he said he was going next year on the *Heron*.

181

They picked the ship they was going to go on next season—when they hadn't finished this one.

The ships they wanted to fish on, that led to waters they fished in. Fort liked it around Princess Bay in Maryland. "Good fishing, good waters," he said. Hammet fished as far north as Montauk Point, he liked it around there, it wasn't rough seas. Rough seas brought Blu into it. He was against Delaware Bay. "The water deep, hard on the net, the tide runs strong. Tide so sharp it will blow the purse boats together till you have to pull them apart with the big ship. Hard to anchor if you have to, because you may be working in a hundred fathoms. You'll spend five or six hours getting out into those waters and the same time getting back with a load if you get one."

Everybody jumped on Cape Hatteras then, plenty fish there, but plenty danger. Lift said, "Fish off the Cape in bad weather and your mother may be a childless woman." He was right too. The Sailors' Graveyard. By it being way out in the Atlantic, liners, cruisers, freighters take their bearings to and from the Cape. Pilots and captains of liners an hour away from the Cape, but coming toward it, will worry because they know it's a cemetery of drowned ships. Some places you'll see the mast of a ship sticking up a few feet, rocking in the wind, like a dead man's hand waving for help. A warning buoy nearby. Here and there markers to show where a ship is below, but the mast or the hull may be near the surface. I've seen an ocean liner grounded there, like a big city, settled in ten or fifteen feet of mud, five hundred yards from the beach, waiting to be hauled out, or waiting for a big sea to free her. Many shrimpers gone down hereabouts; catch your net on a shrimper, that's the finish of your net. Around those wrecks plenty eating fish, sheepshead, bass, blackfish, drum. You'll see hand fishermen with their boats tied to the top of those wrecks, they'll be fishing there. More sea treachery there than any other part of the East coast. I've fished there half of my life, seen dreadful times. The deep sea makes a deal with the winds that blow, the currents play tricks with the coast line, a nasty sea come up in a minute. You got islands and sounds connected in a steady line for two hundred miles, all along the Carolinas. The waters on the ocean side and in the sounds have plenty menhaden, so you maneuver for them in shallow waters. Pamlico Sound, that's a great forty-mile-wide stretch of water that goes from Cape Lookout up past Cape Hatteras. If you enter the sound from the sea through Ocracoke Inlet you go through a narrow slew, the nine-foot shoals, rough water in any northerly wind, the ship dragging bottom all the time. Diamond Shoals, that's right at the Cape, the water varies from two to three feet to three hundred feet for a twelve-mile stretch. You got paths to go through there, else you have to go around twelve miles to cover a few hundred yards. The menhadeners all make those short cuts. Just beyond the shoals the ocean drops down a mile into the mountains underneath. Where there's danger there's sometimes treasure, and one of our menhaden oil treasuries is right there. So the Carolina and Florida fleets work here summer and fall. In the fall the ships go way out in the big sea for the Amagansett and Chesapeake Bay fish that come down here fast to go off coast for the winter.

Cape talk set the men going on sinkings, wrecks, fires they been in or knew of, crews that gone down, crews that got saved. Somebody pointed at Noah, "He was on the *Parkins,*" about the worst sinking in menhaden history.

Ronay said, "I was on the *James Gilford* when she turned over." But he didn't have a chance to tell of it because Hammet jumped in. "I was on the *Cosette* when she sank, but we all got saved." I came in with how I was on the *Hathaway,* a steamboat, when that went down, and still here to tell the story. Fort started to say, "That *North State,* when that went bashoom . . ." but Westley cut him off, "The *Beckwith* sinking, that was worse than the *North State.*" Somebody else threw in how nasty it was when the *Long Island* went under. Genty, he was on the *Carolina* when she went to the bottom fish. Another started to speak of the *Lynn Haven,* and Carters got him from where he was squatting on deck and said, "Don't mention that *Lynn Haven.* I was on that when she burned to the water. I know that one like nobody."

"Hold on," I said. "They didn't all go down." I told them of twenty ships I been on in my days, and practically all but one or two still going. I been cook on one, dry-boat man on another, mate on a third, bunt puller on all of them. "We had some close times, but the most of them I been on, they still going—like this tub."

With all the water in the forepeak, the ship moseying so almighty slow, I didn't like to hear the men worry too much about ships that gone down, so I sent one or another about tending the nets, cleaning the small boats, sweeping the deck. "I don't mean to break you men up," I said, "but that net needs pickling very bad." The four seine and ring setters went aft to salt the net. That net is hungry for salt. Eats thousands of pounds a week, like the fish eat plankton. On the factory property back by the docks they got a big salthouse, just keep loose salt in there, it looks like a mine. That salthouse has to be filled two or three times a season with salt to feed all those nets and boats the Thorpe Company owns. On the nets and small boats on just one ship like ours they'll use forty sacks of salt a day. The nets will rot overnight if they don't keep pouring salt on them, and water on the salt.

I ordered Carib, "Keep the deck clean. Get after it." That's the striker-boat-man job.

"Clean out them purse boats," I told others. Water and mud and slime is on the bottom of those small boats after they make a set. There's a two-inch plug in the bottom of each boat. You sweep all the dirt out of that plug. I may do it or get a man or two to help me. One way or another, you watch the whole ship, keep the men as busy as you can. Different ones, for an extra half cent on a measure of fish, they got certain ship duties. But there's plenty of hours after a catch when it's not a thing for some of the bunt pullers to do. Then they'll play cards, talk, read, sing, hang over the line, worry one another, cuss out the captain—and maybe me.

"That sonofabitch mate, he's always siding with the captain against us! He's no goddamn good neither!" I've heard them say it. And I don't claim to be no angel with the men when I got to make them go do something. I've tommed many a man or helped tom a man. Tomming a man (that's from the tom weight) is throwing him overboard, usually from the purse boat, and wake him up that way. Been tommed myself.

In the crow's-nest captain yelled all over the sky the pogy call, "Fish! Fish! Big pla-a-a-a-y!" He pulled the rope that set the bell to ringing all over the deck. But the pilot knew enough to keep going. The ship was loaded. The captain often did that when he saw the red line, even when we had a shipful. Just felt like hollering when he saw menhaden, it was such a lifetime habit. A bunt puller said, "The captain is in his juice and his juice is operating." Some of the younger men that been to the big cities or in the service, they used jive lingo. A man said, "I think I'll get on my double deuces and broom to the foreign seases." Means he's headed for the galley for something to eat.

Jive and jabber down the coast, every part of the ship all silver-gray now, rusty with fumes. The tom weight, it looked sick. Walls of the galley, inside and out, they sweated with ammonia silvering. It was so hot we could smell our shorts and shirts burning, like when a woman sprinkles water on clothes and irons it: the same smell. The Lord said it was nothing in the world as good as a good fish and nothing in the world as

185

bad as a bad fish. He was right about that. A bad fish, the whole world want to get away from it. We would like to have been free of the funkiness we breathed in place of air, but we was tied to it, like a farmer's feet to the earth.

Well past Sapelo and Doboy sounds now, just even with Altamaha Sound. Groaning along low in the water. One pump busy spitting water overside from the fish hole and another hard at it clearing the wash out of the forepeak. Splop, splop, splop, over the rail. Noontime, and the smell coming out of the galley and the voice of McNally, "You can just let your mouth water for this baked fresh fish we going to have in a few minutes." It would be just the way McNally promised too. Fresh eating fish we got in the morning haul. A fisherman likes fish. That's all they is to it. I even think menhaden is a fine tasty fish, but most land people don't agree. You get the finest roe in the world from the menhaden.

"You hear that Cooking Devil?" one of the bunt pullers say. Even with all that water around in the sea and more than we wanted in the forepeak and sweat rolling down our skins, just let the Cooking Devil talk about his cooking and our mouths would make *more* water!

Early in the afternoon Eppes flew his Piper Cub over us. He was grounded yesterday, plane trouble, he said. We told him where we been all night and picked up this deckload. Eppes said the fish were schooling heavy down by Nassau Sound in the Mayport vicinity. He had sent most of Thorpe's menhadeners into these waters for today's fishing but flew up this way to see what was doing.

Captain Crother said, "When you get back to the office tell Thorpe our ship is taking water like the wood done turned to sponge."

After Eppes dipped and headed south Captain Crother said, "Harder to figure out those fish this season than I ever known it. They playing hide-and-seek with every captain in the fleet."

The menhaden, mostly it's a summer fish, begins to school around northern Florida and Georgia in March and April. Comes in from deep water. Seamen on cruisers, commercial boats and shrimpers thirty and forty miles out, they'll see rushes of menhaden heading in from different seas, all the way from Florida to North Carolina. The fish come in close, swallow the animal and vegetable skim in the water, grow and move upcoast. They keep columning in toward the beach all spring, and nobody knows exactly where they coming from. At first in small numbers, like they're sending out scout patrols. They may be small fish then, two and three inches long, and no bigger than five or six inches, but by May—if it's a season when they're showing—they'll be coming in hundreds of thousands, millions. Eat their way north, and by May and June the whole coast up to New York be swarming with them. Be so many they will keep about thirty menhaden plants going full blast out of twenty menhaden ports.

Some places and some times the menhaden will settle in great patches, close to shore, solid in the water like an army, army of the sea in multimillions. Ten, maybe fifteen menhadeners can gather over a mine of ocean oil like that, pick them up by the hundreds of tons. The ships be close enough to each other sometimes to yell across decks. Then the fleets go out daily, work on the great pools of fish puddling by the beach, keep bringing them to dock.

Frost hits in the northern waters, even before then, the menhaden start back down-coast. Some will be three and four years old, they made the trip a few times without being webbed in. They'll be eighteen and twenty inches long, plenty oil in them. Everybody wants to get them. They'll school south now, pick up on all that skim that flows off the hill down to the sea, the plant life, the dying insects ground up by the waves, all the small matter that makes oil inside the pogy. But

187

the pogy is particular. He hunts, like everything else. Won't
eat everything that gets into his mouth, throws out lumpy stuff
that won't get past his gill rakers. He's got no teeth, can't
chew, just takes in what can get through the sieve in his
throat.

When the autumn journey down-coast starts, the big oily
ones, and schools of smaller ones too, head for Chesapeake
Bay, then on to the Carolinas. Some start to move off coast, out
into the deep waters. But there's lots of eating for them in
warm Carolina waters. The Carolina coast is splattered with
menhaden ships then. Ships will be there from Florida and
come down from Virginia to get in on the last big take of oil
fish before the cold Thanksgiving weather comes and the fish
get scarce.

You get those big fish in your net, they'll stay there, they
won't thunder as easy as the smaller ones will. Won't work so
hard, either, once you net them in. But you got to go way out
for them sometimes, into the storm waters, the deep fathoms,
catch them quick and get back before sudden winds and high
seas sweep you up on the shoals. What you try to get now is
the big fish that don't stay around to get caught, but move
steadily southeast off the coast into deep waters to hide, or
spawn, or be gone for the winter. You'll see those eighteen-inch
menhaden, traveling fast, in big schools ten or fifteen miles off
Cape Hatteras. They'll keep right alongside the big steamers,
and you very seldom catch them. They'll be gone overnight.

By Christmas not much bunt pulling going on anywhere in
the menhaden fishery. A few schools be around in the deeper
water and below, but you don't bother with them. Hard to
get at, even the fathometer may not locate them.

Winter, it's a truce. The fish have sounded. The ships are
at the piers for repairs.

Where are most of the menhaden schools then? What they
eating? What depth they at? Nobody knows. Marine science

don't know. The menhaden industry itself asks the questions
but don't much try to find out. You don't ask how a banquet
is put together. You just fill up on it. All they really know of
the pogy's habits, he hangs his hat all the way from Maine to
Brazil, surfaces, sounds, spawns, moves as he will. Summers
here, winters there.

Fishermen once believed that menhaden popped up out of
the bottom mud, like flowers. Spawned in the ooze below the
water and budded, like blossoms on trees, in the spring. That
idea been given up. Now they think temperature is the main
thing in the life of the pogy. They'll show in hot summer, be
scarce in winter. Be plentiful in warm coastal waters, quit
northern waters early. Any place where the temperature drops
below fifty degrees, the menhaden are going to leave out. And
it seems they spawn all over.

Every fisherman, every captain and mate got their own idea
how the fish move, where they can be, what drives them, how
they spawn. They'll figure it out from the trouble they had
catching them. I think that when they get ready to spawn it
makes no difference where, they just spawn—in close, far out,
in the North, and in the tropic waters.

Once, off Long Island, I saw them spawning. We headed for
a big red smear offshore. They were milling around in big
circles, a white and red grainy look to the pool. They moved
so much you couldn't make a set on them.

In Gulf waters off Louisiana I've seen big beds of small pogy
one or two inches long, just hatched, moving like rafts, whirl-
pooling about, making for shore. Sand from the bottom
whirled up to the top from forty feet below from all that working under water.

On a grown menhaden the roe, white and red, will be big,
four or five inches long. Two and a half million eggs in one
roe. Us menhadeners got a saying, "A pogy is full of roe and
a captain is full of promises." Makes a wonderful roe for eat-

ing. Fishermen that catch pogy like to eat it, it tastes like a herring, but they can't get land folks to eat the fish. You can't take too much of it, it's oily, it'll make you sick. But us fishermen, we eat it right along. We take them, split them, take the big bone out, salt them, and let them dry. Wash them off, put it in a pan and shove it in the oven and bake it, and eat it right out of the hub. We keep them salted at home, like salted pork. They'll stay a long while, we'll eat them in the winter when we're not working and money is slim.

Just a week ago a smart young fellow from the marine laboratory at Miami Beach, he came aboard the *Moona Waa Togue* and asked me questions about what I've seen at sea. A young white man in his thirties, he went about ship with some instruments, studied the gas, the water and oil, like a doctor. He called the pogy by a name I never heard before: *Brevoortia tyrannus*. A whale of a name for the little twenty-million-dollar-a-year pogy. That was the scientific name for the fish, he said. There was a half dozen different kinds of menhaden, but not much difference between them except in size and color, but some oilier. Especially in the Gulf, small, fat, but real oily ones there.

This fish, it has almost fifty different names. Around here we call it menhaden and porgy, but we shortened the word "porgy" to pogy. Around North Carolina, shad or fatback. Hardly ever know it as menhaden about there, mostly just shad. In Connecticut, bony-fish. It is a bony fish too. Maryland, Virginia, Delaware call it alewife, bug-head, bug-fish, menhaden. That's because sometimes there's a bug, a parasite, in the head of the fish in those waters. Around Long Island it's mossbunker, or just plain bunker. Even heard it called "the Atlantic schmoo" because it's so fertile and gives so much of itself to everybody.

But it all goes back to the Indians.

They first used the fish for fertilizer when the tides threw

them up on shore. They took a fish, put it at the root of each
cornstalk, found that it enriched the soil. So that the red man
had in his corn the strength of the sea and the soil. He called
it *munnawateaug*, something that fertilizes, makes to grow.

Indians called it poghaden too—poghaden to porgy to pogy
—and it's pogy for us in the region from Florida to Texas.

Off Sea Island Beach a shrimper came toward us. This
shrimper, the *Miranda* out of De Leon, floated up close. We
knew the crew. Their pilot motioned with his hand and said
through his fist that menhaden was schooling a few hundred
yards away, deep under water.

"We got a full load," I told him. "Can you handle some
pompano?"

"Sure, we buy it from you."

The *Miranda* came right up to our starboard.

Some of the crew went to the icebox, where we stored the
pompano, and brought them out on deck. We had caught
about fifty of them in the last set we made this morning.

"We pay you twenty cents apiece," this shrimper said when
he saw the size of them.

The bunt pullers threw the pompano one at a time over the
rail onto a net on the shrimper's deck.

I reached across the rail for a ten-dollar bill. "See you in
town, Hoagley," I said.

I told the men as soon as the captain came down from the
hawk's-nest I'd get him to change this bill, we'd split it equal
among the whole crew. Just come to about a half dollar apiece,
but a little something extra. A small racket some of us menhadeners work with a few of the shrimpers, because we not
supposed to catch eating fish and can't sell them when we do.
But a shrimper can unload them for a profit at the markets.

By it being impossible to keep an eating fish out of the net
when you raise up pogy, and nobody wants to throw a good

191

fish away when you do catch him, this matter been in the courts for a century. Never going to be solved either. Menhaden nets have been burned with acid, ships set afire by food-fish fishermen, but dammit, every time you haul in fifty tons of menhaden, there's a mackerel or two going to be in there, and sometimes a few hundred bluefish. Yet in most sets it's practically all menhaden you bring up.

But nobody makes too much off the fish except the captains and the companies, so these piddling side deals over one or two kinds of eating fish go on from time to time. We get along good with the shrimpers, may live next door to them, and anything they earn they're entitled to. Because shrimping may be the most dangerous fishing in the country, more even than menhadening. They drag deep bottom waters at night mostly, use a 110-foot spread net made of linen like our nets, sometimes go way out in the Gulf looking for the ten-inch long "golden shrimp." Or stay out on freezer boats for six months, hold their catch till shrimp freighters come pick up the haul. A lonely, dangerous life. Their boats deathtraps, broad, flat-bottom, made of second-rate wood sometimes. A shrimper's deck, it's a wilderness of ropes. Heavy seas swamp them, carry them under. Many lives lost in that fishery year round. So us menhadeners and shrimpers, we're sea brothers.

That pompano deal, that set off a card game in the galley and another up by the bow. For an hour and a half fifteen of the crew gambled. They gambled to see who would go home with the most part of that fresh money that came on board. The winner of the game in the galley, Louisiana Bob, he drew cards with Carib, the winner of the game up by the bow. They had cornered three or four dollars apiece. That much wouldn't mean anything great to either one, but if one man went home with seven or eight dollars, that meant something. Louisiana Bob won.

The crew went fore. Some sat below the pilothouse, others hung over the bow rails, looked straight out to where ocean and sky met on the windward side, and land and ocean on the lee. Sunlight still very mighty. A man's shorts dripped with sweat. The men complained of the funkiness, always somebody muttering about that. The fish gave off a steam that wasn't mentioned even in the Bible, it burned holes in their faces. *Can a man gather up fire in his lap and shall his clothes not be burned?* That oil, it's true fire. We heard Cooking Devil consoling the dog. "Poor Jubilee. Her eyes crying from the fumes. She don't know what ails her."

Lawyer held out his arm and he pointed his finger into the eastern sky. Because big space, big water all over, that sometimes gave the men big eyes to try to figure out where they came from, where they going, Lawyer asked, "What lies beyond there?"

I humped my shoulders. "Nothing but the water and then more land. Then maybe some more sky."

"I don't mean that. I am asking you, what do it mean? Where we going? Why? What come after this?"

I answered, "Maybe it means nothing. Maybe it means just we are here, either make the best of it or do better."

Lawyer: "No, that still not what I'm talking about. You talking about what we got, what we ain't got. That's all right, but I'm talking about what's beyond this world, why we are here. What's the reason for this hard work just to get fish—or become part of fish?"

The other bunt pullers got in on it. Hammet said Paradise and Fire lay beyond, like it said in the Koran, depending on how you did in this world. Lift said nothing was beyond this life and no good reason for its cause, everything just *was* and *is:* to hell with it, enjoy yourself.

Lawyer kept at it, he wasn't satisfied. "I don't mean all that Sunday-school stuff. To hell with hell. Whose idea is this? Is it

193

going somewhere or not? Ain't there no answer to living—beyond working and fighting over your color?"

Lift: "Ain't that enough?"

Lawyer: "No, not for me. I want to know what goes below the fathoms, beyond what the chart mark off and what's to the other side of the sky."

I said we wasn't rightly made to find the final answers. Maybe the right thing that knew the answers wasn't to be found on land or sea or in the sky. "We ain't got enough eyes. Maybe we had a thousand eyes, like a fly, it would help to see and know more. Maybe we had all the arms of a squid and could use them like we use our hands, then we could make more instruments to find out more. Maybe we had a sense of smell like a dog, or could feel as much each instant as a whale —if we had all that, and we would be something different, maybe we could see into the web of it all. And maybe even if you had all that and you was that kind of a being, you would still only see a longer line, a farther distance, a bigger sky. You still wouldn't see the beginning or the end. Man's job, it's to live here in what is and what might be and not in a world of why. You live in a world of why, you will *never* touch bottom, you will *never* reach the horizon. You will beat yourself out, and God, He'll laugh at you!"

Lawyer said, "Mate, you may be right, but I like to think about it."

I told him out front to find out the *why* of the big mysteries we would have to have stars for eyes and look with them through space. Have to have a sense of smell to smell out all the gases in the sky. Senses to see and hear all the stars buzzing around and figure which way they grinding. We would have to have enough stretch in ourselves to lay down a hand from a billion miles away and touch the crow's-nest of the *Moona Waa Togue*. We'd have to have a brain as big as everything we see right now—then we might get at *why*.

194

Rev and Hammet, they didn't like my thinking. "You getting too far away from the Roots," Rev said. Rev meant the Bible. But not all the crewmen are religious. Some don't like that talk one bit and they will blame colored troubles on the Bible. They'll tell Rev to go give that spiritual stuff to the captain, *he* needs it, but *they* don't need it. Yet most will go to church on Sunday and most be ready for a disputation over what the Bible say.

Lawyer: "Rev, did Christ have a brother?"

Rev: "I believe He did."

Lawyer: "No, He didn't."

Rev: "What makes you say that?"

Lawyer: "Because if He had another brother there would be two Christs. Because Jesus was supposed to be the Son of God, so if He had a brother, there would be two Sons of God, and so two Christs."

Rev: "Why don't you stick to the way history done showed it? It showed that only one Christ been lived."

Lawyer kept hammering: "And if Christ had a sister it would still have been two Christs, because she would have to be the Daughter of God."

Rev: "Watch out, Lawyer, pretty soon you get yourself way over into blasphemy."

Lawyer: "It ain't nothing like that. It's a matter you think out what you hear. You hear so much, if you don't think about it your head be a mess."

Rev: "That's what I think—your head a mess right now."

Lawyer: "Look, what I believe, it's got to be showed to me. Tennessee ain't far from Missouri, you know."

Ronay agreed with Lawyer. "The Lord want a man to think. Otherwise a man got no difference from a beast. Lawyer got the right to his opinion. That Bible is a crossword puzzle sometimes. What *you* think fits ain't what *someone else* think fits."

Billy Ritchie, he said Ronay was right and he knew how to

get a fight going over chapter and verse any time he wanted. They asked him how. Ritchie said, "Is it true or ain't it true that the Bible got a saying in it that every tub must sit on its own bottom?"

Rev jumped all over the deck, he said the Bible wouldn't use no language like that and he never came on it. But Billy Ritchie said, "Aw hell, Rev, that Bible don't stop at nothing!"

Rev: "But not what you said, 'Every tub must sit on its own bottom.' You got to find that in the chapter and the verse before I go with it!"

Two or three men, they took out their pocket Bibles and hunted around for it. While they hunted for that, which I never knew nobody to find, somebody else asked a more important question: Did God hear a sinner's prayer?

Rev gave the opinion that the Lord wasn't interested in a sinner's prayer. He quoted from the first chapter of John, "It is true that God hear it not a sinner's prayer, but if he be a worshipper and do what He commandeth, then He hear it.

"Therefore," said Rev, "He don't hear a sinner's prayer."

I said I thought God *ought* to hear a sinner's prayer.

Rev said, "Mate, you make the rules for the Big Ship too?"

I told him he ought to know me better than that. But he cut a notch off me. Sometimes the men think I'm too close to the captain. Rev said, "You heed the Bible, Mate, and don't waste your sympathy on none of them sinning captains. They got a special place for them when *they* get *there*."

Hammet, he went with Rev about the Hereafter going to take in fellows like the captain. They did have a special place for something like him that cussed all day long, worked the men to death on ten sets some days, stayed off to himself because his skin told him to, got such a big share on each measure of fish, guzzled in the crow's-nest, and lorded it around like *he* was the one made the world in six days instead of Allah. Hammet said, "The way my Book tell it, Captain

Crother going to the Fire. First they going to scorch him and boil him, then give him cold water to drink, then scorch him again. That's the Muslim hell. They do things by two and two to make it have good effect. And he'll burn *forever*."

Rev never liked the competition he got from Hammet. Hammet knew a little about Muslim and quite a bit of the Scriptures. Rev argued with him over how long was forever. An old argument. Rev said forever would be as long as you could feel yourself burning. That might take just ten or fifteen seconds, and then you be just a wisp of smoke—and that was forever.

Hammet said the way be believed about it was that you keep burning once you got to That Place.

Rev said, "No more than if you would keep drowning once you drown. Once you drown, you drowned. It takes a few minutes and that was forever."

"No sir," said Hammet. "You go to the Fire, you burn for a long time, till the stars burn out. You keep burning and you keep feeling."

Lawyer said, "I wouldn't even wish that on Captain Crother."

The men asked Hammet to tell about what happens if they do good on earth. Hammet had told it many times and they always liked to hear it. So Hammet said, "If people follow Allah they going to go in halls above halls till its way up high, and a river flowing below a forest, and it's beautiful, and when you get there you got a companion forever to gaze at you with a loving eye. And wine there too."

"Tell us about Omar Khayyám," they asked.

Hammet would let them have it, quote a few stanzas from the poet that the fishermen liked to hear. They even liked that better than the Koran, because who in the world don't like a jug of wine, some fresh-baked bread, and the right party out in the glade somewhere?

197

Hammet, he was very critical of the New and Old Testaments. The right way was with Mohammed. He and Rev be having some hot fusses over that. The men liked to listen. Sometimes Hammet got a man or two over on his side about one thing or another, especially when he would say how Muslim didn't pay no mind to color.

Genty, he jumped in by Hammet's side. "This Bible ain't necessarily so. It say there you shouldn't eat hare, the hare is unclean and you shouldn't even touch his dead carcass or you'll be unclean till evening. Yet I have shot and eat rabbit meat and liked it and what it meant by evening I never found out."

But Lift told him what it meant. "It meant you got through that day with your eating just by a hare."

Talks like that, on the sea, I found out from it no matter how a man thinks, how one is going to differ from another, that the Good Book means life. It's not what you find exactly in the Book. You can find whale, shark, pogy, and plankton in it. It's that the Bible is a raft in the world because it shows how man been looking for what's good and what's right even if he ain't always found it.

Not quite dark when we dieseled into St. Ann's Entrance early in the evening. But the lights went on in our rigging, in the pilothouse, and at stern.

The big ranger on the hill, it blinked every twenty seconds, showed us how to come in, because at night you depend on lights. We were going along the jetties, they give you a straight cup to come in by. The captain, he was sober now, him and me both behind Fitch, helping him with the buoys, spars, cans, markers between the lighted buoys.

Sometimes in high tide like tonight the water will cover that bank of rocks, then you follow the lights, cans, spars. Can buoys, there's no lights on some of them, but you can see them at night, like shadow on shadow. Miss on these signals, you're in trouble. Running the channel buoys, the inland signal system, that may be the biggest trick on the water—at least in our seagoing—except living through a big gale way out.

Fitch knew his way, but a pilot can stand help when the dark comes on in that narrow waterway. The channel choppy, we had to watch every ripple. We were low in the water, full of fish, and slowed by that half-filled forepeak. By that fish hole being so powerful fumy, gull, pelican, gannet by the hundreds convoyed us in.

Captain or me be saying, "Occulting light, Mister Fitch. (You're in close to the bar then.)

"Fixed light, watch it." (That's a permanent danger spot. Could be rock, ledge, anything.)

"Better put your wheel to starboard a bit . . . Straighten out . . . Right on, Mister Fitch."

In and out the narrow line of the bar. Try to stay where you've got twenty-eight or thirty feet of water below ship. Get off that narrow course, you'll hit banks, shoals, rocks, or be in shallow. Those spots are like sharks' teeth, ready to snap the keel of your ship, stove her.

"Red can." (Red and black cans between the light buoys. There's a number on each. In case you get in trouble you can radio where you are. Those cans and buoys are on each side of your ship, they're your fence: stay inside them. We got to get to the end of the jetties, turn into Alta River, down-river to the docks.)

"I'll take her from here, Fitch," the captain said. "You knock off."

Captain took the wheel.

Short light and quick on it a long flash; head straight for that. Spar buoy, that's sharp, like a pencil at the top; deep water there, that's fine. Reflector buoy, lights that say go ahead, come in by it.

Those lights blinking, blinking, they're eyes you're glad to see.

"Temporary buoy, Captain. Watch it!" (It's stationary, the light don't blink, we're close to a shoal. The channel only a hundred yards wide here, shrimpers coming toward you on starboard, passing you on the port, one menhadener coming in two hundred yards behind us, a motorboat not far off, bells ringing in some of the buoys to herd in the menhaden and shrimping sheep.)

The water licked up the sides of our ship to the deck. Inshore, from the docks at the menhaden plants, they could see us low in the water, like we had the biggest load of fish of the season. No way for them to know of the half-full forepeak.

The men stayed up by the bow, tense, tired, ready to jump off, stand by while the fish went through the suction rig, over the ramp, into the factory. (I'm beat out too. When night come you go through the town from such a fishing trip, your shoulders will curve, like the davits that hold up the small boats. Get in the house after a day like this, go to the icebox for a pitcher of ice water, you won't be able to pick it up. That pitcher weigh just a few pounds, but it feel like the tom weight.)

Captain said, "Mate, take her to the dock."

I slid the *Moona Waa Togue* down the last quarter mile of the Alta to the Merrick Thorpe piers.

The line tenders, they jumped off the bow rail with the forward spring lines, tied her up at the front. I brought the ship broadside to the dock for mooring with the stern spring line.

Laden as she was, the ship didn't bob at dockside. Just stayed settled, very quiet, tired too.

But we were fast.

And we were home.

A factory foreman came up by the ship, looked over the load, and called two pier hands. "Get that rig down in her belly!" The workers took the nozzle end of a long pipe and slipped it into the fish hole. The pipe a foot wide, it led over a ramp along the pier, up an incline that brought it to the factory fifty yards from the water's edge.

A powerful draft came through the pipe. You could see and hear the menhaden pulled into the suction rig. Made pumping, whooshing, hard-working sounds.

First the fish go through a three-way catch basin, a big steel turnstile. Each basin, that's one measure, holds ninety-six gallons of fish. That might come to more than a thousand fish in a measure. We figure three thousand fish to a ton. Each time that turnstile switches and shows a measure of fish been picked up, a bell rings. That registers a share of fish.

The fishermen keep track of each ring, figure out their earnings then and there. Company bookkeepers stay right by the turnstile too and count bell rings just as the bunt pullers and the rest of us do. That way we all check on everybody else and it's not going to be no argument over how much fish been caught. (Though we have had such arguments.) Captain, he supposed to get around fifty cents on a measure, the most of anyone, and that's why he can make fifteen to twenty thousand a year. Engineer and me get seventeen cents on a measure. Pilot and cook fourteen cents. The bunt pullers ten cents on a measure, and a one- or two-hundred-dollar bonus at the end of the season if they work the whole season. Bunt pullers, in a good year, they'll make from four to six hundred dollars. Sometimes a few hundred more.

A deckload like we brought in today, that will bring the bunt pullers eighteen to twenty dollars for the day. Fine, except a deck-loaded ship don't happen every day. But by the bunt pullers never having got a guaranteed salary they could live on, they like the sharing system best. That gamble makes them hope for and look for the big deckload. Captain, he'll start out early in the morning, "All right, men, today's the big day. Going to get us a million fish!" We all steamed up. The big catch. The men yell back at him, "All right, Captain, fish us hard. Keep the net in the water!" The sharing system been in for a generation, took the place of a wage system when wages brought less than what sharing got them. What the men would like is a bigger share on each measure.

Right after each bell rings, that fish gets dumped into a raw box, then goes on a ramp into cookers. Goes through the whole wooden factory. All in one operation. Plant stretches a few acres, and from all over its insides you can hear the sounds of the fish being pressed, cooked, refined, ramped around. Steam blowing out of windows. Smell going up over the whole plant and settling over the town of De Leon. "Ma, get that smell from the pogy plant. Bix making money tonight!" Trains and trucks rolling right up behind the factory, carting away meal and oil.

Maybe thirty-forty factory hands work all through the plant, help the machines hurry the fish along the cooking belts, watch for something to go wrong, helping the scrap along, leveling it off where it piles up, unloosening it if it clogs the belts. They live at the factory yards, have a two-story building where they sleep and eat. They depend on the fish we catch. They'll give us just as much trouble if we not catching them as Merrick Thorpe. They see us coming in some nights without fish, they'll yell, "What's the matter, you fellows go for a vacation? If you don't catch them we can't grind them. You want us to starve? What's the matter, you can't raise them?"

Sometimes one of us on the ship will work for a while in the factory, or a factory hand will try out as a bunt puller. I once worked in the factory for two seasons. I'd dip a sweet potato in that oil and eat it. Liked it real good, it kept me well, but got back on the sea as fast as I could.

The fish go through big screw presses. Fine oils come out on screens, move into special basins and tanks. Different grades of oils—liquors, stickwater, gurry oil. No part of the fish go to waste. Even the gooey sludge at the bottom of the cookers, they carry it away on trucks, make glue of it. Shafts and belts keep the fish moving till the oil is separated from the scrap. The scrap is dried, gets fired into scrap houses, then it's packed in bags. The bags are tied by hand and carted off in trucks to trains. Oil pours right into big storage tanks at the edge of the factory. Then it's piped into trains that run behind the factory along the river. You can hear that train whistling and chugging day and night when there's plenty of fish in the works.

The machines grind out about eighteen gallons of oil from a thousand fish, but less if the fish are less oily. Ten million small fish will make a hundred tons of scrap for meal, fertilizer, bait. The figures get bigger and bigger in the menhaden fishery. They'll catch a billion or more fish a year. All done by bunt pullers like Bob, Blu, Fort, Lift, Westley, Carters, Noah, Rev, and me. I'm a bunt puller. Always a bunt puller. I pull bunt every time I fish, think of myself first and last as a bunt puller. Because I may wind up, not a mate, but just pulling bunt somewhere. The bunt pullers, they hold up the whole fishery on their shoulders; carry the factories, the ships, and the meal and the oil that's used in more than two hundred different ways, in just about every industry in the country.

In the earliest days the main thing they used menhaden for was fertilizer and bait for other fish. Around 1800 or so, in Rhode Island, they began pressing the oil out. Cooked the pogy in big kettles, squeezed the oil out in a clumsy way with rocks and levers. Later they put holes in the bottom of tubs, pressed the oil out the holes. Mixed the oil with mineral oil and used it in miners' lamps. After the Civil War they came in with hand-operated screw pressure machines that saved more of the oil. Then big hydraulic steam-powered presses that catch *all* the oil. A while back they discovered the scrap from the fish made good eating for fowl and animals. Now the chickens get it all over the country, and when you eat an egg there may be menhaden in it. It's fed to most of the animals on the farm, mixed in the other feeds, reaches everybody's plate through the back door. But the oils, that's where the most uses are. Solubles, vitamins, antibiotics, they get all that out of the stickwater, the leftovers of the oil. Use the oils in tanning leather, making rope, and in paints as a drier. They put it in soap, inks, insect sprays, linoleum. A lubricant for most anything that needs smooth going. Make steel and aluminum castings with it, calking mixtures. For waterproofing on all kinds of clothes you wear; for plastics; for metal treating. Mix it into putty, put it in brake blocks in autos. Plenty of it goes into lipstick. Kiss her and you kissing a little fish oil too. Freeze it, heat it, change it. Everybody been just about swimming in menhaden oil and they never known it.

As soon as the fish count ended, the crew came up to me. I was at the edge of the pier by the ship. A few feet opposite the fish hole. I stared at the ship. Plenty on my mind. The same thing the crew worried about. They had Carib to talk for them. "We not going out tomorrow, Bix."

"Not going out?"

"No. We not leaving out."

"What go down?"

"You know what go down."

"If you don't tell me what go down how I'm going to know?"

"If you don't know what go down you ain't the mate we been believing you was."

"She be shipshape before we leave out again."

Carib said, "We want this woman put in dry dock. She knocked up and she needs fixing."

He was right about the ship's condition. I wasn't anxious to go on her tomorrow myself, not unless something very serious be done with her. But you get to be an old salt and ship on these waterlogged menhadeners as long as me, a leak ain't going to overly fright you.

The men jumped all over me.

"Put her in dry dock!"

"She need a week's overhaul!"

"You and Captain Crother see Thorpe. Tell him to parcel us out one man to a ship on the other ships till the *Moona Waa Togue* fit to go out again!"

"*Put her on the railroad!*" A railroad is a structure they build by the pier to hold the ship up out of water while they make repairs.

I told them out front I didn't believe Thorpe would take the ship off the waters for a week at this time of year unless she already gone under and nothing else he could do.

"Well, we not shipping!"

"Let *him* catch fish!"

"*Mate,* you with *us* or you with *them!*"

They had me then. Right over the barrel a mate is over all the time. Besides, I didn't like the ship's condition any more than they. "I see the captain right now, men."

I headed for the office where the captain was. The office is a one-story wooden building fifty yards behind the factory. Only men work there. No women. Practically no women in the whole menhaden industry. Not around here anyway. It's a man's work. During the season when fish are brought to port at night the bookkeepers will work nights too because plenty figuring got to be done.

I told the captain what the men said. He switched the tobacco plug on the right side of his face over to the left and said we best talk to the chief right off.

Captain and me, we waited till Thorpe came back from the processing plant. He always piddled around there to see if anybody was taking it easy. He'd walk over by the pier, see a fish there, and say to a man, "Pick up that fish. It's worth twenty-five cents." Always cussing out his captains if they didn't bring in fish. "I seen you do better than that only last week, Crother. You brought in four deckloads. Why you laying down this week?" Crother would tell Thorpe of the luck of the sea and the seasons, the same thing Thorpe himself always talked about. Sometimes Thorpe worried about the competition he got from Flint, Keegan, and Brodhead, menhaden operators with piers and plants right next to his property. He'd yell at Captain Crother or some other captain, "We can't let Brodhead get all the fish! Somebody else got to make some money. There must be some money in that ocean for me!"

He walked up and down in his wooden room talking like that, then he'd sit down hard on his hard wooden chair. He got used to hard seats sitting in the crow's-nest of fishing boats the early part of his life, so the office chairs were as hard as the plank you sit on in a crow's-nest. He came up in the menhaden business the hard way, pulled bunt, ran the ship himself, even pressed the oil out of the fish with hand presses till he got the money to buy machinery. Then he bought up ships, till now he owned a fleet of twenty-five menhadeners, the oldest ones in the whole fishery. He bought them after some of the bigger men began building their own. Worst thing that bothered Thorpe, he feared other businessmen would come in and take the fish business away from him. If people came to look at ships or the plant, he didn't like it. "Keep them out! Too many people get to know about pogy, we'll have every businessman in the country wanting to grind up fish. Anybody comes to see what we're doing, tell them how many people gone bankrupt in this business." He'd tell that to his bookkeepers and they'd say, "Yessir, Mister Thorpe, we'll ease them right out

fast as we can." He was right about the number of bankrupt-
cies in this business in the last generation. Maybe thirty in all.
The sea and the seasons broke them. Till now there's only
about thirty reduction plants. Maybe a dozen operators own
them and one or two operators got most of the ships and plants
in their hands.

When Thorpe got back we told him what the men said.

"What you mean, not shipping out?"

"They want the ship put in the railroad."

Thorpe, a short, stocky man, looked like a workingman in
his shirt sleeves, he about blew his top. Stamped his right foot
on the wooden floor. That wood was in much better shape than
the floor of our ship. Some people, if you ask their opinion,
they'll answer with a decision. Thorpe, that was him. "I never
saw such independent sonsabitches in my life. What the hell
they want, the *Queen Mary* to catch fish with?"

I told him what the men thought. They wanted the ship
dried out, the weakened hull planking removed and new
boards put in, the keel thoroughly inspected and fixed if it
needed it, a good calking job, and a few coats of copper paint.
The whole ship to get a once-over.

He said he ought to fire every goddamned one of them, and
he gave me a hard look too.

I told him he best take a peek at the ship. "You been a captain and a fisherman in your time too, Mister Thorpe."

The president, he moved up and down the room like he
walked a deck and he was the captain of the deck he walked.
Which he was. Figured and figured.

"Them fish just beginning to school," he said, like he been
personally insulted by the men *and* the fish. "This no time to
put a ship in the railroad."

He turned to Captain Crother, gave him an eye with whips
in it. *"Where in hell they get the idea I should farm them out
on the other ships while the* Moona *being fixed?"*

"They done thought up that one by themselves," I said.

"They done thought up a sonofabitch! Ain't *no* menhaden ship afloat needs more than twenty-three men, and I ain't going to put twenty-*four* men on *my* ships even for *ten* minutes!"

Captain Crother and me both told him again to please come take a look at the forepeak.

Thorpe gave his left palm a serious punch with his right fist. If he'd have punched that hard at the hull of the *Moona Waa Togue* right then, the ship would have gone down at the dock. His eyes lit up like electric lights in a rigging. That's a very outstanding light in the dark. He swore he get this ship in shape by morning. He put *every* carpenter in port at work on her *all* night. "This an emergency measure," he said. Said he call up Flint and Keegan and Brodhead, the other menhaden operators, and borrow their carpenters, masons, and painters. "Work all night. Put the big pump on her right off. You tell them to be here at five o'clock and the ship be as good as she was when the season started."

Even when the season started the *Moona Waa Togue* had lots of water on her kidneys.

I told the captain on the way out I didn't think the men was going to like it. Wasn't sure myself I wanted to go out on her any more till she was fixed and fixed right.

Captain Crother, he had faith Merrick Thorpe could really get the ship in floating order by morning. Back on the pier he talked to the crew and gave them the same picture that Thorpe showed to him of the special work going to be done on the ship all night long. "Mr. Thorpe going to put seven or eight men working on her. This the height of the season. I think we ought to stand by the company and do our best."

Even I couldn't talk to them that way. I wasn't sure. All I knew, I was a menhadener a long time back, and my job, it's to catch ocean oil.

The men had some hush-hush among themselves for a few minutes.

Carib, he came up to us alone. "We be here in the morning, Captain Crother. Like you say. But if we don't like the way the ship look below the water line we not leaving port."

Fifth Day

JULY 15, 1949

DEW all over the ship, spray from the sea as we went through the cup of the jetties. Go out of a morning on a menhadener, you don't wash your face in no sink the way you might on land because it's no washbasin on board. Your morning wash, it's that sea spray that keep blowing a little against you.

It was no sign of any serious weather change. The sky clouding over, and a little muggy, nothing more.

All the other Thorpe ships been out for hours, gone since before sunup. But they didn't finish fixing the *Moona Waa Togue* till nine o'clock. Then she floated high in the river again, the water line where it should be. The seams looked like new where they been weak. A heavy tarring over the new

213

in-planking, over the fresh calking. The forepeak dried out. The fish hole dry as a bean.

Merrick Thorpe, he was at the pier when we slipped away. "She's as good as new," he said. "I told you I was a man of my word." He looked down the river toward the ocean. "Eppes says they coming back already with fish. It's no reason why you can't deck-load her."

The plane spotter, sometimes they called him "the flying fisherman," he been flying around off the coast because menhaden was out there in a few big schools. The fish had moved out of the Mayport vicinity, gone north, and were five or six miles off Amelia Island.

Genty, he didn't like the fast repair job. He mumbled over the deck as we went out along the jetties. Said it was going to take more than fixing this ship by searchlights to make her seaworthy. He beefed that if we had a real captain he wouldn't be bulldozed by Merrick Thorpe and wouldn't take us off the beach till the boat be fixed right. Two other bunt pullers hung out with Genty, and all did some hard eyeballing at me and at the captain. I knew it was a quick repair done, but I been on this ship so long and seen her float and work and keep coming home so regular that I didn't have Genty's fear of her.

The Arizona bunt puller, he eased over by the hatch. He climbed below to take a look around.

He came back up out. I asked how the forepeak looked.

"Oh, it looks all right." But his mind wasn't changed any.

Captain Crother had overheard Genty faulting him and me and Merrick Thorpe. He passed by Genty, and the bunt puller couldn't keep matters from him no longer. "Captain, you think this ship going to take us home?"

From chewing Half and Half the captain had a fine set of yellow teeth. Claimed that the tobacco pickled his teeth so they wouldn't spoil. The captain, he was no man to save his words, he showed Genty his yellow teeth. "You didn't have to

214

come out! You can quit tonight if that's the way you minded!"

"I wasn't talking about quitting. I just think the ship should have been put in dry dock and fixed clear through. That calking was still wet when we left the dock."

"Ships under me don't go down. I ain't never lost no ship. We get home, and bring fish too."

But Genty stayed with it, said next year he might go back on Captain Hornbeam's ship. "He got a good ship, built since World War II."

The captain got tired of it. He looked through Genty hard till he saw the coast line the other side of the bunt puller. "There must be a good reason why you not with Captain Hornbeam now."

Genty said he left Captain Hornbeam's ship to get a penny more on a measure with this ship and the Merrick Thorpe Company.

Captain spit some brown juice over the rail. He passed by the bunt puller, "It was us that got the bad penny," and he climbed up on the flying bridge by the pilot.

The bunt puller wasn't no bad penny, just a worrier. On these ships you should worry. He just shouldn't have got so free with the captain. He done that before. I usually go between the captain and the crew, and any man that by-pass me, he's going to meet the captain's cusses. The only way to go before the captain is together in a group the way Carib done it.

Maybe the words with Genty bothered the captain. Or the whole troubled week. Thorpe been nagging him about those two lost nets, that's ten thousand dollars. Another bad break like that and the captain could get tossed out right there in the middle of the season. Could be Mrs. Thorpe been after him too, which she always was. He went from the pilot's quarters to his own room, tinkered with the fathometer—and with a bottle of bourbon. I knew he'd wind up shutting off the fathometer and staying with the bottle.

215

Genty and his two friends, they stayed aft and beefed about the ship. When I came by Genty said, "Mate, we all may just get up and leave this captain and this ship."

That kind of talk, I heard it before and always handled it this way: "If you don't like the captain, fellows, that's one thing. But stay on and help *me*. Help *me* raise them."

"You all right, Mate. It's that sonofabitch captain."

"Just this damn old haunty ship."

We moved out of the bar, headed southeast, went rung up, till we could see two miles away the masts of the menhaden ships where they settled in a loose huddle for making sets. The sun practically all covered up by now. Looked like we might get a bit of rain.

One way or another I got to keep the crew regular. Keep them on just as even a keel as the pilot keep the ship. Else a bad mood can spread over the crew and make it so they won't be able to haul in fish if they do set on them. By Genty keeping up a steady grumble and taking on like that, it wasn't nothing left for me to do but act.

I usually count on Blu, Fort, Rev, and Lawyer, maybe one or two others, if any crew trouble coming up. I looked at Genty with my left eye and winked steady at the others with my right. I couldn't have talked to them any clearer with my mouth. They started moving up besides Genty.

Genty, he was by the fish hole, staring down the hollow. Kept rolling his tongue under his nose like a porpoise rolls under the bow. "When I get back to port I may just walk down the road and stop in at the Brodhead menhaden plant and ask them do they need a good bunt puller and has they got a good straight boat for a man to go out on . . ."

Somebody behind Genty put their arms around him very fast, lifted him off the deck. So that somebody else grabbed him by the legs. Another jumped on him around the middle. They carried him to the rail, till all of a sudden the Arizona bunt puller, he went flying smart as a gull overside and down into about fifty-five feet of good clean salt water, ba-S-H-O-O-O-M!

Almost the same instant bells rang on the ship so that the *Moona Waa Togue* slowed right down. Then backed up.

Captain Crother, he saw the whole thing from the bridge. He may could have figured it was because Genty was upsetting the crew and a stop been put to it.

'Cause I gave him a damn good wink too.

The same men that tommed the bunt puller, they threw him a line. Hauled him back up over the stern.

Nobody laughed much at all.

No one said nothing.

A menhaden ship, it's got discipline. And must have if fish going to be caught. The crew got their beefs about the captain and the company. Captain Crother could be a sonofabitch four fifths of the time. And which he was. But in this world you got to see the shades of a thing and do what you going to do in the right way. Once we all shipped out and the men agreed the boat was fit to go on, Genty shouldn't have carried on the way he done.

Maybe we should have listened to him and turned back. But the way it seemed then, we had to make him easier to work with.

That's what we thought at the time we tommed him.

Right then and there and for some time to come there wasn't a quieter man on the ship than the Arizona bunt puller. You would of thought they cut his tongue out.

The *Guilfoyle*, the *Jason Harding,* and the *Captain K. Y. Hornbeam,* they passed us on the way back to port, full of fish and singing men. The voices came across the lee toward us— "I've got a girl in Georgia, hey, hey, honey, I've got a girl in Georgia, hey, hey, honey, Who's going to help me to raise

217

them, hey, hey, honey, So I can see her before the sun go down."

A half dozen ships still making sets all in this area about a half mile around. Spread out one from the other in a loose star design. The *Captain Fischer,* the *Lorna Deene,* the *Oxford,* the *Howland Higgins,* and *Colonel Lorelard.* Mostly old ships, one a converted sub chaser; two of them been sailboats at their beginnings, like us. None more than one hundred and ten feet long.

Those ships looking so fine with fish up by the rails, that set the men talking about maybe the streak of bad luck going to end, the fish going to school hereabouts for the rest of the summer. Some said the fish must have come up from St. Augustine waters. Others figured they came in from deep waters. No telling of that, but it may could be meal and oil from here on in.

Three menhadeners, they went back in as a race. Prow by prow as they passed by us, horns tooting. First one docked be the first to get unloaded. The others have to wait two or three hours. But such a run, it's more to see who get across the line last. Because loaded menhadeners ease on like old women going home from the market with big bundles under the arms, on the back, and on the head.

Eppes, he flew over us, told us to follow his flight, he'd dip his wings where we could make a set.

Captain, he was very woozy. Barely able to get into the purse boat. I had to about run the set-making, tell the captain boat which way to go, where to stop. Carib, he had trouble signaling to the captain too. Lucky the fish so plentiful, because Captain Crother, he was no help.

"Bix, raise them for me. Raise them, old man."

He just sat on the bow of his captain boat and watched while the bunt pullers brought them up.

The men beat their feet between pulls on the webbing.

Drinking out the wine,
  Oh, drinking out the wine, wine, wine.
                    (Pull)
Oh, drinking out the wine, the whole wine.
                    (Pull)
Oh, you ought to be in heaven ten thousand years,
  Drinking out the wine.
                         (Pull)

Could be they was singing that for the captain's benefit, he been drinking out so much bourbon. One quart, maybe two quarts.

Maybe they just sang that chantey because it happen to come up.

Oh, if my mother ask me,
                    (Pull)
Oh, tell her that death done summons me.
                    (Pull)
You ought to be in heaven ten thousand years,
  Drinking out the wine.
                    (Pull)

Pull in water and wave and heat, till the linen cut the lifeline in your palms deeper, harder. Each bunt puller with those three lines in his hands, deep, like rivers, in the blood of their palms. One say to another, "Man, your hands are blooded up. Them blisters as big as boils." And the other answer, "You telling the whole truth now, man."

No chance to get back into port ahead of the other ships. We only had the fish hole half full anyway. May as well stay out and deck-load her.

So we stayed on, into the afternoon, while all the other ships gone. Pulled in four sets all told, till the hole was filled and

219

the rails were high with fish, and the crewmen larking over a twenty-dollar day.

Plenty trash fish in the fish hole, crabs, starfish, catfish, all kinds of bottom fish. Must have been really hilly and weedy down under to have all that in it. Threw the trash fish to the air pirates. They was appreciative and yelped plenty thanks at us, till we saw something come out on top of the fish that we never care too much to bring up.

"Look! Octopus!"

There he was, swabbling around on top of the pogy. A fellow so blown up that the center of him looked big as a big man's belly. Spidery arms, each may could have been three feet long and fat as a snake, sticking out eight ways around him, and his two big eyes looking at us shore folks that raised him up. The crew gathered around the fish hole. It wasn't often we pulled in an octopus worth looking at. Most are quite small, weigh only a pound or two and no trouble to nobody. You throw them away as trash fish. Pelican and gull very happy to get them.

This fellow, he shriveled up fast.

"Where's he going?"

"Look like he's coiling to jump, or something."

Seemed to me he was trying to slip under the menhaden and get out of sight. Kept pulling in his arms, wrapped them around himself, made himself small. Maybe he let out water.

Soon he looked small enough to grab, no bigger than a five-pound bag of potatoes. So I reached in, put both my hands around him, and pulled him out. He may could have weighed between ten and fifteen pounds.

Sat him on the rail of the fish hole.

He didn't do nothing, just perched there like a hunk of quiet.

I always heard it said if a big octopus grabbed you, you couldn't easy get loose. But here, he wasn't bothering me at all.

Just drew himself in, and it looked like he either gave up or played dead.

"Look what the mate got!"

I put this catch in a ten-gallon tin can, left the can by the galley. Figured I'd take him home tonight and try octopus on the table for the weekend.

We started northwest back to port. I went about ship duties, had some of the men to help out around the deck and up by the fish hole and clean out the purse boats. Took a look in on Captain Crother. He laid out on his bunk just about beat out. Old, soaked up in water and bourbon, leaving the rest to me and his crew. "Sleep it off, Captain. Fitch and me take her in."

A half hour passed till there was this commotion by the galley. Cooking Devil, he was hollering and bringing the men around him and pointing at that tin can. It was squeaking and hawking. You couldn't hear no other sound on the ship for the metal sound of breaking that came from where the octopus been stocked.

The fishermen stood by, watched the can expand and change shape. The tin spread out, kind of lowered and flattened a little. Plenty going on in there.

Cloy-o-o-n-n-g!

The tin broke at the seams.

The next instant that octopus, this time blown up again, like when we first saw him, he done bust right out of the can. The split-up can fell apart with a racket that sounded like pans rolling. Like a big chicken had cracked open a big tin egg and trouble hatched.

Octopus, he looked around, rolled his eyes fore and aft. He started for the rail, reached his arms up on the wood just like he knew there might be a purse boat down the other side for him to jump into. Knew the ship better than a green man would.

It comes a time a man got to show off.

221

I went for him. Grabbed at him to pull him back on deck.
He gave me the eye.

I grabbed him by one of his arms, figured I would lift him
up and smash the center of him down on the deck. Then I
found what a terrible thing a good-sized octopus is. The Lord
gave him plenty of arms to go plenty of rounds with anything. He had the strength of the ocean and the secrets of its
deepest parts right there in his eight tentacles and the suckers
on the ends of them.

He whipped one of his long snakes around my back but
used the rest of himself to stick to the deck. He played a slug-
ging game, going to stand his ground. His whole center seemed
stuck to the deck, like suction, and that gave his one arm
around me good leverage.

I couldn't budge. This snake arm of his went right around
my arms and back. The nozzle end sucked right into the
muscle of my right forearm. Like he'd made a study of men all
his life and knew just where to grab them.

"The mate found him a match!"

"I ain't fighting this thing! Get him off! Cut him off!"

I sat down on deck, put my foot against his center, between
the eyes, and pushed. Pushed so hard my circulation was cut
off, because that one arm still gripped me. He shot another one
out so as to go under my legs and come up around in back of
me and twist around my neck. Fast as a housefly would fly over
the same course.

That woke the men up.

Someone closed in with a knife and slit off both snake arms
that the fish had around me.

But two more arms went around me. I was helpless, numb.
Each time they sliced off one of his arms the nozzle of his ten-
tacle where it was sucking on my body went pop and left a
blister there.

In a few more seconds that octopus wasn't the same man.

They had cut off all his arms and run a few knives down through the center meat of him.

I stood up, wanting my strength back and not having it. Real mad, at him, and at myself.

That damned thing, there it was, all cut up, his arms laying all around, still the center of him was busy trying to live.

I picked up what was left of him and heaved him overboard.

That's when I lifted my eyes straight up. Because it was raining. The whole sky heavy. The sun gone.

Hungry ocean, you see how hungry she is when she takes in the rain. The top laid out flat, like something with its mouth open, long waiting for a rainfall. And the water that fell landed in the biggest blotter God created.

Some of the men, they was glad to see it. The weather been so drearyful hot for days, they welcomed a cooling. Others headed into the galley for some coffee to celebrate the weather change.

While I scanned over the sky and looked at the beach and tried figuring how long before we'd reach the channel, I heard all of a sudden a whoopee from all the men, stem to stern. I joined in it myself. One loud outcry, all together, because all together we found out something. I knew right off what it was, but the newer men yelled, "What's that?"

"You feel what I feel?" . . . "Yes, I feel what you feel!"

"This ship exploding?"

"No, it's nothing like that," I called out. Calmed them. "Just a ground somewhere." The wet conducted it all through the deck, through the rails into all the wood. The rainfall and the water around the fish hole and the slopped-up decks, water all over, that carried the current almost everywhere.

Most of the fellows, they was barefooted, and almost anywhere they were on deck, that ground was bound to reach into them. They couldn't move for the sensation. I warned, "Keep

223

off iron!" I was barefooted too. Got a steady little electric feel. Nothing great, but it could frighten people that never felt it on ship before. I hadn't known this to happen since last year.

I hurried aft to the engine room. The rain had wetted up the stairs going below, and I could feel a throbbing through my feet and legs, light and steady, but not enough to hurt. I yelled below, where I thought the trouble might be, "What going on down there, Stovely?"

He hollered back nothing, nothing going on. He didn't know the ship had electric jitters. It was dry all around him and he wasn't touched.

I told him there was a ground somewhere, the whole ship shivering.

The engineer, he said he knew it didn't have anything to do with his Diesel. He slowed down the engine and ran upstairs behind me.

We looked over the pump motor on top of the engine house. He said to check all the electric lights, look in the galley, on the steward's deck, check the forepeak, try the rigging lights.

I sent the bunt pullers flying over the deck till they meddled with every wire and light. Still that electricity throbbed through everything. "Hustle, men. This can get worse." I didn't know whether it could or not, but anything to find the spot.

Fast as they got over ship they called out, "It's not in the pilot house." "Forepeak okay." "Rigging wire all right." Till almost every place where it was wires, bulbs, pumps, motors been checked.

All except the galley.

McNally, he stuck his head out the doorway, he said, "If you-all don't find the trouble soon I'm going to be tickled to death."

Stovely, he ran in there, messed around with all the connections. "Here it is," he said, "the cook done it." He started working on a bad socket.

Cooking Devil, he been doing a lot of shifting of the skillets, till some steel or tin in his hands touched a metal socket, and the circuit grounded. Salt water, it conducts electricity, and the wood of the *Moona Waa Togue,* soaked up for generations in every sliver, with the sea, together that made the ship a natural conductor.

The shock lifted.

The men came into the galley for coffee and talk. Stovely, he gave us what to talk about. After he finished his fixing he said, "That grounding ain't nothing to the shock we all may get any day now."

We knew what he meant. He meant the electronic thromping horn. They working on that in many laboratories. Been making headway with such in Scotland. Farming the seas, they call it. Working to raise fish by magnets, by lights under water, by conduits. The fishery, it's been full of that talk for years. That's the companies' dream, an electronic thromping horn. Maybe put up channels in the ocean and siphon the fish right into shore, into suction rigs at the docks, suck them right into the factories.

"Sure won't need bunt pullers if that come," Lawyer said.

"Won't need mates either," I said.

Stovely said, "Hell, they might not even need captains or engineers if it come to that. You put the right magnet into the sea and thromp the fish straight up to shore and into the factory, they won't even need a rowboat."

Sometimes the men didn't want to believe all that was going on in the laboratories. But we heard so much of it, it was in the menhaden trade papers, that it's no more any doubt. The companies would like to cut out crews, ships, and sharing out with bunt pullers if they could. It's only a few years ago they didn't use planes, fathometers, nor radio in this fishing. Since they caught onto electronics and radar the fishery can't wait

225

for the Pied Piper of the pogy to be invented. They driving men in laboratories now worse than the captains drive their crews.

And yet all that talk ended with the men busting into a Lulu chantey, like they believed it wasn't nothing ever going to take the place of laying a net, making a set, and pulling bunt.

That singing brought Captain Crother to the galley door.

The commotion over the grounding, that had raised Captain Crother out of his bunk. He been on deck in time to put his hands on the rail and get the trembles. He was a barrel of salt over it. Blatted and cussed like a hungry pelican. Sure was *some* week. "Every goddamn thing happen!"

He found words never been used before and he used them. Tossed an empty bourbon bottle over the side and yelled at McNally, "What the hell you doing in there, *anyhow?* Ain't you got brains to keep forks out of the sockets? What you put a *fork* in the *socket* for?" The cook hadn't done nothing like that, just shifted the skillets wrong.

Stovely went back to the engine room.

Captain Crother, he didn't mean to let nobody stop him now. His eyes was red with staring at the sea and finishing a bottle or two and keeping quiet so long. He must have been having hard dreams of Merrick Thorpe, the way he took on. *"Goddamn! You-all make me sick and you make the boat sick! I'm all a-tremble like this ship been a-tremble! You goddamn crew, you!"*

The men just fell off to the sides, went up by the bow and stood there taking the drizzly weather, hung over the rails, cussed out the captain's drunk. "Same old thing. Captain got a load on deck and a load on his gut."

The captain, he stood midships, starboard side of the galley.

Rocked a little more than the ship did. He spoke direct to each man with one question he fired at them all. "HOW MANY CAPTAINS IS THEY ON THIS BOAT?"

The fishermen looked on the captain like a sulky child when he did like that. One or two might say, "Just one captain, Captain Crother, that's *Captain Crother.*" The captain, he liked to hear that.

"JUST ONE CAPTAIN!" he hollered at the sea.

Captain, he had a line, a twist, a turn in his face for every year he lived, like the slab side of a cut-down tree. Now he showed all his rings.

He sat on the rail so that a little roll might carry him overside, and he said, "I want to ask you-all a riddle."

"Ask the riddle, Captain Crother."

The crew crapping him up good now and he too lit to know it. He thought he had them in his hip pocket, where he had his bottle of bourbon before, but the crew got some kicks out of his carrying on.

"I want to ask you this riddle: HOW MANY CAPTAINS IS THEY ON THIS SHIP?"

And all the men answered together, laughing inside so as to split, "Just one captain, *Captain Crother!*"

"*The fish-catchingest captain they ever was!*"

The captain liked that.

He stuck his head in the galley door. "I ain't forgetting what *you* did!"

McNally, he didn't pay him no mind.

Captain sure had put away a lot of fluid. In all my shipping with him I never seen him quite like this.

He made it to his feet and started piloting a course aft toward the engine room. He got back by the engine-house staircase, he called below, "Stovely, you want a drink?"

Stovely didn't want no drink.

227

"Stovely, I want you to have a drink with me because we going to web in a shipful of fish. We ought to have a drink on that, Stovely."

The engineer, he didn't answer.

The captain put his right hand in his back pocket and faced fore till we all saw his eyes showing some kind of forgot look. "That's funny," he said, "I thought I had a pocket there."

It was raining pretty steady now and the sea took on a little. A roll or two went under the ship and jogged the captain and all of us. Still he stayed on his feet.

Captain Crother, he couldn't see for looking. He reached his foot out very easy, touched the deck a foot or two in front of him. He said, "I believe *that* spot is still shorted."

The crew laughed right out front now, the captain was so downright pickled and funny-acting.

The smell from the pogy hole went up right next to him. But he was so high he didn't know what was before him, just didn't see all that load of fish at his feet. His face got serious and he said to us what he said once or twice before a few days ago, "You-all thinking hard of me because we ain't catched no fish?"

One of the crew thought he might be able to get something across to the captain. "We got fish, Captain Crother. There *it* is." And he motioned at a hundred tons of it.

The captain looked into the fish hole. He pointed at all that menhaden packed between the hatch coaming and the rail on the port side, and he said, "We going to deck-load that whole section sometime."

The captain's footing wasn't none too good.

The men just stayed out of his way.

I told him, "Captain Crother, you best go lay down. Fitch and me bring her in."

He gave me a woozy look, like he was trying to see through to the bottom of waters fifty feet deep.

I steered him up on the steward's deck into his quarters. He laid down hard on his cot.

"You hear them fish hawks?" Carib asked me. He stood by me at the bow as we cut northwest toward St. Ann's Entrance. Carib's look followed the way the birds turned.

I said nothing.

"They hollering fit to scare their own selves."

I just listened and watched how they flew beachward.

She had grayed over, from as far as east is from west and north is from south.

"Can't see the hill, can you?" Carib asked.

It wasn't no use to make an answer to that.

Carib kept after it. "The land done gone out of sight."

Just a few minutes before we could make out the hill four and a half miles away. St. Ann's Bar, it was just a mile northwest of here. If we could get there we got it made. That's ten minutes more.

I pointed at the sea off the weather side. Fish all around, they grabbed at the air. Different fish, not just menhaden. All over the top. They snapped, gulped at the air, and went under.

Some fish behave like that when a weather change coming. Maybe the wind miles away affects the water, carries signals along the bottom or over the top. Maybe the fish smell a change in the sea like man do on land when the sky gray up. The Lord gave most fish good smelling sense. Maybe they feel water movement in their scales. Maybe their scales run a little like radar, take in and give off. Whatever the cause of their sense, the fish got it, like the ocean got it.

"Hawks heading for the hill, Bix."

I answered him nothing.

"Going to the ponds and woods."

Any time a steady man like Carib worry about weather, that's to be taken serious. Carib, like me, he seen spout and

229

sundog, gale and hail, all that the wind and sky mix up in this big bowl of salt soup.

Carib, he just about demanding me to say something. "You realize the shore no more!" We couldn't see the coast for the way the clouds lowered their bullheads on us and settled between us and the hill.

Wasn't nothing to say. Going as fast as we could. Same old six-seven miles an hour, straight for St. Ann's Entrance. Could see the flashes of Cyclops Tower lighthouse. Powerful revolving light, 160,000 candle power, something to head for.

The crew, they went over the ship about like always, watched the fish hole, talked with one another. Just anxious to get in. (Menhadeners, they don't look for sea trouble or any other kind. When they're finding fish, that's about all they'll see. Many a time the men been so busy making a set that they won't see a black cloud coming up in the sky. Then if it looks bad they'll have to let go the fish, hustle back to the big boat, pull the purse boats up in the davits, and get home fast.)

Till it started real hard raining.

They noticed that quick enough. Some jumped into the galley, called for coffee. One or two stayed on the windward deck, saw about what Carib and me been seeing, and took the rain on their skins. "Mate, tell Stovely to push that governor. Let's get in."

Westley, he looked up at the balloons of cloud and he said to Rev, "Who emptied out the bottles from the sky?"

That struck Rev's light side, and he fixed up what Westley said and put a little music in it.

"Who emptied out the bottles from hea-a-a-ven-n?"

Lawyer put his face out the galley door, felt the rain, heard Rev jiving up what Westley had said. Lawyer passed it on to the men in the kitchen.

"Who emptied out the bottles from hea-a-a-ven-n?"

The men are going to look for what to cheer themselves

230

most of the time, especially if a little poor weather butt in. So
Fort, he was standing next to Lawyer, he put his twist on it:

"And let the rain fall dow-w-w-n?"

Genty, he got in with his idea:

"Who? . . . Who? . . . Who?"

The whole galley rang with it, so that Carib and me, up by
the bow, we heard all that good nature.

> *Who emptied out the bottles from hea-a-a-ven-n-n,*
> *Who emptied out the bottles from hea-a-ven-n-n,*
> *Who emptied out the bottles from hea-a-ven-n-n,*
> *And let the rain fall down-w-w-n-n?*
> *Who-o-o? . . . Who-o-o-o? . . . WHO-O-O-O?*

But they didn't know what Carib and me knew. That what
whupped up out beyond was a little something more than just
a rain emptying out of a sorry sky.

Because whatever it was, she was bearing a sea with her.

"It's a blow coming, that's for sure, Bix."

Nothing to do but keep going, look and wait, and figure a
course when we see what the wind and the wave going to do.

A sea like this working up, if you knew it was coming, you
wouldn't even go out. Not in our kind of fishing. Get a spell of
bad weather that lasts a week, you stay home a week. I been
in some winds I thought I was never coming home. Sometimes
you had a hint the night before. Maybe the sun gone down red
in the bank, there's a wind behind it; then, come morning, if
the sun rise bright red again, watch out, that's a blow on the
way. If you go out then, the sky may get dark, she go to raining and driving so hard it look like night coming on right while
it may be only seven-eight in the morning. You get in that,
shoot back into the channel quick.

But this time, no such warning the night before. None all
morning. Nothing but the kind of rain that will bring the men-

haden whupping to the top till it's like pellets of water falling on the surface to tell you where fish are schooling.

Eppes, he was gone, back to the hill and grounded. No chance to see him and his plane when the sky darken.

I ran up on the steward's deck, told Fitch to have Stovely ring her up, get to the bar fast as we could.

I picked up the radio phones, reached the office. They said the Coast Guard talked of a local storm around northern Florida and Georgia. "Just a squall," they said, "but hustle in."

Back on deck I could see how one man's squall was another man's gale.

It began with the wind saying whrrrrrrr, whooping.

Then we took a long ride high up on a swell. Maybe five hundred feet till we reached the peak and slid down the other side. If it's any more like that and they coming in from deep water, we going to have a tough.

Because that's the big sea.

Still nothing to do but full power ahead and worry a bit. Maybe we shouldn't have tommed Genty. Might have been bad luck. Maybe I shouldn't have fought that octopus. Maybe the grounded wires, that was an omen and we should have hopped to it. You get the Lord's mouth cussing down at you and you wonder whether you done some little thing wrong instead of some main thing—like going out on a doomy old ship. If you got a secret little luck charm on you, you'll grab it now.

This big liner, maybe South America bound, she passed us by just as another swell lifted us. Big boats, they been slipping by us steady. For them this blow-up be no great matter. They'll weather it out. They're ships. We're riding a mess of slivers held together by time and the Lord and our seamanship. Nothing more. Look up at a fifty-degree angle, we could see the helm of this ship maybe a hundred yards away. A seventy-five-degree angle, see the tops of her smokestacks. She tooted her horn, but plenty of sea between us. Maybe they wondered what we doing in this sea in this tub. Nothing else they could think of, seeing us flipped up on the water by the swells like we was a raft.

From then on we didn't know whether we'd ever see ships *or* people again. The sea getting harder, blowier.

Ours is a round-bottom ship, but we got a keel there, it's supposed to steady us in bad weather, keep her from rolling too far. But the *Moona Waa Togue,* she was no more on an even keel. The danger now, if the ship roll too far until the keel come out of water and catch air, we may turn over. If she rolls sixty to seventy degrees, she can turn back, but if she catches air while she's doing it, she's overbalanced, we gone.

The purse boats swinging in the davits, they get to singing in a happy, squally way, as if they going places. And they might. The minute strong wind starts, those small boats crave water: squeak and crack, whack and thump in their kleafs till they're either griped down fast or go overside.

"Carib, see you can get someone in the galley to help you gripe down those boats."

If the mate boat tear loose and go in the drink, that leave the captain boat, four tons of weight, on the other side of the stern, enough to off-balance the ship and help capsize her.

Fort, Blu, Lawyer, Kirwan, Hammet, Rev, and Booker came out of the galley—they'll stay on deck with us in a bad time. "Tie them down, men. Quieten them!"

The dry-boat man, he stood by the starboard rail and pointed east till, if his finger had anything in it to fly out, it would have hit England. Pointed to where you couldn't see nothing but sky and water and couldn't tell where they met. Might have been a second sea. And which it was. Rolling at us from the northeast. Worst direction for a blow to hit a menhadener on the Florida coast.

Nature speaks in signs, a whole language nobody ever done

traced. The wind, she'll puff down on the sea, the sea answer with a wave: a fisherman don't know what the talk was between them, but if the blow is hard enough and the wave tall enough, that man may feel fear in his heart. We felt that fear now. Carib and me, and the men by the purse boats.

That first smash, it can do more to a man and a ship than worse hits that will come later. The surprise, the shock, the worrying and waiting over. Then bla-a-a-m, she smack your hull so you can hear the ribs and the stanchions talk back hurt.

Could be for a second or two the whole ship was about out of the water.

A board twelve feet long that we use to build up the fish hole coamings when we deck-load the ship, it snapped out of its place, flew over the mast like a kite. Lifted to weatherward, balanced way up for a few seconds like a gull would float with its wings stretched out. Lifted up another fifty feet, then spun straight down, turned all the time like a top, and dived into the sea smart as a kingfisher.

By that board breaking out, all the fish between the coamings and the deck rails, they went overboard in the same flash. Thousands of fish, tons, it washed back in the sea in a wave's toss of its head. Went overside and left the decks as clear of fish as before we brailed them on deck. Pogies all around the ship. Some washed back on deck, rolled across it, went into the water again on the other side.

But losing ten-twenty tons, that was good. A heavy boat, she'll ride the sea, but if she's too heavy she'll bust right on through the crests, take in sea with each plunge.

"Quick, get a tarpaulin over that fish hole!" It was still full to the waist with menhaden.

If we didn't get canvas over that hole real quick to stop the fish from getting tossed out and keep water from coming in, we lost before we have a chance to get control of the ship. Water in that hole, you start worrying. It'll swing you from side to side, keep your ship off keel. If the sea beats your sides at the same time, the ship may break in half.

Didn't let them rest. "Get that canvas across the fish hole!" Egged them on to get around the hole and pitched in on the work.

Hammet, he dropped his corner of the tarpaulin and started back to the galley. Must have decided he couldn't stay on deck no more. The others followed him. Because wind, rain, and wave beating on us like the skirts of fifty thousand women, you couldn't tell what. Carib and me finished pinning down the canvas. Now the heavy stern going to help balance the ship. No chance to lash down anything else loose on board. Carib's rowboat up by the bow, at the foot of the steward's deck, he had tied that down good before the weather got too bad.

Sometimes so much happens, you can't think. You can be the captain or the mate, but if something is happening, it's happening to you too, and you can't think clear.

I had an idea I should get up there by Fitch, thought I should try to wake the captain, figured I ought to get on that radio too. But couldn't act for trying to keep my feet.

Thick as that sky was, Cyclops Tower, now it was blacked out. Couldn't see light nor dark. Couldn't see the edge of St. Ann's Entrance.

All I knew for some certain, we yawed into one wrong hollow after another. Big old sea, she roared, with all that filled it.

Even when we floated straight in good water, if we had a load on, the water line came up to just a few inches below the rail. Now the sea was all over the deck, rolling from one side to the other, whichever way the ship take a wave's fancy.

Till this big roller, and powerful wind with it, came at us green and broad as grass on the breast of a hill.

But this wasn't grass, and we not on the hill.

This blow, wide as a street of houses, it came straight down at the *Moona Waa Togue*. Whupped and twisted over the ship and tore the mast off, split it right out of the partners at the galley floor.

The seventy-foot pole, it slapped down crosswise, landed just a bit fore of the ship's center, like the clouds had swatted a fly. Fell athwart the ship, straddled her on both sides.

The middle of the pole, it locked in the smashed wood walls of the galley. About thirty feet of her top part pointed to windward, and the thick lower third laid abeam to lee.

Crow's-nest busted off the mast as it hit the sea.

All that in the huff of a wind's twist.

A flash in your life like that, it's going to teach you what the Lord meant when He said He was a wrathful Lord. He must have meant that mostly for sea fishermen. Especially for cooks that leave the hill.

Because nobody ever saw what happened to Cooking Devil.

McNally, he could have been slingshotted by the mast out the lee side of the ship when the pole snapped next to him. Or he could have been washed out the galley by the sea that rolled in on us along with this windfall.

He been standing right next to the mast, where he always stood, just sorry he couldn't dish out coffee because the sea was so high, just those words, his last words, and nobody saw him in the air, on the deck, or even hit the water.

Just gone. As lost as shelled corn.

Because of this that happened to the cook, the men in the galley figured that might be the worst place to stay. They been tumbled together with the table and benches, and lucky nobody else hurt. When they untumbled, got on their feet, saw McNally was gone, they got high with panic. Hollered and called for me. McNally! He overboard! Gone! Where the cook? And like that. All crawling over the mast and piling outside on deck.

They looked at the big pole sprawled across the deck, which it did lay out in a frightful way to look at. Each end of the pole, like leeboards, dipped into the sea with every bend of the boat. The rigging, it scattered over the galley and deck, and some lines dragged overside in the water. The rails on both sides partly torn out, just open deck on each side at midships.

Some held onto port windows, planking, lines. Others stared into the sea for a sight of the cook. And a few started for the forepeak.

"Mate, take us in!"

"Beach her, Mate! Give us a chance to swim for it."

The same men that helped gripe the purse boats and lay the tarpaulin, they still stayed on deck to look the storm in the face. Grabbed for what to hang onto, twisted their heads and necks fore and aft and to both sides to watch each trick of the wind and wave. Westley, he wouldn't get out of the galley, but felt safer laying on the kitchen floor hanging onto that fallen mast. Two fishermen, they watched out for young Roger as well as they might, held him between them while they made for the forepeak. The other fishermen, they jumped from one thing to another to get along that narrow deck without going overside. Crawled, held each other by the legs and arms, and moved when the ship's roll gave them a chance to inch along.

All that yelling to go with it. There's a minute when even tough men that been in rough spots before, they'll holler and beg out like all the scare in the world planked itself inside their ribs. Take us home, Mate! Undo this Lord's work, Bix! Wake up that damn captain!

"I carry you home, men!" But no idea how I'm going to do it. Just I held onto the stairs to the steward's deck. Wondered how I'm going to get to the side of Fitch, because I was sure something happen in the pilot house. The ship just snaking through the water. Rev made a grasshopper's jump by me and

237

I heard him yell through that thick weather, "Lord, Lord, we asked for fish. You gave us a serpent!" That's how the ship pitched, like a serpent going through reed, headed no-place in particular, just romping.

"Get us home, Bix!" "Mate, Mate, do something!" "Why the boat twisting?"

One bunt puller, he said, "I rather look at a man in the face with a .38 than see that sea coming at me again!"

He was talking of a big rubber-tire roller, thick like a million rubber tires right next to each other, rolling their rubber toward us, and the wind roaring at us to get down in the forepeak or jump off the ship. Oh, the wind talk to you like that, give you crazy ideas.

A sea like that, it don't look like water, it look like something grabbing you. The roller comes to you shaped like a big round hand, the top of the roller like white fingertips, and a hollow of water in front of it, till this big hand reach at your ship.

I yelled back at this fellow that thought the sea was worse than a bullet. "If I go I'm going looking!"

But he scrambled for the hatchway and about fell in the forepeak.

It's times when you may think the weather may be the Lord. After all, you living in this world, and all there is in this world is weather. In a blow you'll call the weather the Lord and pray Him to carry His wrath somewhere else. A deep-sea man still wouldn't call this a gale. But for us in a menhadener, it was serious, and we called such weather a blow. In a regular nautical blow the wind going to run forty to fifty-five miles an hour, and what they call a whole gale, fifty-five to seventy-five. But the gust that took our mast, that was gale-hard.

The men falling along the decks now, piling out of the galley. Trying to reach the forepeak. That's where half the crew will head in a hit. Below, where they won't see the pitch of the sea, where it's dark and they can pray it out. Because

238

some fishermen, they're not seamen and no help on deck, and might just as well be under the hatch. On the way by me this bunt puller said, "Bix, you going to need some prayer, and that's what we going to do." Prayer don't get corn out of a field or a ship out of a valley, but if a man *want* to leave the deck, that's good enough for me. "Good! Them that can pray, *pray!* But them that will stay on deck and help me, the Lord going to bless them most of all!"

A wild high sea, it's a hard experience, gives a man a hard thought. Genty, he made it by me on his way to the forepeak, gave me a crazy man's look, pointed his finger at me. *"I told you so!"*

I wondered what else he was going to say. He kept looking, which showed he had more saying.

"Hogs! Hogs!" he yelled. He might have meant me, or Merrick Thorpe, or Captain Crother. *"Money the root of all evil!"* Like he was the first ever to say that.

"Don't you talk to me that way about money," I hollered back at him, hard as I'd throw something. "I don't want nobody telling me money is evil. *You just have an evil time getting it!"*

He carried that with him down into the forepeak.

I held onto the staircase that went up to the steward's deck. Held and tried to see the picture and figure what best be done.

Sometimes you know right off you're going to live through one of the big deals in your life. You'll make it—or you won't. It's bad when you have a flash few seconds before your work begins, before you start fighting out of it. But there's an open space then that you got to close, got to study what to do, which way to go. A few seconds to feel the breath itself going to hang on what you decide. Look coastwise, seaward, then straight up. Feel the ship under you holding, holding, like weak wooden muscles against a sea of meat. Because a ship, it's a little like a person. Man and ship both, hit them once or

twice, they'll fall from it, but sometimes they'll take on fight
and stubbornness. Could be something like that goes through
the timbers of an old ship under strain. The slivers stick together. The beams and bends, the stanchions and coamings,
the hull and the heel, they try to hold against whatever want
to tear them apart. That's how it seemed to me the *Moona
Waa Togue* carried herself now. Like she was with *us* against
the sea and the wind.

In a minute like that, in a high sea, you'll get some idea how
many ways it's to look at a thing. On a menhadener, at such
a time, nobody going to speak of just two sides to anything:
it's a thousand sides if you could know it all.

A ship in a coast rage, she rides in arithmetic each instant.
All dimensions, to and fro, up and down, side and side,
through water and the foam of your own senses. The ship
lists to port, it can look like the sky goes downhill. She veers
to windward, the *Moona Waa Togue*'ll slide you back to lee
till you see just water on one side of you and sky everywhere
else. You can't make a worm walk on its tail, but a wild sea,
it can just about make a scraggy old ship stand that way.

I was two-three steps up the staircase to the pilot house. But
I got tossed back on deck hard and far. The ship, she had gone
straight up, butt down, stem up in the air. I was looking for
her to come down straight. But when she fell, she fell capsize-
way. The sea got her on the starboard and pushed down the
portside till the port deck was overwashed with sea. When
she was down in the port the sea slapped her midships from
that side, caught the hull between the engine room and the
galley. Instead of the ship going back up, she trembled from
side to side. Couldn't go either way, but wobbled. At a time
like that you apt to feel like you being eat for a sandwich by
wind above, water below. You free and you held down. You
in space and you rooted. You soaked but you ain't drowned.

That pounding, it shook all of us like it shook the ship,

wobbled each of us in our pivot like it wobbled the ship. I been thrown over by the galley door, till I smelled meat burning.

I sniffed.

Carib, he was by me, hanging onto those fallen ratline ropes.

"You smell what I smell, Carib?"

We ran into the broken-down galley.

Westley, he been hanging onto that mast and some broken beam pieces, till we got caught in the tight of this two-way sea. The wobbling had shook him loose. Threw him up on the galley stove. That stove is going most of the time, and she been going before the blow hit.

This bunt puller, he was laying on that stove just about paralyzed. Singed all over his left side.

We pulled him off the stove, tossed him down on the floor alongside the mast.

Nothing we could do but let him lay.

We snaked along two-three hundred yards, just sea and chance taking care of the wheel. That was the time for customers in heaven, and the Lord, He may have done lost it.

I about fell up the stairs, like climbing a house of falling cards while they're falling. Water over everything, all over my body, drenched shorts and shirt. A time to be wearing our oilskin coats, but the blow, it came on so quick, only a few got ready.

I rolled into the pilot house.

Like I thought. Fitch, he was crawling on the floor as if he was trying to find a way out, or a way in, or get back on his feet. Stunned as a cow hit in the head with an ax. He been lifted off his feet by one of those broadsides, must have landed on his head, and ever since, the *Moona Waa Togue* been making a pretzel's pathway through the sea.

I figured what have to be done. On the hill we say, "A mile around the road is shorter than half a mile across the field."

The same now, out here on this wild meadow. St. Ann's Entrance, it was just a few minutes northwest, but the wind, it was from the northeast. No way to make the entrance without running in the trough of these swells. Be capsized quick if we try. So, make no path for the entrance. If we turned head on into the sea and started bucking the northeaster with a weak Diesel engine and a battered ship loaded with fish, that water may sweep over the bow every time a swell come our way.

Only thing to do is tack about, make a complete turn, and put our stern in the way of the northeaster wind. Let the blow carry us down-coast, maybe beach us.

I grabbed the wheel. Started twisting it to take us southeast. A longer way but a likelier sea. That going to put the hill a far piece off—maybe ten-fifteen miles from us—but nothing else we could do.

Fitch, he came from his knees onto his feet. He was babbling how he been knocked over. I hollered for him to help me at the wheel.

His senses came back on him and he helped me tack her around due west. We caught high water on the stern for it, wallowed in a deep hole, but had to chance it. Wheeled her bow southward, till all of a sudden the ship, it jumped forward like we had a new engine. Which we did, because rollers hitting us alee.

Now, ride into the hill.

That hill looked sweet now, like a ripe melon that hollers at you from the other side of the fence.

Let the sea drive us.

Go for the coast on the swells.

I signaled orders to Stovely to cut down the engine, let the sea do most of the work.

"Hold her due southwest, Fitch."

"Got it made, Bix."

I looked in on the captain to see whether he could get up and help out. He's an old salt in a storm, knows his business, better in a blow than me. If he be on deck at a time like this, there ain't a better mariner in the fishery. Besides, I didn't like to have all those men's lives on my head and on my judgment. Which it was now.

Thought maybe the big sea had shook him awake, but even his own mother never saw him sleeping so peaceful. Most passed-out man I ever beheld this side of the grave. I shook him hard, but he wasn't no more use to us now than the fish that been swept overboard.

He was so drunk he'd left the fathometer on. It may could have been on for hours. It showed menhaden below.

I looked in at Fitch again, he said all in hand, so I went down on deck.

Sometimes it looks like everything want to go overside, go down where its troubles be over. Some of the men be just about set to drown, and anything that ain't lashed down on board act like it's about to put on wheels and roll overside. Even now, in all this sea and noisy wind, I wasn't so much afraid of the big ship as those purse boats. Even griped down fast, with plenty of line, still they groaned to die out of their kleafs and go see bottom.

The same half dozen men still on deck, hanging onto whatever was nailed down. "Shall we go below, Mate?"

"No! You men pull that net out of the purse boats. Throw it on top of the fish hole. Put it right on the tarpaulin!"

They knew what I had in mind. Knew I was getting ready to use those purse boats if we had to and didn't want no net taking up room that men could have.

I ordered Carib to the steward's deck. Stay by that radio, keep talking with the Coast Guard. But a pogy boat way out calling for help, that's lonelier than a voice crying in the wilderness, for the man in the woods, he don't have to sink.

The ocean got an appetite like the Lord, eats from the coast, drinks from the sky, draws strength out of her own deepest parts. You see how hungry she is when she takes in rain, swallows up the wind and thunder, takes anything the sky have to offer. Take us in if we give her the chance. She slapped and drove us, poured over our stern, hit us behind like a fighter in a ring clinches and beats on the back of the other's neck. Wind and sea for a motor, and they drove us as if we had sails. Those blasts from behind, they carried us up like you pedaling to the top of a hill on a bicycle; slapped our lazaret, lapped up the sides, tried to make out of us a "ship sunk here" mark on the Coast Guard's chart.

The men hanging onto the lines, the bitts, the dunky, the galley beam pieces. And all that's to hear, if you can make out something they say, it's "Mate, Mate, get us to the hill!"

Just barely made out the line of Amelia Island off our starboard. If we could move due east we could beach her somewhere on Amelia Island sand. The water only five feet deep there, not rocky. Ground her there, and when the ship break up we may be able to walk or swim ashore. Sand and mud bottom, we got a chance. But we couldn't.

We were scudding southeast, beach-bound fast, straight for Nassau Sound maybe ten miles below. That's shoaly water, dangerous in a blow, breakers way out in the sea, high bars of hard sand and coral. If we get pushed down into that coast, our only chance it's to get in the purse boats and hope the Coast Guard pick us up.

I felt my way back fore, didn't trust my legs at all, but went foot by foot from one deck piece to another till I reached the forepeak. Could hardly open the hatch. Wind howling over my back so it wrapped my shirt around my head and I had to tear the shirt out of my eyes.

Genty, he came up the ladder, stood on deck, and saw we

was headed southeast for the beach. Couldn't nothing ever
please him. He pointed at the shore, just about faulted me for
the blow, and yelled, "Strong ships gone down on breakers,
Mate. Where you taking this sick old wood?"

"No other place *to* take it!"

A few of them in the forepeak, they was right down on
their knees, in water up to their hips, calling supplication to
the Lord. I could hear them under me, "Lord save us, we been
good fishermen, save us," and like that. Someone lifted something it seemed to me straight from the Book: "Lord, leave us
pass through the gates. Cast up, cast up a highway for us
tillers of the sea. Remove away Thy great wet rolling stones.
Lift up a pathway for our ship!"

That's what we needed, a Moses to part this sea, give us
sand to walk on. But we had no Moses. Nothing but fishermen's luck now, and just what seamanship we had to get us
close to the hill.

The ship took a big drift to one side, till the water in the
forepeak rolled up and drenched them. One man, the Georgia
bunt puller, he was pretty beat, he called out, "Good-by,
Mate!"

I don't like to see a man show up like that in a bad time, but
of some twenty men and the mess boy, they are going to come
out all kinds. I said, "One thing, Carters, if you go down out
here, they can't bury you and say anything bad on your tomb-
stone."

Tried to sense it into them. "You-all best come out on deck.
Hang onto the lines. This forepeak can't hold much longer."
Still they wanted to stay below where they didn't have to look
at that sea.

For the next thirty minutes we rode the crests of these hills
till we left behind the fifty-sixty-feet water line and passed into
thirty-forty-feet depths.

I kept figuring the rise and fall of the ship, that would bust loose the mast, tear it out of the galley walls that was cracked up by it when it fell. But the pole laid out long, like lee arms there to help.

Each time any of us went fore or aft, we had to step over it. Each list of the ship, you saw the ends of the mast seesaw up and down on the water.

Yet it seemed to me the way the long wood stretched out, dipping in and raising out of the sea, it may could have helped keep the ship afloat like wooden wings. Because we were shipping water in the forepeak, taking it in through the timbers around the fish hole.

The hull on each side of the fish hole, it stretched and closed like it was lungs breathing. Let a timber or two snap, water fill up the engine room, and we go down by the stern.

Raced in the coastal waters till the rain stopped and the sky looked clearer, so that it showed the shore sharp about two miles off the starboard bow.

But behind us it was still those swells coming in from deep seas, backing up Stovely's engine, like a thousand more horses. The whole *Moona Waa Togue* nosing ahead, mast amidships, like a cross headed toward the altar of the hill.

"Try them pumps," I yelled at the hands on deck.

The ship humped so they couldn't hardly work around the pumps. Hammet and Rev, they went below to handle the forepeak pumps, and Blu and Fort, they stayed by the fish-hole pump.

Water in the bilge of a ship, it can bide its time.

Hammet, he came up out of the forepeak. "Mate, this ship, she filling fast."

Rev came out behind him. "Mate, she going down by the head."

"Get them men up on deck!"

But just then they all came scrambling out, wet as fish, one after the other. "Them planks opening up!"

"Mattresses floating around in there, Bix!"

Still they all noticed one thing. "She's clearing!"

It was clearing, too, the kind of blessing that can come too late. The sky showing here and there blue.

No stopping the *Moona Waa Togue* now. In fact, no reason to stop her. Going to smash on the sand sooner or later if we keep going. Hard sand and bars from here on in to the hill. The keel bound to crack open the minute we hit.

Carib, he came rushing down the staircase of the steward deck. I was by the bow, trying to study the coast, see how best to go in.

"Don't beach her, Mate! Coast Guard on the way! Keep her in the water!"

I looked up and down the coast but didn't see no sight of a Coast Guard boat.

When a ship piles at sea she really piles. Fort came running to me. "Bix, the stern under water!"

Wasn't no use waiting to see whether we go down by the head or stern. The thing to do, *get off*. The way it looked, the ship wouldn't last to go to pieces in the breakers, but the danger, it was already on us out here now.

That fish hole, it been too fat with pogy for too long. Too many full deckloads been carried in that stern part. The oil and ammonia been eating the poor wood. The timbers been crying with salt tears for most a hundred years, and the wrinkles of the seams, they was opening and the ocean weeped in.

I told Fort to go get Stovely and tell him to shut off the Diesel and come up on deck before the ocean wash in there.

The sky getting lighter, lighter. Even the wind settling down. Yet sometimes you got to watch out when you get what you want or all you want, because fattening hogs don't have much luck. Here we was, coming toward the hill, the way we wanted, but the clearer we saw it, the more there's nothing

247

else to see but a crack-up straight on. Breakers less than a half mile away, see them raising up like buildings one-two stories high.

Two sea armies been battering that beach, one from far out, one from close by. The big graybacks from far off, they had slugged over the bars, over the sand hills below these waters, and got run in with the foam worked up by the onshore blow.

That's when the coast look uglier to you than the far-out sea. Because the breakers, they're the last blow of the ocean before the sea meet the force of the hill. And the hill, it's still powerful enough to hold back the sea.

You don't know what the ocean plans. You don't know how strong or weak your ship is—or your crew. You don't know how fast the Coast Guard cutter can go, and you don't know what twist a ship going to take as it comes to the hill. So much you don't know, something may even happen to favor you.

That's what we just now found out.

In life, the worst that can happen, it's to be caught in the middle—in just about anything. Mostly it's bad at sea too. But this once, caught between the stern swells that had softened down and the breakers ahead, we got the benefit.

This powerful backwash from the beach, it was a fence that we couldn't pass. It lifted us up on a bank of water, pushed us backward. Made our stern yaw, so that we broached to.

The *Moona Waa Togue,* she wasn't in our hands no longer.

She was having her own fight with the breakers and the hill. The coast showing off its might.

She turned and tried not to go to the beach.

She tried to head off into the sea.

Wheeled around and wanted out into deep water, till our bow faced the northeast.

A ship hate to go to the hill.

It hate the hill and love the sea because it's made for the sea and not for the hill.

The *Moona Waa Togue,* she didn't want to die, she floundered off these backwashes.

Fitch, he was still at the wheel, he kept the bow pointed northeast.

The sea evening out. The big swells from far out, they was dying down.

This Coast Guard cutter, it showed from the south about a mile away. Bobbed up and down like a cork, but a fast-moving cork.

The men hollered joy. But I had to cut that in half. If we waited for the Coast Guard it might be too late.

"Man the purse boats!"

It wasn't a man in the crew that didn't see we had to make it first in the small boats, because water now all over the deck and just anybody's guess whether she going under by stem or stern.

The whole crew waded aft to where the ring and seine setters were lowering the small boats.

We carried the captain and Westley into my mate boat. Captain never knew what was going on.

Jubilee, she jumped into the captain boat without being told that's what she should do.

The water, it was even with the stern deck. The small boats just about slid off the back into sea about forty feet deep.

Motors in both boats, they got going. For a second or two the boats washed close to each other, hit, then broke away.

We headed south, slow, to meet the Coast Guard. But we watched the *Moona Waa Togue,* how her fish-loaded stern settled. The engine room, that must have filled, because the bow tipped up. She drifted in those hollows, wouldn't go into the breakers. Just parts of the deck showing, the broken galley, the steward's deck, and the mast laying out like a long arm saying good-by.

Genty, he was in my boat, his tongue speaking like a finger

pointed at us. "I *told* you so!" Kept saying he warned us and we paid him no heed.

I looked at him fair and square. "That's right, Genty, you done told us. You beefed about it, we paid you no heed, and we *tommed* you besides."

Even in all that uncertain sea the men had a place for a laugh. Someone said, "It just prove sometimes there's a lot of meat in a lot of beef." And Lift, if he had his way, he said, "Hell, Genty deserve *tomming* the *next* time we go out too!"

Yeah, man! Everybody said it.

The *next* time. That might be tomorrow or a few days later, soon as we get a new ship. But most of us be right back on the sea. Maybe one or two might stay to the hill, but that's all. Bad times, bad weeks, a gale, a lost man, or a bad season, that don't mean a menhadener leave the fishery. Catch fish is what you do all your days if you a real old chaser of the red line. If it's in your blood you don't never want to stop hunting those moving islands.

The last few days the fish been schooling real good, and if it go like this the next three months we can still catch fifteen million fish. I could just about have told the crew then and there the ship we be having out in a few days. The *William C. Drawes*, a safer boat than the *Moona* if they give her a good going over.

Because storms pass. Ships may float, or wrecks go down, or make shore, crews live or drown. But men and fishermen, they got to go on, got to farm the sea. Go in the morning and back at night. There's oil in the ocean, and only work going to draw it out. Life in the sea and a crew got to raise it.

So it's going to be no time before us crew look back at this just as something to talk about.

"Sure would like to get into the hill and get this water out of my soul at Front Street Bar."

"We be there tonight and clean them out," I said. That's what you do after a bad time at sea. Put the ship in a whiskey bottle.

This Coast Guard cutter, she coming toward us fast, prow like a knife a quarter mile away.

Behind us and to port the big ship seem to be cracking up in the middle, her backside all under.

You get a sad heart watching that. Nobody want to see anything go down that done good service for two-three generations. And make you worry some too. Old boats, old men, they going to sound. Twenty, thirty, forty years ago I wouldn't have noticed a week like this like I do now. I've had many a five-day run of sea trouble. When you young you can take it better. You got hard muscles to climb that mast, get out on the boom, jump from one boat to the other. The blood run through you then like the Gulf Stream run in the ocean. Everything feel hot and fine and you got a big life on the open road of the coast.

But now it settle down to something a little different. The hardness of the way. Like they squeeze menhaden hard to get the vitamins and the oil out of it, that's the way you squeeze your living before you get the meaning out of it.

I am old, full of days and seas. Maybe someday soon I can't get a mate job. I may be hanging around the docks like old Noah. No pension for me, no work, just stiff arms and legs, the oil gone out of me like out of the pogy. I be saying to the young fishers of menhaden, "I remember when the *Moona Waa Togue,* she did thus-and-so right off yonder apiece by Amelia Island."

Look at it that way, the sea is a sea of tears.

It may could come to that and it may not. Maybe if I stop to think of this sinking today and see how most of us come through it, and if I tell the whole truth, I got to say, "It's been a sweet life to me, sweet and lucky. I caught more fish than any man could count one by one in a lifetime. I done my work for myself and for everybody else. The oil flowed from my hands out over every road into the whole country."

Did you ever poke down as far as the springs of the sea? Ever wander through the bottom of the deep?

I done it.

In the whole of my living as well as my fishing.

You working for that small house so as to keep it. Where life begins and where it supposed to end. If there's food to eat, clothes to wear, papers and rags to chink into the window cracks in the winter—and love in there—and a little time to think—that keep you going, and you go to keep it going.

It's with the others about as it's with me. Fish and fight, Lulu and Eveleaner. Because the race, it got to go on. So that our sons grow from seed to sapling to great trees.

The sea that calls down everything, says welcome to anything, she saying welcome to the *Moona Waa Togue* now. Sea may be hard on man, but good to herself. Feeds herself with everything the world spill her way.

These old menhadeners like the one going down out there, sometimes the men call them hell ships.

The hell ship, *Moona Waa Togue,* God knows how many menhaden she borne ashore since after the Civil War—now she going to her due rest.

First we saw the mast bust loose out of the broken galley. The thinner end, where the crow's-nest had been, it shot up in the air ten-twenty feet, like it been sprung loose, and fell out flat on the water.

Her bow turned up, like a slanted hand and a fist calling to the Lord to keep her afloat.

But the Lord of the Sea is a Lord of Wrath, and He turned down the last prayer of the *Moona Waa Togue.*

It seemed to me she gave a last little motion, a flick, like a wink.

Could have been the hook or a line slipping across the hawsehole, or the way a wave smit her.

But I took it to be a wink.

And I winked back.

The old menhadener, she slipped under.

Down she went.

Till a great wave came along and showed where a minute before the old fisherwoman held her prayered hand high.

A few seconds later we felt that same swell move under our purse boat.

That's all she wrote.